Morgan
Morgan, Rosalinda R.
The wentworth legacy /
$18.95    ocn987620739

**DISCARD**

## The Wentworth Legacy

Also by Rosalinda R. Morgan

BAHALA NA (Come What May)

The Iron Butterfly

# The Wentworth Legacy

Rosalinda R. Morgan

# The Wentworth Legacy

Copyright © 2016 by Rosalinda R. Morgan

All Rights Reserved.

Published in the United States of America

First Edition

ISBN - 978-0-9890017-7-9

Kobbe Books

*The Wentworth Legacy* is a work of fiction. All names, characters, places, and incidents are products of the author's imagination or are used fictitiously. Any resemblance to actual persons, living or dead, business establishments, events, or locales is entirely coincidental.

This book is dedicated to my husband,

Matthew Morgan.

Author's Note

The Gold Coast of Long Island is notable for the history and variety of its mansions, but travelers to that beautiful section of Long Island will not find *Wentworth Hall* among them. *Wentworth Hall* and all connected with it, and the events which take place there, exist only in the imagination of the author and of her readers and have no connection with any person past or present, living or dead.

R. R. Morgan
August 2016

*"Be still, sad heart, and cease repining,
Behind the clouds the sun is shining;
Thy fate is the common fate of all;
Into each life some rain must fall,-
Some days must be dark and dreary."*

Henry Wadsworth Longfellow

# The Wentworth Legacy

## Chapter 1

He walked quietly into the entrance hall where only one light was turned on. The whole house was dark except for the table lamp which was dimly lit casting a shadow across the hallway. As he walked in, a light yellow piece of paper caught his attention right away. It was staring him right in the face as he opened the door. It was placed neatly on the silver tray on the entrance hall table in his home in Knightsbridge, an exclusive residential and retail district in Central London within walking distance from Hyde Park and Harrods. It was odd that there was something on the silver tray.

Mr. Granger, his butler, a man of medium height about 5'10" with a round face and bespectacled and an air of authority, delivered his mail to him on the silver tray when they came in during the day but usually nothing at night. He remembered telling Mr. Granger not to wait for him when he left his house earlier that evening to go to the 1927 Spring Ball at Grosvenor Square. He knew he would be very late. It was now almost two o'clock in the morning. Mr. Granger must have left the yellow piece of paper on the silver tray knowing he could not miss it when he came home.

Spencer Wentworth had too much to drink at the party and too inebriated to comprehend what he saw. With difficulty, he picked up the yellow piece of paper gingerly, opened it and tried to focus his eye. It was a telegram. He started to read.

The telegram said, "COME HOME STOP URGENT STOP". Just five words, so powerful in their brevity. He stared at them and frowned, his mind slowly absorbing what he read. It was not what he expected to see coming home late at night. He read it one more time. "COME HOME STOP URGENT STOP", it said. There was no explanation and no denying it was urgent. It said so. He looked at the signature. He thought it might be from home, from his father, George Wentworth Jr. but it was not. The telegram was signed by their family lawyer, Alistair Prescott. *"Why would Prescott send me a telegram? What could be so urgent?"* He wondered what it all meant.

He put the telegram in his pocket and turned on the sconce light on the stairway. Then he switched off the table lamp light and went straight upstairs to his bedroom. He could not do much tonight and decided to deal with the telegram in the morning when he would be sober.

Upon entering his bedroom, he took off his clothes and draped them on a chair by his secretary desk. He took off his cufflinks and his pocket watch and placed them on his bureau. He sat by the edge of his bed and took off his shoes and donned his pajamas which Mr. Granger had laid on his bed earlier and got ready for bed. He felt tired and exhausted and just wanted to go to sleep.

He turned off all the lights and slipped under the bed covers. As soon as he hit the pillow, he forgot about the telegram and went right to sleep.

A few hours later, he woke up with a start and rubbed his eyes. It was still dark. He wondered what time it was. He closed his eyes again but could not go back to sleep. He opened his eyes and he stared at the ceiling. He suddenly remembered the telegram.

He got up, turned on the light on his night table and walked to the chair where his clothes were. He remembered he put the telegram in his pocket but could not remember what was in the telegram. He turned on the light on his desk, retrieved the telegram from his pocket and read it. "COME HOME STOP URGENT STOP", it said. He placed the telegram on his desk.

He walked toward the window and opened it. The night air was cool. He could feel the breeze on his face. The crescent moon was casting a shadow on the landscape. He stared at the pattern of the opposite rooftops and walls of the nearby buildings, barely able to recognize their familiar outlines. Aside from a couple of night stragglers on the street walking by, the street was quiet and empty.

He thought of home but unpleasant thoughts came circling in his mind. He thought of reasons why the family lawyer wanted him home. He wondered if it had anything to do with the death of his grandfather, George Wentworth Sr. It had to be. He was sorry he missed the funeral. That was the last time when he received another telegram, a few months ago. It was from his father informing him of his grandfather's death. His father said there was no need for him to come home so he stayed in London. Now the lawyer wanted him home and it was urgent. "Why?" he wondered.

    Spencer Wentworth, a tall, lean, and handsome young man, in his mid-twenties with blond hair and deep blue eyes and a penchant for expensive clothes was a scion of one of the fabulously wealthy families in New York. He loved to party and had never done any work in his entire life. He grew up in a privileged environment with all that money could buy. His father, George Wentworth Jr. was the only child of George Wentworth Sr., the founder of Wentworth Bank. His mother, Margaret Ashforth Wentworth, a beautiful debutante from Tuxedo Park when George Wentworth Jr. met her at her Debutante Ball and married her within the year of their acquaintance, also came from a prominent old money family in New York.
    Spencer and his family lived in Meadow Brook on the North Shore of Long Island in a huge estate called *Wentworth Hall* situated on a high elevation surrounded by over 500 acres of land where one could even see the Atlantic Ocean on the south shore on a clear day. *Wentworth Hall* was built by Spencer's grandfather, George Wentworth Sr. They also had another large house in New York City on Fifth Avenue near Central Park and a winter residence in Palm Beach, Florida. The Wentworth family belonged to several private clubs, most notably the Piping Rock Club, the Meadow Brook Country Club, Knickerbocker Club and Colony Club.
    Spencer Wentworth, aged twenty-five, and his sister Emma, four years younger than he, always lived in luxury. They grew up with a nanny, a tutor and a governess always watching their every move. Their house was managed by a butler, assisted by a housekeeper and a cook. Under their management, there was a large staff of servants in all their houses: footmen to help

the butler, upstairs and downstairs maids who took care of the maintenance of the house, stable men to take care of the horses and the stable, gardeners to take care of the grounds and chauffeurs to manage the garage and the dozen cars that replaced the horse drawn carriages and have them ready at will for the family. Work at the house started in the early hours of the morning, before members of the family left their beds. In the hierarchy of a large household, the scullery maids, parlor maids and chamber maids scuttled about, removing the remains of the previous day's fires in all the grates, polishing, dusting, so that when the family arose, everything was ready for them and work continued till the family retired to bed.

Spencer and his sister, Emma, were tutored at home before he went to boarding school at aged eight and Emma went to Miss Potters School for the Girls. From boarding school, Spencer went on to prep school in New Hampshire and on to an Ivy League school like all men of his social standing would do. Spencer went to Harvard as expected of him, a Wentworth, like all men in his family did.

Before the 1920s, few people other than the children of the wealthy attended college and then they were almost universally men. In the 1920s, effectively freed from tradition by World War I, young people began flooding into colleges – to learn, but also, for the first time for many, simply to have fun. By the end of the decade, 20 percent of American college-age youth were on campuses. Few women did. Emma went to Vassar College later on. A popular limerick of the time went: *She doesn't drink. She doesn't pet. She hasn't been to college yet.*

Three years ago, after his college graduation from Harvard, Spencer left the United States and sailed for Europe on a grand tour in June 1924. Although he went away to boarding school since he was eight years old, his sojourn abroad was the longest he had been away from home. At boarding school he could always go home on holidays. Going away to Europe was another matter. It was too long to make the crossing and so he stayed in Europe. He spent his days enjoying the life of a bachelor with plenty of money to spend whatever his heart desired. With his good looks and never ending supply of money in his bank account, he was able to mingle easily with the moneyed class and the aristocracy.

Spencer wished he was home when his grandfather died. He was very close to his grandfather who was instrumental as to why he was in Europe enjoying the good life. It was his grandfather who insisted he take the grand tour of Europe after his college graduation. He was of the opinion that a young man of his stature should. It was expected of him. It would be a great education for him to see the world. Harvard education was not enough, according to his grandfather. His grandfather told his parents that he would finance his sojourn in Europe and money would be deposited in his bank account every first of the month and so he sailed for England on the *RMS Olympic,* the largest ship in the world at that time.

Being the most luxurious transatlantic ship and the first in a new class of superliners at that time, *RMS Olympic* made her maiden voyage on June 14, 1911 and arrived in New York seven days later on June 21, 1911. The press gave her extensive coverage and she attracted much attention from the public. After her arrival in New York, *RMS Olympic* was opened up to the public and received thousands of visitors and even more spectators came to watch her depart from the New York harbor, for her first return trip.

*RMS Olympic* attracted the rich and famous of the day during its run including Charlie Chaplin and Prince Edward, then Prince of Wales among the celebrities that she carried. One of the attractions of the *RMS Olympic* was the fact that she was nearly identical to the *RMS Titanic* which sank after hitting an iceberg on her maiden voyage. Many passengers wanted to experience the voyage of the ill-fated sister ship of *RMS Olympic*. Spencer was one of them and enjoyed his voyage to England three years ago.

For his first year abroad, he visited most countries in Europe except Germany. He went to England, France, Belgium, Spain, Portugal, Monaco, Italy, Switzerland and Austria, enjoying various cities along the Mediterranean coast, hopping from club to club, going to art museums, attending concerts and operas and having a great time. He was playing the field and women flocked to him like bees to honey where ever he went but he refused to get hooked with somebody for too long. He met plenty of expatriates from the States doing mostly the same thing as he did. He enjoyed the night life in Paris and Monaco tremendously. He found life at the Riviera to his liking with the more intellectual attractions a city had to offer.

In the first half of the 20th century, the Riviera was visited frequently by writers and artists, including Edith Wharton, F. Scott Fitzgerald and Pablo Picasso. While Europe was still recovering from WWI and the American dollar was strong, wealthy Americans started arriving. Edith Wharton wrote *The Age of Innocence* at a villa near Hyeres, winning the Pulitzer Prize, the first woman to do so. F. Scott Fitzgerald first visited with his wife, Zelda in 1924 and eventually stayed at Saint-Raphael where he wrote much of *The Great Gatsby* and began writing *Tender is the Night*.

Spencer loved Italy with all the arts, the museums and the opera which he started to enjoy tremendously. He went beyond Europe, to Istanbul and enjoyed and admired the exotic atmosphere of the place. He spent a couple of weeks in India and visited the Taj Mahal. After his trip to India, he went back to Europe and stayed a month in the south of France, then on to England again where he wandered in the countryside and fell in love with it.

While touring the Continent for a year, he discovered he liked England the best. The English countryside reminded him of home with its sloping vistas and grand houses with fabulous gardens. The City of London was a vibrant place and he enjoyed the social scene there and loved hobnobbing with the elites of London society. He was in a constant whirlwind of social events which made him stay. He decided to settle in England and rented a house in London where the social scene was more to his taste and within a driving distance to the countryside where he was welcome as a house guest in some of the great houses of England.

Now that his grandfather was gone, will the money still be deposited in his bank account? He was certain his father would make sure the money would be there. What if he was wrong? What would happen to him abroad? He could not continue his leisure life, hopping from club to club without the money from his grandfather. It was his means to luxurious living. The thought of not having enough money made him so depressed. Maybe that was the reason. Maybe the money would stop. He never thought of that before. He suddenly felt vulnerable and homesick. Maybe it was time for him to go home. He had been away for too long. Three years seemed like a lifetime. He had lived in England for two years of his three-year stay abroad. At some point, he contemplated on living in England the rest of his life but of course, life was unpredictable and constantly changing.

It was unexpected that he was summoned to return home as soon as possible and it left him no choice. At first, he did not think he wanted to go, but after some thoughts, he decided it was best to go home and find out what the telegram was all about. He suddenly realized that he was getting old and it was time to settle down. There were more things in life than the pursuit of empty pleasure. He had sown his wild oats. Enough of that already.

Time to get serious. Yes, he wanted to go home more than he realized. Once he made up his mind, he went back to bed and finally fell asleep.

The next morning Spencer woke up with the sun shining brightly. He got up and walked to the window. People were up and about and he saw some people already strolling towards Hyde Park. He could smell the spring air. Spring blossoms were appearing everywhere.

He turned around and aimed for the bathroom. He saw Mr. Granger had already drawn the water for his bath. He undressed and dropped his night clothes on the tiled floor. He dipped his toes in the warm water and sank into the tub.

After his bath, he put on his morning clothes which Mr. Granger had laid out in his dressing room and then he headed hurriedly downstairs.

"Good morning, Granger," he greeted his butler, a man in his fifties, always attired properly in his butler's uniform and took pride in his job as Spencer's butler and valet at the same time. He loved his position and he was devoted to Spencer who he found to be a very pleasant employer who treated him very well.

"Good morning, sir. Did you see the telegram I left on the silver tray at the hall last night?" Mr. Granger asked.

"Yes, I did. Thank you," Spencer said as he walked past Mr. Granger who was holding the door to the dining room open.

The dining room was a gracious room painted a very pale yellow and was bright with light coming from the morning sun through the open window facing east. On one wall stood a

Georgian sideboard with a pair of silver candelabra on both sides of a porcelain famille rose punch bowl. Flanking the sideboard was a pair of arm chairs in the Jacobean style. At the other end of the dining room was a marble fireplace with a roaring fire giving warmth to the room. Above the Hepplewhite dining table with ten chairs in Queen Ann's style hung a crystal chandelier with a golden wire chain. A couple of hunting scene pictures graced the wall above the sideboard and the fireplace. The table was set for one person.

Mr. Granger had Spencer's breakfast of buttered toast, marmalade, eggs, bacon, ham and kippers ready on the table. Spencer sat on the chair, flipped his napkin, placed it on his lap and started to eat.

He turned to Mr. Granger and said, "I have to send a telegram today and also see if I can book a passage to New York right away."

Mr. Granger's eyebrows shot up. After the initial shock, he asked, "You're leaving, sir?"

"I'm afraid so. I have to," Spencer said and continued eating.

"Does it have anything to do with the telegram?" Mr. Granger asked suspecting it had something to do with it.

"Yes. Our family lawyer wants me home. It says 'Urgent'."

"Urgent? Did it say why?" Mr. Granger was curious to know.

"No. No explanation. Anyway, I have decided it's time to go back. I hope I can get a passage on the *Olympic*. I love that ship. It's the same ship I sailed coming over three years ago." Spencer picked the last piece of bacon from his plate and chewed it.

"I heard it is like the *Titanic*," Mr. Granger said solemnly.

"It is, but better and safer. They put in so many improvements after the *Titanic* sank to improve safety. The number of lifeboats was increased from twenty to sixty four and extra davits were installed along the boat deck to accommodate them," Spencer said.

"It's terrible there were not enough lifeboats on the *Titanic*."

Spencer nodded. "I agree. They learned a big lesson from the disaster. An inner watertight skin was also constructed in the boiler and engine rooms to create a double hull. Five of the watertight bulkheads were extended up to B-deck, extending to the entire height of the hull. I understand improvements were also made to the ship's pumping apparatus."

"That's nice to know. It makes one feel at ease and worry free."

"Exactly. The ship also has plenty of amenities that I enjoyed. The first class section has a Georgian-style smoking room, a Veranda Café decorated with palm trees, a swimming pool, Turkish bath, gymnasium, and several other places for meals and entertainment. If you ask me, it has the most luxurious accommodation among the ocean liners. It's a home away from home. Maybe even better."

"That's wonderful," Mr. Granger said.

"I understand even the second-class facilities include a smoking room, a library, a spacious dining room, and an elevator. The third-class passengers even have reasonable accommodation compared to other ships. Instead of large dormitories offered by most ships, the third-class passengers of the *Olympic* travel in cabins containing two to ten bunks. Facilities for the third class also included a smoking room, a common area, and a dining room."

"That sounds terrific."

"Yes, it is," Spencer said as he picked up his cup and drank his coffee.

Seeing Spencer almost finished with his breakfast, Mr. Granger asked hesitantly, "What are you going to do with the house?" He was afraid he would lose his job. He liked his employer, a fine young man, kind and generous.

"I have not made up my mind just yet. I would most likely break off the lease. I don't know if I am coming back. Not for a long time anyway," Spencer said and took another sip of his coffee.

Mr. Granger looked down, not knowing what to say. He felt depressed. He knew at this time in his life, it would be difficult for him to find a job much less a good employer like Spencer Wentworth. It did not escape Spencer's attention. Spencer realized his butler was worried about losing his job.

Mr. Granger and his wife, the cook, had been in service at his house for two years since he leased his home and were conscientious employees and Spencer liked them. They were highly recommended by a friend who worked at the U.S. Embassy who knew Spencer's father back in the States. Mr. Granger and his wife used to work for a young American couple who was recalled back to the States. At their first interview, Spencer took a liking to Mr. Granger who seemed very pleasant but knew his place in the house hierarchy. Spencer hired him immediately and the Grangers took good care of him and he appreciated their loyalty and service.

"Granger, if you are worried about your position, I will try to find you and your wife a job with my circle of friends when I leave for the States. You should not worry about that. I will give you a very good reference," Spencer said.

"Thank you, sir. That is very kind of you. I do appreciate it very much."

"You're welcome."

Mr. Granger beamed broadly. He noticed Spencer had finished his breakfast. He came closer to the table, cleared Spencer's plate and gave him the morning paper. He stepped back and left the room.

Spencer picked up the morning paper, glanced at the headline and stood up. He headed to his study and drafted a letter to his solicitor in London, then left it on the silver tray on the hallway for Mr. Granger to have it delivered before he went out to answer Prescott's telegram and book his passage to New York.

## Chapter 2

Leaden gray clouds hovered across the sky. The wind was still blowing hard but the rain that had fallen hard in the morning had slowed down to a drizzle. Spencer Wentworth had left his London home in Knightsbridge in heavy rain to go to Southampton to board his ship which would take him back to the United States. The morning was cold and damp and he could feel the chill dampness even underneath his heavy wool coat but it did not dampen his spirit as he looked forward to coming home after three years abroad.

At the pier, passengers started arriving with their huge amount of luggage. They brought trunks covered in leather. The rich had their Louis Vuitton luggage and trunks, some with checkerboard pattern braced with wood. They brought extension suitcases for transporting dresses, gowns, tuxedos, and business suits. They brought large boxes built especially for footwear, and these smelled pleasantly of polish and leather. They carried smaller luggage as well, mindful of what they would need while aboard and of what could be left in the ship's baggage hold. Passengers arriving by train could check the most cumbersome bags straight through from their cities of origin to their staterooms or to the baggage hold of the ship, with confidence that their belongings would be there when they boarded.

Passengers wore their best clothes. The dominant palette was black and gray, though some young passengers had cheerier outfits like red jackets. They brought diaries, books, and other items to occupy their time. They brought cash and letters of introduction. The wealthiest passengers carried their jewelry of various precious stones - diamonds, sapphires, rubies, and pearls which they left in the purser's vault for safekeeping until they needed them. Everyone seemed to carry a gold watch. Some men carried a pocket watch.

Spencer found his way amidst the huge crowd at the pier where men in topcoats, fedoras, and caps and women with large hats mounded with sewn-on flowers carried their umbrellas, bags and other belongings outside the terminal. Toddlers and young children all bundled up in heavy coats held on tight to their mothers or nannies. At the far side of the building, the *RMS Olympic's* hull loomed above the wharf in a black wall of steel with the funnels spewing braids of gray smoke into the mist above, getting ready to depart as thousands of well-wishers gathered along the wharf.

The RMS Olympic had several levels of passenger accommodation. Passengers were divided into three separate classes, determined not only by the price of their ticket but by wealth and social class. However, no class was neglected.

Those traveling in first class, most of them the wealthiest passengers on board, were prominent members of the upper class and included businessmen, politicians, high-ranking military personnel, industrialists, bankers, entertainers, socialites, and professional athletes. Spencer was booked in first class traveling alone. Some first class passengers also traveled accompanied by personal staff – valets, maids, nurses and governesses for the children, chauffeurs and cooks. They were given a list of first class passengers, a "who's who" of the rich and famous of the upper class, which gave them an idea of whom to socialize with, especially rich bachelors for their daughters. Spencer was a target of some mothers looking for a prize catch for their daughters. The first class passengers enjoyed luxurious cabins, some were equipped with bathrooms. The two most luxurious even included a private promenade deck. They enjoyed a number of amenities including large dining rooms, a lavish Grand Staircase, a Georgian-style smoking room, a Veranda Cafe decorated with palm trees, and several other places for meals and entertainment, a salt water swimming pool, electric and Turkish bath, gymnasium, a squash court, and a barbershop.

Second class passengers were middle class travelers and included leisure tourists, professors, authors, members of the clergy and middle class English and American families. The ship's musicians traveled in second class. They were not members of the crew but rather employed by an agency under contract to White Star Line. Second class passengers had their own library, a spacious dining room, an elevator and the men had access to a private smoking room. Second class children could read the children's books provided in the library or play shuffleboard on the second class promenade. Some traveled alone or in small family groups. Several groups of mothers were traveling alone with their young children. Most were going to join their husbands who had already gone to America to find jobs and having saved up enough money could now send for their families.

Third class or steerage passengers were primarily emigrants moving to the United States looking for a better life. They enjoyed reasonable accommodation compared to other ships. They had their own dining facilities, with chairs instead of benches, and meals prepared by the third class kitchen staff. Rather than large dormitory-style sleeping areas offered by most ships, they had their own cabins. The single men and women were separated, women in the stern in two to six berth cabins, men in the bow in up to ten berth cabins, often shared with strangers. Each stateroom was fitted with wood paneling and beds with mattresses, blankets, pillows, electric lights, heat and a washbasin with running water, except for the bow cabins which did not have a private washbasin. Two public bathtubs were also provided, one for the men, the other for women. Passengers gathered in the third class common room where they could play chess or cards, or walk along the poop deck. Third class children played in the common room or explored the ship. The class also had a smoking room.

The *RMS Olympic* was the lead ship of the White Star Line's trio of Olympic-class ocean liners whose name ending with *ic,* was part of a ship identification system paralleling Cunard's *ia* suffix. White Star Line's trio of Olympic-class ocean liners were *RMS Olympic, RMS Titanic,* and *HMHS Britannic.* All three of the Olympic-class ships had nine decks, seven of which were for passenger use. All three vessels sported four funnels, with the fourth being a dummy which was used for ventilation purposes. On the one hand it was a decoration to establish a symmetry in the ships' profile; on the other hand, it acted as a huge ventilation shaft.

Two did not have long service lives and were lost early in their careers. *RMS Titanic* sank on the night of April 15, 1912, after hitting an iceberg in the North Atlantic claiming more than fifteen hundred lives. *HMHS Britannic* sank on November 21, 1916, after hitting a mine laid by the German minelayer submarine U79 in a barrier off Kea Channel in the Mediterranean during World War I killing thirty people. Unlike her younger sister ships, the *RMS Olympic*, the lead vessel, enjoyed a long and illustrious career and had a career spanning twenty-four years. This included service as a troopship during the First World War which earned her the nickname *"Old Reliable"*. Her captain was knighted in 1919 for valuable services in connection with the transport of troops.

Each ship could accommodate a maximum of sixty-four lifeboats. However, only 20 boats were installed on *RMS Olympic* and *RMS Titanic* during construction to avoid cluttering the deck and provide more space for passengers. Shipbuilders of the era envisaged the ocean liner itself as the ultimate lifeboat and therefore imagined that a lifeboat's purpose was that of a ferry between a foundering liner and a rescue ship. Despite the low number of lifeboats, both *RMS Olympic* and *RMS Titanic* exceeded Board of Trade regulations of the time. Following the sinking of *RMS Titanic*, more lifeboats were added to *RMS Olympic*.

*RMS Olympic* was the largest transatlantic ocean liner in the world for two periods during 1911–13, interrupted only by the brief tenure of the slightly larger *RMS Titanic*, and then outsized by *SS Imperator*. *RMS Olympic* regained the title of the biggest British built ship ever constructed and held the title until the commissioning of *RMS Queen Mary* in 1936. She was built by Harland & Wolff in Belfast, Ireland during the early 20th century. The maiden voyage was captained by Edward Smith who would lose his life in the *RMS Titanic* disaster. Designer Thomas Andrews was also present for the passage to New York and return, along with a number of engineers, as part of Harland and Wolff's "Guarantee Group" to spot any problems or areas for improvement. Andrews would also lose his life in the *RMS Titanic* disaster.

    Spencer boarded the *RMS Olympic* to take him home to New York. Once aboard the ship, Spencer was led by a steward through one of the three elevators behind the lavish Grand Staircase on to his luxurious cabin, a stateroom equipped with private bathroom on B Deck on the starboard side. The steward told him he can have his meals in the ship's large and luxurious dining room, in the more intimate A La Carte Restaurant or at the Café Parisian giving the first class passengers more options for their dining pleasure. He deposited his small suitcases and made sure his trunks and shoe case had arrived. He thanked the steward, gave him a tip before he left. He tested the locks on his suitcases and trunks and then went back out to join the crowd on the A deck promenade which was wide open along its whole length.
    He went up the Grand Staircase with two rows of stairs bisected by a middle railing, at the foot of which stood a statue of a putti on a plinth holding a torch lamp. There was a set of sweeping railings above a fancy grillwork starting from the newel of carved acanthus leaves. At the center of the top landing surrounded by paneled walls below the domed ceiling stood prominently an elaborate niche for a wall clock. This type of Grand Staircase was built only for the Olympic-class ships, along with three elevators that ran behind the staircase down to E deck.

He saw family and friends of passengers were allowed easy access to come aboard without question to see passengers off. He looked out to sea and it was rough and metal gray. He wished it was better weather to cross the Atlantic. But it couldn't be helped. Weather was always unpredictable and so was life. You could not know what would happen next. It happened to him just as suddenly as the weather changed. He had not envisaged coming back to New York this year although once in a while he missed home and wanted to go back. He still could not believe that within a matter of days, he would be in New York.

As the whistle blew and the stewards ordered the visitors to disembark, Spencer began to relax, knowing he would be home in six days. He was totally drained, mentally and physically. The last few days were hectic trying to get everything in order before his unexpected departure. The break-off of his lease to his home at Knightsbridge was left to the care of his London solicitor, the shipment of his belongings to New York which he gave instructions to Mr. Granger on what to ship and the rest given away, his bank account to be closed, all those had to be taken care of. He sought the help of some trusted friends to help him out with the details of his leave-taking. He found a job for Mr. Granger and his wife and gave them a hefty bonus for which they were grateful and they wished him good luck and safe crossing.

Leaving England was a hard thing for him to do. He was getting used to a life of leisure. He loved the English countryside and he was fascinated with the English ladies of the aristocracy. With his impressive credentials, a man with deep pockets and good looks, he was constantly invited to parties and mothers of the English young ladies were vying for his attention to get him to their parties to be introduced to their daughters. As his association with the British high society broadened, he found English women were more reserved than their American counterpart but no one seemed to capture his heart. He did not think he had found the right woman to share his life. He was having such a grand time and did not want to be tied down with anyone. Still the invitations kept on coming and at the start of the London Season, he was incessantly being invited to fancy balls.

Spencer was glad to be able to book a passage to New York on the *RMS Olympic*. So in a cloudy spring afternoon in early April 1927, Spencer stood with his face toward the wind, gripping the rail of the *RMS Olympic* as it set sail from the White Star piers of Southampton. With the wind blowing vigorously, he looked sad and nostalgic about leaving. He knew it would be a long time before he would set foot on English soil again if ever.

As the *RMS Olympic* steamed on, the usual shipboard tedium began to set in, and meals became increasingly important. On the first day of the voyage, passengers had to adapt themselves to their assigned table mates or dined alone. Unaccompanied travelers, like Spencer, faced the prospect of being seated among tiresome souls with whom they had nothing in common. One would likely met a pleasant fellow or beautiful maiden if one was lucky. Sparks could ignite and romance got kindled or one got dumped. If you're unlucky, you could encounter a boor and be miserable the entire voyage. But the food was always good and plentiful, even in third class. In first class, the food was beyond good. It was lavish. First-class passengers were offered soups, hors d'oeuvres, and a multitude of entrees and desserts at each meal.

The ship was supplied with plenty of liquor - several cases of Canadian Club Whiskey, Black & White Whiskey, Plymouth Gin, French red wine, Chablis, and barrels of stout and ale. Passengers drank and smoked a lot, a significant source of profit for the White Star Line. There were thousands of cigarettes and cigars from Havana, Manila and the United States. For the many passengers who brought pipes, there were several hundred pounds of loose tobacco in 4-ounce tins. Some passengers also brought their own. During the voyage, the scent of combusted tobacco was ever present, especially after dinner.

Spencer did not mind sitting with strangers at his assigned table. It was one way to meet some new acquaintances. It was on his second night at sea when he was having dinner with a new group of passengers when all of a sudden, someone said, 'Either I am getting a little drunk or it is getting rough.' They looked at each other and found themselves leaning sideways in their chairs. There was a crash and sound of falling cutlery, and on their table the wine glass all together toppled and rolled over, while each of them steadied the plate and forks and looked at one another with expressions of deep horror.
Silence followed the crash, then a high, nervous babble of laughter. Stewards laid napkins on the pools of spilt wine. They tried to resume the conversation, but all were waiting as the next great blow and it came heavier than the last. The ship rocked from side to side. Some women in their table started rising and saying good-night. The dining room was emptying fast.
Another climb, another drop. The stewards were at work straightening things up, shutting things down and putting away unstable items. Spencer left with two couples and aimed for the lounge. On their way to the lounge they had to cling to a pillar. It was almost deserted when they got there. The band played but no one danced. There were a few passengers reading books, a few playing bridge, some men drinking brandy and smoking cigars but most of the guests had disappeared to their cabin. Then the two couples decided it was time to call it a day and Spencer was left alone there. He decided to walk around the ship on one of the covered decks where the wind howled and the

spray leaped up from the darkness and smashed white and brown liquid against the glass screen. Then he decided he might as well go to bed.

He went to his cabin with the boat swaying back and forth. It was no better in his cabin. He did not sleep well that night. He turned with each swing and twist of the ship. She was rolling now as well as pitching and his head rang with every creak and thud. All he could think of was the *RMS Titanic* and hope and pray to make it to New York.

The next day, the wind had dropped a little but it was still blowing hard and there was a very heavy swell. Spencer decided to go to breakfast. He went around the promenade but it was hard going. When the ship rolled heavily, he held on to the rail. He could see the grey sky and the black water outside. The howl of the wind was now subdued. There were few people about that day. Only the brave souls were about but they did nothing except sit rather glumly in their armchairs, drank occasionally and exchanged congratulations on not being seasick. A web of life lines had been stretched across the lounge, and they seemed like boxers, roped into the ring.

By the fourth day at sea, the wind calmed down. The sun came up and passengers came out strolling on the deck. For the most part of the days remaining at sea, Spencer wanted to be alone till dinnertime. He would sit on deck with a steamer rug over his shoulders reading or just staring at sea and wondering what lay ahead in his future. He would give some extra cash to the steward to obtain him a good seat. The quality of mid-ocean wind and sun was curiously invigorating. Sometimes, he would take a break from reading and enjoyed watching some of the games being played on deck during the daytime. He found it quite entertaining and relieved some of the boredom he found agonizing.

In the evening, there were concerts and talent shows in the first class lounge. The room was large and warm, and carpeted in maroon and beige with two grey marble fireplaces with curved mantelpiece in the front and rear walls and a curb of a pierced scroll-and-shell pattern. The lounge was described as "a magnificent salon, pronounced by many persons as the finest room ever built into a ship. It is more suggestive of a state apartment in a palace than a room on shipboard." The room was decorated in the Louis XV style based on interiors at the Palace of Versailles. The walls were paneled with finest English oak carved with delicate *boiseries* decorated with scrolled floral-and-shell ornamentation. At the entrance to the First Class restaurant, there was a revolving door, a feature that only appeared on *RMS Olympic*, which needed a way of keeping sea breezes out of the room.

As the days passed, he began to enjoy his voyage more and more, and found acquaintances such as one does on an ocean crossing. Unhappily, the voyage was nearing its end. Before the crossing was over, Spencer Wentworth like most young people in first class had discovered that third lounge was far livelier than the stuffy respectability of their own public rooms. All the most attractive girls in the ship seemed to be in third class and they were having more fun at their party. However, just as the young men in first class were trying to go to the third class, some bold young passengers from the third class were trying to sneak into the first class. All they needed was a dinner jacket and the audacity to break the barrier.

How ironic could that be? Spencer began to see the difference between the social strata of society. He was never exposed to this situation before. The things that he took for granted, he found out was very important to some young people. He also discovered that the less privileged class had more fun in life that the upper class.

Spencer together with a couple of young men of his age found some young men from the third class to trade places and so they sneaked in to the third class. It was awkward at first but as the music got louder and livelier, they forgot their inhibition and joined in the fun. The dance got wilder as the evening progressed. By the time, they left the third class and met their counterparts to retrieve their jackets, Spencer could not care less if he got his jacket back. He had the most wonderful time of his life which he would always remember.

## Chapter 3

As the *RMS Olympic* continued on its way toward the New York Harbor, Spencer Wentworth crossed the huge hall with its luxurious carpeting and splendidly decorated for the first class passenger. He aimed toward the door leading to the outside deck where he would join some first class passengers enjoying the last few nautical miles of the voyage. As the ship entered the New York harbor, the fog was low but not as thick as the fog that enveloped London when he left his London home to come back to New York. Spencer could barely see the outline of the Statue of Liberty. He still could not hear the pulse of this astounding city from across the water.

Half an hour before sunrise, New York, the most garish of the Atlantic ports, was beautiful as seen in the distance from the waters of the harbor with the fine mist softening the outlines of the new modern tall buildings. No city port in the world could compare to New York Harbor against the magnificent backdrop of the new towering superstructures that dominated the landscape. It was an impressive sight to behold as you enter the harbor.

The foghorn whistled and he knew they finally arrived and he would be in Meadow Brook soon.

Meadow Brook . . . Yes, Meadow Brook and *Wentworth Hall*, his childhood home.

Spencer sighed with relief that they made it to New York unscathed in spite of the one-night storm across the sea. He was glad to be coming back home to *Wentworth Hall,* the 40-room mansion on over 500-acre estate built by his grandfather. He could not wait to know what was so urgent that their family's lawyer, Alistair Prescott, summoned him to come home.

Alistair Prescott, their family's attorney, began his career at a small law firm but rose to prominence when he opened his own law firm and became the counsel for some of the famous business magnates who lived in the area on huge estates on the North Shore of Long Island during what was known as the Gilded Age. These businessmen owned palatial residences propelled by the tremendous fortunes earned in railroads, shipping, steel, oil and coal. Alistair Prescott also represented some of the old money, names who occupied pages of the Social Register like the Wentworths. Alistair Prescott lived nearby in a 20-room brick house on 100-acre spread in Cove Meadow named "The Lilac Walk" appropriately named for all the lilacs grown along the driveway.

The New York harbor was busy more than ever with the bustling sound and activities as when Spencer left home three years ago. New York was still beastly loud and fast. New York, the least smoky of big cities was just beginning to stir up, suddenly awake. The water was opalescent under a gray sky, cool and dim, slightly ruffled by wind that followed the ships from the sea. A few streamers of smoke flew above the city. The body of water was large and so the rising skyline did not appear to be towering above one as when they looked up close by from the street. The impression was of long buildings stretching down to the water's edge on every side, and countless low black wharves and piers. But as you get closer, they grew and grew until they seemed to soar up into the heaven. Tugs, steamers, ferry boats, sailing boats spread near the harbor as the *RMS Olympic* entered the harbor with the superb maneuver of a skilled captain of an ocean liner. A New York Port Authority tugboat came out to join them and guided the *RMS Olympic* safely to its berth. Amidst the beauty of the majestic building and the silver expanse of the water, the city seemed like a fairyland until you looked down at the water closely and instantly you knew that New York was real and dirty with all kinds of debris floating by.

New York was noisy and frantic like all big cities. The noise, bustle and frenzied pace of everything made Spencer realize that New York was quite different than the other cities he had visited in Europe. It was this frenetic activity which made New York vibrant and appealing to the best and brightest of the world and contributed to it being the financial and intellectual capital of the United States. From the rich diversity of its inhabitants and the new immigrants coming from Europe contributing to its vitality, New York would set the pace for

American and global change. It was in New York that everything seemed possible through modern thinking emancipated from Victorian restrictions by the "war to end all wars". Population changed with new immigrants coming in, and of vast importance, the economic boom. Along with these catalysts was the arrival of modern technology that brought about the bicycle, Model T, radio, electricity, electric appliances, motion pictures and towering skyscrapers.

    Spencer took the Grand Staircase to the lower deck where several passengers were streaming to get off the ship to be reunited with welcoming friends and relatives. He went down the gangway alongside those passengers on the first class. Once they stepped on to the dockside, they headed towards Immigration where Spencer joined a long line of passengers. As he came out of Immigration with so many passengers milling around, he wound his way toward the crowd looking for Paul Conley, his family chauffeur. With a multitude of people around, it took him a while to find Paul who had been waiting for him outside the custom section of the terminal.

    Paul Conley was dressed in his chauffeur's uniform of khaki with black trim and his chauffeur's hat complete with white gloves. He had a few wrinkle lines on his forehead but his facial expression was the same. He looked almost the same as Spencer remembered him. He was still the most jovial man he knew.

    "Hello, Mr. Spencer." Paul saw him and greeted him, always with his first name. When he was a young lad, Paul used to address him Master Spencer.

    Paul Conley was an older man, now in his fifties, and had been in service with the family as far as Spencer could remember. He was of Irish descent and spoke with his Irish brogue which was endearing. He and his wife were the oldest members of his family's downstairs staff. His wife was the cook and they lived in the chauffeur's cottage on the Wentworth estate in Meadow Brook.

"Hello, Paul," Spencer greeted the chauffeur and they shook hands. "How are you? How's everything at home?"

"I'm fine, Mr. Spencer. How are you? Everything is fine at home. The cook can't wait to serve you your favorite desert."

"The chocolate soufflé! Mrs. Conley made it so perfectly. I can almost smell and taste it now. I'm glad to be back."

"She knows you like it so much so she made it today for your homecoming. We missed you, Mr. Spencer. You're away too long."

"I know. It seems ages and I was ready to come home anyway when I got the telegram from Mr. Prescott."

A boat steward in his white uniform was coming in their direction with a couple of Louis Vuitton trunks with S.A.W. initials on it. Paul saw him pushing a trolley with a couple of trunks Pointing to the boat steward coming their way, Paul asked, "Mr. Spencer, are those your trunks?"

Spencer turned around and saw the boat steward with a couple of trunks. He looked at the trunks and saw his initials on it. *S.A.W.* for Spencer Ashforth Wentworth. "A" stands for Ashforth, his mother's maiden name and his middle name. He wanted to make sure they were his. With so many Louis Vuitton trunks on board the ship, you never knew which one was yours.

He nodded. "Yes, they are mine," he said to Paul.

Spencer motioned to the boat steward.

"You may leave them here," Spencer said.

The steward was about to place the trunks next to Spencer. He looked at Paul and said, "I can take them to your car, sir, if you want. Where are you parked?"

"Over there." Paul pointed to a parked Green Model "A" Town Car. They all walked together to the waiting car. Paul and the boat steward put the Louis Vuitton trunks on the rear of the car.

Spencer took some money from his pocket and gave the boat steward a tip.

"Thank you, sir," the boat steward said.

"You're welcome."

"Good day, sir."

"Good day and thank you."

Spencer hopped on the passenger seat in back of the car and Paul took his driver's seat. Spencer could smell the newness of the car.

"How long have you driven this car?" he asked Paul.

"Just a month, Mr. Spencer. It just came out of the factory. Your father was one of the few lucky ones to purchase it. Ford just introduced it in February."

"Great looking car."

"It is and it drives beautifully."

They drove through New York City. They had only gone few blocks from the terminal and already the city was teeming with activity. All around them, people moved fast and heedless of the traffic. Men darted in and out hurriedly across intersections, dodging oncoming cars and carriages. A man entered a coffee house with a newspaper tucked under his arm and they could smell coffee roasting and biscuits baking from the street. Another man came out of the coffee house eating his sandwich as he walked briskly toward his destination. A woman wearing a fancy hat and carrying a shopping bag came out of a store and walked fast. Spencer kept reminding himself that this was New York, his hometown where everyone was in a hurry.

As they drove their way up Tenth Avenue, they saw vast freight yards and factories that lined the street and the frenzied activities around them. Teams of horses drew huge rolls of paper to printers' shops or bales of cotton and wool to textile mills. They passed slaughterhouses with their malodorous smell as well as soap factories with their dizzying fragrance. There were delivery men loading their wagon with newly made home furnishings. They heard the men shouting orders to one another in various accents like a bubbling Babylonian in the Bible. In spite of their bustling activities, New York was nothing like London. It was still young, a new city where every street and building spoke of speed and modern ways. It was the city of the future, a city of commerce. The new buildings with their soaring architecture bespoke of progress and ambitious goals.

Ahead of them, a wagon laden with building materials moved so slowly heading for uptown where most construction was going on. They heard more cursing and yelling from drivers as they fought their way through Eight Avenue into midtown. Slowly, the factories had now given way to neat, well-kept shops and huge houses. New mansions were sprouting everywhere. Spencer's family owned one of these big mansions on Fifth Avenue. The house stood back from the avenue and was approached by wide steps leading to an iron-grilled entrance. Spencer was not going to his home in the city but going straight to Meadow Brook. His family wanted him home at *Wentworth Hall* in Meadow Brook.

They drove to the Queensborough Bridge which was built just over ten years ago, into Long Island under a light shower. Spencer caught a glimpse of the Steinway Piano Factory sign. They passed wagons carrying newly minted pianos from Steinway Piano Factory for delivery to Long Island customers with new found money. Paul slowed down, then picked up speed the moment they reached the Frederick Floyd Parkway, the road leading to Long Island.

As the green Model "A" Town Car roared up the Frederick Floyd Parkway, the rain had stopped and the sun began to filter through the gray clouds. Paul, the Wentworth chauffeur for some twenty plus years, knew the road like the palm of his hand, anticipating the bumps and twists, slowing when necessary and picking up speed when there was a clear stretch of road before them. Spencer gazed dully at the surrounding landscape. His mind turned to the telegram he received from his family's attorney. *Why did the attorney want him home? What was so pressing that he had to come home immediately?* The answer, he would soon find out. Alistair Prescott did not explain. Spencer was intrigued and the timing was right. He was getting tired of London and was wanting to go home anyway.

Paul drove quickly along the parkway and after an hour, they were already well beyond Mineola and headed toward Westbury and making good time. The traffic now was relatively light. Spencer settled back in his seat and closed his eyes. In an hour, he would be home in Meadow Brook. They passed Westbury into Jericho, past the Meadow Brook Country Club where his parents and other members of his family enjoyed watching the polo matches or went fox hunting.

Meadow Brook was a wealthy village in the town of Oyster Bay. It was located between Jericho to the south and Oyster Bay to the north. In the last century, Meadow Brook was a farm and woodland backwater but changed drastically as wealthy millionaires built immense estates in and around Meadow Brook with sweeping vistas and a whole cadre of servants to maintain the high standard of living. By the mid-1920s, there were so many huge estates in Meadow Brook, a part of what would become the North Shore Gold Coast. The North Shore is the area along Long Island's northern coast, bordering Long Island Sound where the terrain is hilly and the beaches more rocky than the flat land and sandy beaches of the South Shore. The South Shore is the area along the Long Island's Atlantic Ocean shoreline.

A couple of miles further north, they entered an imposing gate, one of the largest set of eighteenth century iron gates in Long Island. This one of a kind gate was imported from England when the senior George Wentworth, Spencer's grandfather, built his house here surrounded by over 500 acres of rolling landscape. Since England encountered hard times after World War I, some of these national treasures of England found their way onto American soil into the hands of wealthy Americans amidst some protests from the British. The intricate design of the magnificent gate was superbly crafted by skilled artisans, there was no mistake about it. There was a big "W" on the top of the gate with both the beginning and end of the letter turning in a curlicue like the swirling curve of an unfurling fern frond.

They entered the gatehouse, a brick building with an arch opening in the center acting as *porte cochere*. There were four mullioned windows on either side of the arch. The arch had a keystone at the center on top which gave it an elegant look. At the top of the roof in the center of the building was a cupola, a widow's walk with railing around it and two chimney pieces on both ends of the roof. A trio of dormer windows with the eaves looking like eyebrows stared at you as you arrived. A moulding of egg and dart design graced the eaves. There were some plantings of shrubs and trees on both sides of the driveway leading to the gatehouse.

They continued the two-mile drive, with the road twisting and turning like an enchanted ribbon as they went along. They passed long meadows with grass swaying in the wind. In the distance some trees, oak, maples, hemlock, elm and pine trees were scattered about. They passed a colonnade of trees whose branches nodded and intertwined with one another and formed a canopy and darkened the drive. Then the drive opened up to a clearing. They drove through rows of pleached hornbeam trees shorn to perfection as they neared the house leading to the cobbled courtyard of *Wentworth Hall*.

"Mr. Spencer?" Paul slowed the car and glanced at the mirror.

"Yes, Paul. What is it?"

"I just realized you haven't seen the house with the new extension. The house that you knew had tripled in size."

"No, I haven't."

"You'll love it. Your grandfather extended the house right after you left for England. He had in mind a large and impressive estate just like those you see in England. Since the house sits on the highest elevation on the estate, it looks magnificent. The architect made it look like it had been there all the time. I mean the addition blends in beautifully with the original house. You'd think it was always there. He added an indoor tennis & swimming pavilion, several holes of golf on the property, a U-shaped carriage house for his five Rolls Royces and enlarged the gardens."

"Really? Leave it to Grandfather."

"He hired Delano & Aldrich, the New York architects to do the extensive renovation and extension to the original house. They did a wonderful job."

"What happened with Warren & Wetmore who built the house in 1904?"

"I don't know, Mr. Spencer. But Delano & Aldrich are designing plenty of houses around the area and I guess your grandfather liked him. I heard Delano and Aldrich was also commissioned by Mr. Egerton Winthrop Jr. down the road to build a house modeled after Mount Vernon, the home of George Washington."

"Well, I guess that says something," Spencer said.

"There has been so much construction lately. All the new millionaires are moving in and building huge houses. Further down the road, there is a French Normandy style home built for Mr. & Mrs. Benjamin Moore just after you left. I understand this one has a moat around the mansion."

"A moat? What for? Did they think they'll be invaded by the Vikings?" Spencer said with a smile on his face. Paul was amused.

Spencer thought for a moment about this new information from Paul. His grandfather wanted to keep up with the Joneses although he didn't have to. His family had been here before all of them. After all, his grandfather was a member of the Sons of the Revolution. Not many people could say that. Maybe he really liked Delano & Aldrich better than Warren & Wetmore with that grandiose design of which they were well known. That includes the chapel at Greenwood Cemetery where most of the notables including his deceased ancestors were buried and which reminded them that his architectural designed structure would be the last thing they would be in before they went to their grave. Also, Warren & Wetmore designs were too ornate and Delano & Aldrich designs were something new and blending the two designs was quite refreshing.

Paul started saying, "You know, your grandfather always thought of you. He always talked about you when I drove him to the city. He thought you'd love the house since you love England very much. He even hired the best landscape architect, Umberto Innocenti, to design the ground to complement the house. Trees, hedges and ponds were arranged to develop walking paths. Various gardens were installed and planted with blooming flowers and shrubs to provide color at all seasons. The result is fabulous. Since the house is so far from the main entrance and sits on top of a hill surrounded by vast tract of rolling land, it really looks magnificent."

"I can't wait to get to see it."

"We're just a few hundred yards away."

Spencer looked out at the surrounding vista and felt a pang of anguish as he thought of his grandfather. He was sad that he missed his funeral. How he wished he was home during his dying days. He wondered what he was thinking when he added the extension. The old house was grand enough as it was. Why add more to it? Paul just mentioned his grandfather said he would like the new home. What does that mean? He didn't see any reason why not.

There were many regions where there were a lot of great estates. Many major cities had great estates like Philadelphia's Main Line, Pittsburgh's North Side, Boston's own North Shore, New York's Westchester County and the Hudson Valley, Fairfield County in Connecticut, Chicago's North Shore and the list goes on but Long Island was definitely where the concentration of them was, especially on the North Shore. East End resort areas and part of the South Shore in Long Island also boasted some magnificent estates. Long Island's natural beauty, its pristine shoreline and ocean beaches, its proximity and easy access to New York City, and its suitability for yachting and other recreational pursuits made it the perfect place for the leisure class. These areas were the pinnacle of grandeur in all style of architecture and the surrounding acreage with its beautiful gardens that only money could buy.

One only had to look in the Social Register and would be amazed at how many of them owned magnificent homes on Long Island and another home on Fifth Avenue in New York City. They owned large estates on Long Island which they called places, some had palaces in Newport which they called cottages, duplexes on Fifth Avenue which they simply called houses. They also lived on the better streets of America's larger cities, and in the more affluent of these cities' suburbs. Prominent families, among them the Astors, the Hearsts, the Morgans, the Vanderbilts, the Whitneys, and many others had built palatial homes on Long Island. Though Newport was probably the most famous gathering place of the American rich, it was Long Island that possessed by far the greatest and most interesting assortment of houses designed for the rich and the super-rich. Here was the playground for the very rich where they indulged in fox hunting and polo games at the Meadow Brook Country

Club, yachting, fishing, aviation, golf, tennis, and duck shooting.

As they rounded the bend, Spencer saw the outline of the house perched on top of a hill. They were almost near the house. As they approached, he saw the magnificent brick structure, a lovely Georgian-style mansion peeking from another wrought iron gate flanked on both sides with a brick pillar topped by a round ball and high yew hedges flanking the gate. He could see the brick façade with its fluid lines and classical proportions that gave it such perfect balance. Two pairs of magnificent reeded columns of the Corinthian order capitals flanked an archway of the handsome portico with wide marble front steps. There were several chimneypieces protruding from the rooftop of the central building and many more from the adjacent wings. The house with its symmetrical design had an identical wing on both sides. Few steps to the portico lead to the central entrance hall. There were numerous tall shining windows, looking out onto fine green lawns and gardens.

They reached the cobbled courtyard of *Wentworth Hall*. The car drew to a halt in front of the steps leading up to the massive front doors. Spencer looked up at the three-story center block of the house flanked by two large wings. The whole house was rendered in brick and roofed with slate. He peeked through the car window and spoke to Paul.

"Good Lord, I know what you mean. I feel like I haven't left England." He laughed.

"That's it, sir. The inside is as grand as the outside. Your grandfather said it's like an English country estate."

"Well, it sure looks like one."

## Chapter 4

There was a chill in the air though the sun was a golden orb in a clear blue sky. The early daffodils with their bright yellow petals were swaying against the clipped green lawns that rolled down to a nearby pond. Spencer drew in a breath of fresh air. He smelled the sweet fragrance of spring bulbs heralding spring after a hard winter. It rained earlier in the day and even if it was almost noon, the dew from the shrubs gave an iridescent quality in a cool spring day. Spencer looked up at the house and could not help admiring its majestic grandeur surrounded by acres of rolling meadow, gardens and rare specimens of trees just like Paul had told him earlier. The brick façade, flat balustraded roof, five-bay central block flanked by extended bay on each side, with mullioned windows looking more Elizabethan than Georgian architecture made him feel like he had never left England.

As soon as Paul parked the car in front of the portico, the massive front door opened and a few members of the household staff came out to welcome him. They formed a semi-circle in front of the front steps. Spencer saw his mother, Margaret Wentworth in her morning dress with his father, George Wentworth Jr. in his morning coat came out of the house. Following them was the butler with two footmen. Paul went around the car and opened the car door and Spencer stepped out. He smiled and nodded to the servants and walked towards his mother who was standing by the front stone steps with his father by her side. She looked him up and down and saw the changes in him. He was now a full grown man, not the young man who went abroad three years ago. Spencer saw his mother had not changed. She still had the slim figure. His father had put on a little weight.

"Welcome home. It's good to see you back," his mother said. Spencer kissed his mother on the cheek and they both embraced tightly. She then took a step back in order to look Spencer over. His mother thought he looked more serious and cosmopolitan now than when he left.

"You look wonderful," she said.

"Thank you, Mother," Spencer said with a smile.

She looked at her husband who was watching his son and appraising him too with keen interest. Spencer turned to his father and gave him a handshake and then hugged him.

"Welcome home, son," his father said as he released Spencer from his embrace.

"I'm glad to be back. It has been a long time," Spencer said.

Both his parents smiled. His mother came to the conclusion that living abroad or away from one's parents could change any child when they left their nest. They grew up pretty fast. His father thought the same thing.

Spencer looked around and did not see his younger sister. "Where is Emma? Is she home? I was expecting to see her here today to welcome me."

"She's with some friends in Bar Harbor. She apologized she could not be here today but she'll be back this weekend," his mother said. He was a bit disappointed but he let it pass.

"How's everything? The house looks magnificent."

"Very well. Come on inside," George said.

George led him inside as the servants went back to their posts and the footmen gathered his trunks and suitcases to bring inside the house. He heard the butler, Mr. Yates, told the two footmen, Frank and John, to bring them upstairs to his bedroom.

They walked into the huge entrance hall, a room with black and white marble tiled floor and a majestic Waterford crystal chandelier hanging from the lofty ceiling, the light dancing on the multifaceted glass. There was a large marble-topped French commode by the front door with fresh arrangements of spring flowers and a small silver tray for calling cards. Above the table was a Neoclassical mirror flanked by two carved wooden brackets with Chinese porcelain jars on them. As they entered, Spencer stopped and looked around. He saw the great curving staircase leading to the upper floors on the left side of the entrance hall. It was a relief to see that it was not altered with the latest renovation. He simply loved the staircase where he used to slide down on the banister when he was a youngster.

George Wentworth saw the look on his face. "You can go to your room later," George said and led them straight to the drawing room, a gracious room with its understated elegance and good taste, the kind of understatement that could only be achieved by a skillful eye for the very best in American furniture and furnishings, someone who has a vast knowledge of American antiques and know how to use them to their best advantage. The dark polished floor gleamed against the magnificent silk Heriz carpet with muted colors in the center of the room. The drawing room with wallpaper of cabbage rose on a trellis design on the palest of yellow background gave the whole room a sunny, airy feeling of one enclosed in a garden. It was a very comfortable room for anyone to linger and relax.

 Two long sofas, facing each other across a butler's tray table in front of the fireplace, were covered in romantic chintz with beautiful roses of soft pink, and butter yellow on a white background carrying the rose motif from the wallpaper. The Pembroke tables at each end of the sofa held priceless crystal lamps with pale cream pleated shades of the finest silk and rare porcelain bowls filled with fresh spring nosegays of yellow jonquils and blue hyacinths sending their aromatic scents around the room. The Neoclassical fireplace was ornately carved with a caryatid figure on each side and upon it was a pair of antique silver candlesticks holding white candles and in the center was a Cartier's carriage clock. Above the fireplace dominating the wall was an oil landscape painting by Thomas Doughty, one of the artists of the Hudson River School, an artistic movement developed in the United States during a period of roughly fifty years (1825-1875) based on Romanticism and inspired by the wild areas in the vicinity of New York's Hudson River.

 On the further end of the room was a Chippendale cabinet of great beauty, was filled with fine Sevres porcelains. A pair of another landscape painting of the Hudson River School by Thomas Cole graced the wall over a pair of Chippendale chairs upholstered in gold damask flanking the Chippendale cabinet.

Whoever decorated this room had an unerring eye for color and form and skill at placing and arranging furniture which was evident everywhere and yet this was not an extremely feminine room, devoid of useless clutter. It was a gracious drawing room where a man could feel at ease in great comfort amidst its simple beauty.

George Wentworth walked across the room while Spencer and his mother stood by the fireplace. Spencer put his hand near the fireplace to warm them. George Wentworth went to a small console that held crystal glasses and a silver tray of drinks. He picked up three glasses.

George Wentworth turned around and asked his son, "Can I offer you a drink? It's that time of day already. A brandy perhaps."

"I'd love to, Father. A brandy would be great."

He turned to his wife, "Sherry, my dear?"

"Yes, please."

George poured sherry for his wife and brandy for himself and his son. Spencer excused himself from his mother and walked toward his father. He took his mother's and his drink from the console and went back to where he was by the fireplace. George was behind him.

"Welcome home," George said again and raised his glass.

Spencer did the same. "Cheers." His mother smiled and raised her glass too. They all took a sip of their drinks.

George pointed to the sofa and they moved and sat down on the two sofas in front of the fireplace. George sat next to his wife and Spencer sat across the butler tray table on the other sofa. Spencer suddenly realized that Prohibition was in effect. He wondered where his parent got the liquor.

Spencer looked at his drink and asked his father, "How did you get this?"

George knew what Spencer was thinking. "We have the right connections. We know where to get them."

"Isn't that too dangerous?"

"Only if you get caught."

Spencer wanted to argue but decided not to. He needed that drink anyway. He took another sip of his brandy.

"How did the Prohibition come about?" He asked his father.

"If you remember although you may not since you were still at prep school on your last year. It was Jan. 16, 1920. Every saloon in the United States was legally abolished and the manufacture, importation, and sale of intoxicating liquors for beverage purposes were prohibited. This was the result of a battle waged for over two centuries."

"We were not really paying attention at that time," Spencer said.

"If I go back in history, the first laws in America against the use of intoxicating liquors was made in Massachusetts in 1639, and at about the same time in Connecticut. Governor Oglethorpe in 1733 had the importation of rum into Georgia prohibited, as well as the importation of slaves. Then in 1774 the first Continental Congress proposed to the different states the passage of laws to stop the distilling of liquors. Even the United States army got into the act and changed the ration of "grog" to coffee in 1832," George said and took a swig of his drink.

"Really? That's terrible for the soldiers. I bet you they did not like that one bit," Spencer said smiling.

"No, they did not but they had no choice in the matter," George said. "At about the same time laws were passed in some states requiring a license for the sale of liquor. There were other efforts to pass prohibition laws over the years but were soon repealed. In recent years the liquor problem has been seriously considered in all parts of the world." George took another sip of his brandy.

How was it in England?" Margaret asked.

"There seemed to be no problem at least for me. Where ever I went, I could get a drink, granted it was mostly on country homes of my acquaintances," Spencer said looking at his mother.

"I don't think we had a problem at private homes. The saloon is a different matter. Besides, saloons are more and more regarded as a nuisance and a danger to society and the state," George said, then continued. "In 1908 it was enacted that after 1922 the saloons in Great Britain could be closed without paying the owners for loss of license, and that the magistrates could close as many saloons as they saw fit."

"That would be difficult since the British like their pubs," Spencer said.

"Well, here in the United States the Anti-Saloon League has taken the lead in the campaign since 1903, its platform - the suppression of the saloon. It had the support of both total abstinence believers, and also those who, while not total abstainers, are convinced of the evils and dangers of the saloon." He paused, seemed to think harder. "Then on December 17, 1917, Congress passed what is known as the Webb resolution submitting to the states an amendment to the Federal Constitution providing for national prohibition. Mississippi was the first state to ratify followed by other states until the required 36 states had ratified, making the law effective on January 16. 1920."

Margaret said, "With the passage of the Eighteenth Amendment, the sale of alcohol in America was made illegal. However, the Mafia both in New York and Chicago became kings of crime by filling the public's bottomless highball glasses and teacups in clandestine speakeasies with 'hooch'."

"That's absolutely fascinating. Anyway, I'm glad you have some liquor in the house," Spencer said.

"You just have to know where to get it," his father said.

Spencer turned to his mother and said, "I can't tell you enough how great it is to be home again."

"We missed you very much," his mother said.

They heard a soft knock and Mr. Yates entered the drawing room. "What is it, Yates?" Margaret Wentworth asked the butler.

"When do you want us to serve lunch, ma'am?"

She turned to Spencer and asked, "Is 1 o'clock good for you? It will give you time to relax and change your clothes."

"That will be fine," Spencer said.

"Very well, ma'am," Yates said.

"Thank you, Yates." Yates turned around and closed the door softly. He hurried back into the kitchen and gave the order to Mrs. Conley, the cook.

After Mr. Yates left the room, George Wentworth turned to Spencer, "How was the crossing? Hope you did not encounter a bad weather."

"Yes, we did as a matter of fact. On our second night at sea. I met some very interesting people on the ship before we hit the rough seas. It was terrifying."

"Really?"

"When passengers started leaving the dining room, I decided to do the same and headed to my cabin."

"That was smart," his mother said.

"But it was no better in my cabin. The ship was rocking violently. I did not sleep well that night. All I could think of was the *Titanic* and hope to make it to New York."

"That was awful," his father said.

His mother put her hands on her month.

"Do you know that your ship, the *Olympic* almost rescued the *Titanic*?" George said.

"How?" Spencer knotted his brow in disbelief.

"When *Olympic* was about 100 nautical miles away from *Titanic*'s last known position, she received a message from

Captain Rostron, the captain of Cunard Liner *Carpathia*, explaining that continuing on course to *Titanic* would gain nothing, telling the captain of the *Olympic*, 'All boats were accounted for. About 675 souls saved.' Rostron requested that the message be forwarded to White Star and Cunard. He said that he was returning to harbor in New York. When *Olympic* offered to take on the survivors, she was heatedly turned down by an appalled Rostron, who was concerned that it would cause panic amongst the survivors of the disaster to see a virtual mirror-image of the *Titanic* appear and ask them to board. *Olympic* then resumed her voyage to Southampton, with all concerts cancelled as a mark of respect, arriving on April 21."

"I did not know that. That was terrible rejecting *Olympic's* offer to help since she was close by." Spencer was shocked to hear that.

"But something good came out of that disaster," George said.

"I know," Spencer said, aware of that. "Apparently, White Star withdrew *Olympic* from service and returned her to her builders at Belfast to be refitted to incorporate lessons learned from the *Titanic's* disaster 6 months prior, and improve safety. Besides increasing the numbers of lifeboats, they corrected a flaw in the original design in which the bulkheads only rose up as far as E or D-Deck, a short distance above the waterline."

"That flaw had been exposed during *Titanic's* sinking, where water spilled over the top of the bulkheads as the ship sank and flooded subsequent compartments," George said.

"Yes." Spencer said. "In addition, an extra bulkhead was added to subdivide the electrical dynamo room, bringing the total number of watertight compartments to seventeen. I understand improvements were also made to the ship's pumping apparatus. These modifications meant that *Olympic* could survive a collision similar to that of *Titanic* and the ship could remain afloat." Spencer rubbed both his hands on the snifter. He stood up and placed his glass on the marble mantelpiece and put his hands close to the fire to warm them up.

"You said, you met some interesting people on the ship. Anyone I know?"

"Yes, a Wall Street fellow named Bloomberg. I have to go to the city later this week and have lunch with him. I asked him to meet me at the Knickerbocker. Will there be a problem to take him there, he being Jewish? " Spencer looked at his father and see what he would say. He remembered when they used to go to the city, his father always went to the Knickerbocker Club. His family had been a long time member.

"No problem if you take him. I'll let them know to include you in my account."

"Thank you."

His mother looking at Spencer's outfit asked, "Will you change before we have lunch, my dear?" It was more a command than a question. He was in his traveling clothes and he knew he had to change. He could not possibly sit down to lunch wearing his travel outfit. That would be deplorable. His mother would be horrified.

His father nodded his head and said, "You may go check your room now and freshen up a bit and change."

Spencer stood up. "I think I better do that right now. I will change into something more comfortable."

"Splendid idea. Then after lunch we can show you the grounds," his mother said. "We're putting you in the last room on the east wing facing south. You'll have a fantastic view of the grounds. You might even see the ocean from your room on a clear day. It was really built with you in mind. See if you like it."

"Fabulous. Let me go and check it out."

Spencer picked up his glass, took another gulp of his brandy, put the glass back on the coffee table and walked out of the drawing room. He felt the exhilarated comfort and pleasure of being back home with his family at *Wentworth Hall*. He walked towards the curving stairway to the second floor. On top of the stairway, he turned left and walked down the long corridor passing through rows of bedroom doors towards the end. A selection of rare hunting prints graced the wall of the hallway, obviously the favorite pastime of the family. He walked into his bedroom with lofty oyster white ceilings and bluish gray paint on its wall. It felt soothing and restful to his senses. The curtain was pulled back and the room was filled with light and airiness. A slight breeze was coming through the wide opened window facing south. He looked down and saw the Japanese garden just below his window. A parterre was laid down just beyond it with its central axis directly opposite the terrace by the drawing room. Spring flowers were abloom. Hyacinth, tulips, daffodils and scillas were all vying for attention. The roses and perennials were just beginning to green up. He looked further and could see the whole of South Shore toward the ocean.

He noticed the trunks were already empty with his clothes hanging in the closet in the adjoining dressing room. He was astounded at the efficiency of the staff.

To keep a big house like *Wentworth Hall*, the owner had to hire a cadre of servants to maintain the house in tip-top condition. The butler was the head man among the staff. Then there were under butler, footmen and the housekeeper. The housekeeper was equal to the butler and was the supervisor over all the female servants except the kitchen staff. There were upstairs maids and downstairs maids, laundry maids, and a cook and her helpers. Outside there were the gardeners and crew to take care of the ground and the greenhouse, the stable man and his boys to take care of the stable and the horses and a chauffeur and under chauffeur to drive the master and his family in any of the ten cars in the garage, including five Rolls Royces.

His room just suited him fine. There was a huge mahogany four-poster bed flanked by two mahogany night tables, one on each side. A secretary desk was on one side of the room. There was a fireplace in the Robert Adam style across from the bed where the fire was going to warm the room on this chilly morning. A landscape painting by Turner with its misty greens and clear blues was hanging above the fireplace. A pair of Queen Anne wing chairs in light tan leather and a small table flanked the fireplace. Above the mantelpiece was a bronze equine sculpture by Remington. The room felt comfortable and not stuffy at all.

He glanced at the bed and was tempted to lie down but he decided otherwise. Lunch was just a few minutes away and he better not be tardy on his first day at home. That would not go well with Mrs. Conley, the cook. He washed up a little and quickly changed his clothes. He put on a white shirt, a regimental tie, a tweed jacket and put on his riding breeches. He intended to go riding after his parents gave him a tour of the garden. He looked at himself in the mirror. He looked so white. He needed some tan. His blond hair was straight and finely textured. He brushed it loosely across his shapely head and went back downstairs. His parents came back to the drawing room in a short while after changing for lunch.

In no time, they heard a knock at the door and Mr. Yates walked in. "Lunch is served, ma'am," he said to Margaret.

"Thank you, Yates." The butler turned around and headed toward the dining room. They all got up and walked through an adjoining door into the dining room following Yates who stood by holding the door open and closed it after they entered the room.

The dining room was a lovely room with chinoiserie design wallcovering. It faced the south adjoining the terrace. It was bright and airy and furnished with fine furniture from the three great furniture makers of the eighteenth century. The huge Hepplewhite table was set for three with the finest china and silverware. In the middle of the dining table was a floral arrangement of spring flowers flanked by a pair of silver candelabra with five glittering arms. A Waterford crystal chandelier hung above the dining table. On one side of the room was a mahogany Sheraton sideboard with silver tureen in the middle and knife caddies on each side. Above the sideboard was a Dutch Master still life painting of flowers including roses in a baroque style with swirling brushstrokes of the flowers in its vitality that practically jumped at you when you look at the picture. On the opposite wall, there is a Chippendale cabinet which housed a collection of fine Rose Medallion china. A fireplace with rich detailed carving on its mantelpiece graced another wall. Above it is a convex mirror reflecting images of sparkling silver and crystal against the mellow patinas of the handsome furniture.

As soon as they were seated, the butler and a footman came and served them their lunch of quail eggs, small potatoes and creamed spinach. As they were eating their dessert of chocolate soufflé, Spencer brought up the subject which had been in his mind since he got the telegram in England from Alistair Prescott.

Spencer asked his father, "Do you have any idea on why I was summoned to come home immediately? Prescott did not say much but sounded rather urgent. I was thinking of coming back home soon anyway so it did not matter much to me but I was still curious."

"Well, when your grandfather died, there was a provision on the will for you. The estate is not settled yet and will not be until that provision is taken care of," his father said.

Spencer looked up questioningly at his father, "What kind of provision?"

"Alistair will tell you about it. He has all the details. All I know is everything is held up until your return."

"Then I suppose we have to deal with it as soon as possible," Spencer said matter-of-factly.

"I told Alistair you are coming in today. I invited him to come to dinner tonight so he will see us tonight."

"I guess the sooner the better. I don't have anything planned to do today except maybe go riding around the estate sometime this afternoon. Which horse can I take?" Spencer asked his father.

"I'll tell Yates to ask Robert, our new groom to saddle one for you. Sultan might be good for you. He is a bay stallion which we got only a year ago," his father said.

"Is he temperamental?

"Nothing you can't handle. He's a great horse. You'll love him."

"Thank you, Father."

"What time do you want to go riding?"

"Right after Mother shows me the garden. Say three o'clock." Spencer glanced at his mother who nodded in agreement.

"That would be fine. Consider it done."

They finished dessert, rose from their seats and walked toward the door to the terrace. As they walked down the stairs to the garden, the footmen busied themselves clearing up the dining table and getting the dining room ready for dinner later with the Prescotts.

## Chapter 5

Lilly Prescott dressed in a pale green evening dress and Alistair Prescott dressed in white tie and tails arrived at *Wentworth Hall* at around 7 PM. Mr. Yates welcomed them. Alistair Prescott handed him his briefcase which he handed to Frank, the footman, and told him to take it to the library. Mr. Yates then ushered them to the drawing room where Margaret Wentworth dressed in a light yellow evening dress and George

Wentworth and Spencer Wentworth both in white tie and tails were already having their cocktails.

Mr. Yates tapped the door lightly, opened it and announced their guests. Margaret and George put their drinks down and stood up to greet them. Spencer did the same thing. Mr. Yates stood in the background waiting.

"Hello, Spencer. How are you? Sorry to make you come home so soon," Alistair said as he shook hands with Spencer.

"No problem. I was thinking of coming back anyway. I'm happy to be home," Spencer said.

"You look great," Alistair said.

"Thank you."

"How about a drink?" George asked.

"I'll have vodka martini with a twist," Alistair said.

"Gin and tonic for me," Lilly said.

George looked in the direction of Mr. Yates who nodded and went to the console, took some glasses and made the drinks.

Alistair and Lilly sat on the sofa across from George and Margaret.

Mr. Yates came back with their drinks on a silver tray and handed them to Alistair and Lilly.

"Thank you, Yates," Alistair said.

"You're welcome, sir," Mr. Yates said. He turned to George and said, "Anything else, sir?"

"No, Yates. That's fine. Thank you," George said.

Mr. Yates retreated to the door and quietly left the room.

They clinked glasses and Alistair asked Spencer about his sojourn abroad. Spencer gladly told them about his adventures, all the countries he visited and all the people he met. They found his stories fascinating. The conversation continued at dinner which was served at 7:30 PM. Alistair did not want to bring up the reason for the telegram which Spencer was dying to hear. Spencer knew it was reserved for later.

After dinner, George Wentworth led Alistair Prescott and Spencer into the library while Margaret Wentworth and Lilly Prescott stayed behind.

The library was a great room but rather stark compared to the other rooms in the house. Spencer looked around the library seeing it for the first time after his long absence. It looked the same as he remembered it. This was still an impressive room, baronial in stature with its immense high-flung coffered ceiling and grand proportions, its paneled walls of deep mahogany and its collection of leather-bound editions of literary masterpieces. Books were of the greatest importance to his grandfather and he collected the best of them. To his grandfather, the best room in the house was the library at which he spent most of his days while at *Wentworth Hall.* The floor was made of polished oak. Hand-knotted fine Sarouk Persian rugs of vibrant red and ochre on tan background were spread across the polished wood floor. A pair of comfortable Chesterfield sofas, upholstered in leather of ruby-wine color, was positioned next to the huge marble fireplace with a Carrara marble mantelpiece imported from Italy. Above the mantelpiece was the only picture in the room, a formal oil portrait of Spencer's grandfather, the senior George Wentworth done by one of the best portrait artists of the era. Flanking the fireplace were built-in bookshelves from floor to ceiling containing scholarly tomes. The wall on the west side opened up to the enclosed terrace with hydraulic wall that opened up on three sides. One opened to the south-facing veranda, with a panoramic view of Long Island South Shore all the way to the Atlantic Ocean. Another wall led to steps going down to the Italian garden and the other wall led to the front courtyard. On the far end of the opposite wall, flanking the French door to the terrace were more built-in bookshelves with more leather-bound editions. On the corner was a big globe about 36 inches high, along with a pair of deep Queen Anne wing chairs of dark wine leather matching the upholstery of the Chesterfield sofas across the room. Facing the Queen Anne wing chairs was the mahogany desk and chair that belonged to George Wentworth Sr. A Palladian window behind his grandfather's desk shed some light in an otherwise dark room. On the right of his grandfather's enormous desk stood a refectory table overflowing with newspapers, journals and magazines. Opposite on the other side was a French marble-topped chest serving as a bar which held a silver ice bucket and crystal decanters filled with port and brandy as well as leaded Waterford crystal glasses on a huge silver tray.

    Spencer studied his grandfather's picture above the finest marble fireplace. The picture was staring at him and seemed to be speaking to him. Spencer could not help thinking what his grandfather wanted from him. His grandfather who he always adored had something in store for him and he could not wait to hear it from his attorney. His eyes moved around the room and thought the room had a certain degree of masculine dignity compared to the drawing room where the decoration evoked more feminine graciousness. Like his bedroom, the library reflected man's tastes. His grandfather could have spent most of his time here in the library when he was home in the summer unless they were entertaining guests. In the winter time, the family settled in the city at their Fifth Avenue house and enjoyed the social scene in New York.
    Alistair Prescott was watching Spencer intently. He just thought what a big responsibility he would be handed tonight. Spencer had no idea what the attorney had to say. His father was vague about it when he arrived this morning and the attorney did not say much on the telegram either except it was urgent that he comes home.
    Spencer joined his father at the bar and took his drink from George. Alistair joined them. George handed Alistair his drink.

Then George motioned them towards his desk. Alistair took one of the leather Queen Anne wing chairs and Spencer took the other one while his father sat on the opposite side of his grandfather's desk.

"Cheers." Spencer took the lead and took a sip of his drink. The two older men raised their glasses.

Without preamble, Alistair brought up the subject of the will of George Wentworth Sr. He opened his briefcase and pulled out some papers from it. He cleared his throat, took a glance at George who nodded and started reading it. Spencer gave him his full attention.

Alistair began . . .

"*I, George Wentworth, of Wentworth Hall, Meadow Brook, in Nassau County and State of New York, being of sound mind and body do hereby make, publish and declare this to be my Last Will and Testament, hereby revoking all wills and codicils at any time heretofore made by me.*

*FIRST: A. I give and bequeath to my son . . .*

Alistair paused and both George and Spencer waited. Alistair looked at the paper, then looked at both George and Spencer. "This is such a long document full of legal terminology and it will take me all night to read the more than one hundred pages, word for word. It is easier to tell you in simple language what your father," he looked at George, "and your grandfather," he turned his gaze to Spencer, "wanted to do with his tremendous business holdings, large amount of properties and immeasurable wealth." George and Spencer looked at each other without saying a word and nodded their heads. Alistair turned to Spencer.

"As you know, your grandfather was the chairman of the board of Wentworth Bank which his father founded in 1875. In addition to that, he invested heavily in public utilities and by the time he died, he had accumulated a fortune estimated at almost

$500 million in public utilities, making him one of the wealthiest men in the country."

"I did not know that," Spencer said in awe of his grandfather. He looked at his father who nodded. It never occurred to him that his grandfather was that wealthy. He knew his grandfather was rich but not this rich. He was not really paying much attention to what his grandfather did for a living. All he knew was money was not a problem when he was growing up and he went to the best private school and then to Harvard. When he went abroad, his stipend was always in the bank and he spent it the way he wanted to knowing full well that money would always be there. Now he was stunned at the revelation, the enormous figure of his grandfather's wealth.

"Let me explain to Spencer how his grandfather got his money." Alistair looked at George who nodded. "He knew plenty of rich people and George invested in their businesses and some of them became big depositors in his bank," Alistair Prescott said as if giving a lecture on Business 101. Spencer listened intently. "Your grandfather was a friend to big names in business like J.P. Morgan who lives not far from here."

"That I know," Spencer said. "He built that large mansion in Glen Cove designed by Christopher Grant LaFarge just before I left for Europe."

"That's correct. J.P. Morgan owned J.P. Morgan and Co. and chairman of the board of U. S. Steel Corporation. Your grandfather invested a chunk of money in U.S. Steel and the company did very well and your grandfather made a lot of money."

Spencer smiled and nodded. He picked up his glass and took a swig of his drink.

Alistair continued, "Your father had been appointed the executor of the estate and I as the co-executor. The whole estate was in trust to you except the Fifth Avenue house which goes to your father and five million dollars which goes to your sister."

Spencer opened his mouth but could not speak. He closed it abruptly and stared at Alistair who continued, "The income from the trust will go to your father during his lifetime which could amount to about five million dollars a year. Your grandfather is giving you an outright ten million dollars in cash and the rest goes to the trust. All your grandfather's shares of several utility companies, railroad companies and U. S. Steel Corp. were transferred into the trust in your name."

Spencer rolled his eyes, looked up at the ceiling and could not believe what he was hearing. He kept on shaking his head. The number was staggering. He could not comprehend it thoroughly.

Alistair continued, "He bequeathed the Meadow Brook house, this house, *Wentworth Hall*, and its contents together with its 500 surrounding acres to you with the proviso that your parents can have a lifetime privilege to live in the house. Your father will remain President and Chairman of the board of the Wentworth Bank until such time as your father thinks you are ready to take the helm. You have to learn the banking business from the ground up."

Spencer's head was spinning. He was not expecting this sudden responsibility entrusted to him. He had lived a carefree existence for the last three years and suddenly he was thrust into an enormous task. He was speechless after hearing the news. It did not occur to him that he would get the bulk of his grandfather's estate. He was so sure it would go to his father. Not that his father would go to the poor house, they still could live in both houses at Fifth Avenue and Meadow Brook and five million dollars income a year was not something to sneeze about. But he was given the rest which was enormous. He picked up his drink and emptied his glass. He stood up and went to the bar and poured another one. George and Alistair were watching him pace the room. Then he finally sat back down.

"I could not believe Grandfather gave me the whole thing." He ran his hand through his hair and shook his head.

"Your parents are well provided for. Eventually you'll get it anyway so he decided to do it right now. That way, he knew you would get it." Alistair looked at George who nodded in agreement.

"But Father should have them first," Spencer argued.

"He does not have to. Your grandfather had a reason," Alistair blurted out.

"And what was that?" Spencer could not help getting agitated.

"Your father is the president of Wentworth bank and if something happened to the bank, say it goes bankrupt, he would be liable to the creditors. They can go after his money. This way, they can't because the bulk of the estate is in trust in your name. It's solid tight, no creditors can touch it."

Spencer pondered on the idea. He had to agree with that reasoning. Still it shocked him to know that he would be so wealthy so soon. It was a little bit scary. His life changed abruptly. He thought he could continue his frolicking life but with this wealth and the responsibility attached to it, he felt he suddenly should grow up. He quieted down.

When Alistair finished, Spencer emptied his glass, stood up and went to the fireplace and looked up at his grandfather's picture as if asking him, "Why? Why are you doing this to me?" Alistair and George waited patiently. They knew it must have been a complete shock for Spencer to hear all this. Obviously he was not expecting this at all.

Spencer put his head on the mantelpiece. He was thinking hard and fast. Silence prevailed in the room. After a few minutes, he walked back to his chair. He decided to do something. Something unheard of. It was the only way he could think of. They might not agree with him but it was the only way he knew how to tackle his present predicament. If it was inevitable, he had to act quick and now.

"All right. When do I start working at the bank? I want to learn everything I can about the banking industry which I know nothing about," he said with conviction looking at his father.

"Next week is soon enough. I'll have your office ready," George said.

Spencer knitted his eyebrows and shook his head. It was not what he wanted to do. He had other ideas which his father might not agree but he had to do it his way. Spencer said, "No, I don't want an office."

"You don't? Why? I don't understand," George said and looked at Alistair who was also puzzled.

Alistair said, "I don't get it. You don't want an office? What do you exactly mean by that? Where will you be working?"

"I want to start as a teller." Both George and Alistair's jaws dropped. They stared at him. Now it was them who were in shock. They were in total disbelief.

Finally George said, "Are you kidding?"

"No, I'm serious."

"Are you sure you want to do that?" George wanted to make certain that was what Spencer really wanted to do. He could not believe what he was hearing.

"Grandfather was right. I have to learn from the bottom up. That is the only way, I will know how the bank works. Then I can move to be a loan officer in a couple of months. Eventually, I want to work at the finance department and learn how things work in that end," Spencer said with conviction.

George looked at Alistair, "What do you think of Spencer's idea?"

Alistair shook his head. He took a drink from his glass. After a brief moment he said, "If he is comfortable with that, let it be. We'll give it a try."

"I meant what I said. I'll start as a teller," Spencer insisted. It was the only way he knew to learn the banking industry since he had no clue about what banking was all about. All he knew was money went into his bank account and he spent it like water.

George thought about it and finally considered it a brilliant idea worth trying. *What could possibly go wrong? If it does not work and he does not want it, he can always just go to the executive office.* George agreed and said, "OK. It's settled then. You'll start Monday and I will take you to meet Tom Cartwright, the manager at the Fifth Avenue branch."

Alistair said, "Great. One more thing. Your grandfather did something which was smart. He liquidated half of his holdings at some of the companies and the cash is now sitting at your bank. He thought it better to diversify and have some cash."

"How much cash are we talking about?" Spencer asked.

"Ask your father. Several million dollars, I believe." Alistair glanced at George.

'Whew! Why would he do that?" Spencer was curious to know.

"He thought cash was better than a piece of stock certificate. He was probably right with the way the stock market is acting now."

"Hope he was right." Spencer was beginning to wonder the logic of this move.

"With your grandfather, I would not doubt it," Alistair said.

Alistair looked at his watch. "I think it's getting late. I better take Lilly home. The ladies must have run out of things to talk about."

"I would not worry about that. Ladies have plenty to talk about all the time," George said.

"I guess so." Alistair paused. "Now that we have settled everything, I'll start working on the probate." He gathered all his papers and they all went to the drawing room and fetched the ladies.

Mr. Yates brought Lilly Prescott's silk wrap, handed it to Alistair Prescott who put it around his wife's shoulder. Then George, Margaret and Spencer said good night to Alistair and Lilly.

As soon as Alistair and Lilly left, Spencer excused himself. "Goodnight. I think I'm going to bed. It was a trying day."

Margaret noticed her son's sudden need to be alone. "Is everything all right?" She looked at her husband whose expression did not reveal anything.

"Yes, Mother. Everything is fine. I'm just tired from my trip."

"Goodnight, dear. See you in the morning," she said.

"Goodnight, son," his father said.

Spencer gave his mother a quick peck on the cheek and hurried going up the staircase.

George took Margaret's arm and guided her to the parlor. "Poor Spencer," he muttered softly. Margaret gave him a questioning glance.

Spencer entered his room. It was dark except for the soft glow from the full moon outside. He did not bother to turn on the light. He went straight towards the window. He opened it and let the cold air in. He breathed in the fresh air. He looked up at the sky. The moon was a bright orb in the sky casting a dance of shadows over the surrounding landscape. Millions of stars were twinkling above. He looked at the vast landscape. He suddenly thought of the tremendous responsibility that now lies on his shoulder. This land was now his and as a steward of this land, he had to make certain, it stays within the family for future generations. It's his legacy and he promised to work hard to make do his promise.

He looked up at the sky and said, "Grandfather, if you are looking down on me, I want you to help me. I'll do my best of what you expect of me. I promise you that."

## Chapter 6

$\mathcal{E}$mma came home Saturday afternoon. Paul Conley met her at the Oyster Bay railroad station. She could not wait to get home and see her brother whom she had not seen for three years. The moment Paul parked the motor car in front of the house, she did not even wait for Paul to open the car. She came bouncing out to get in the house.

"Where is he? Where is Mr. Spencer?" she asked Mr. Yates excitedly as he opened the front door. Mr. Yates did not even have to tell her. They heard him running down the stairs and as soon as he got down the hallway, the two siblings hugged each other.

"Let me look at you. You have grown up to be a beautiful lady," Spencer said. Emma blushed. She was tall, slim and fashionable. Her blond hair was cut short and she was wearing an ankle length peach dress that seemed to swing with her as she moved. She had a matching shoes to go with her outfit.

"What about you? You don't look so bad. You look dashing," Emma said. "How was Europe? I bet you had a marvelous time."

"Yes, I did but I missed you and your antics."

"Well, I missed you too."

They saw the footman with her suitcases. Emma said, "John, you can take them to my room."

"Yes, ma'am."

"Thank you."

Spencer went toward the drawing room and Emma followed him. "Where is everyone?" Emma asked Spencer.

"Mother went out to play bridge and Father went to see Alistair Prescott," Spencer said.

"Talking of Alistair Prescott, did you find out why they want you home," Emma asked.

"Sure I did. You will not believe when I tell you what happened."

"What was it?" Emma was curious.

"Let me get us a drink first, then I'll tell you." Spencer went to the sideboard and poured himself a Scotch. He turned to Emma.

"I'll have one too," Emma said. Spencer poured one for her. They brought their drinks towards the settee by the fireplace.

"Cheers," Spencer said and raised his glass.

"Welcome home," Emma raised her glass. "So what happened? I'm listening."

They sat down opposite each other and Spencer narrated everything that happened the night after he got home. When he was finished, Emma looked pensive. She thought of how Spencer must have felt with that enormous wealth and the burden attached to it. She loved her brother very much. They were always close since they were little. Finally, she said, "So you really have to learn the business? What a challenge that must be since you don't have a clue what you are going to do."

"Exactly. I have to learn everything about the business. It's the reason why I want to start at the bottom. Maybe I am wrong but that is how I feel. I don't want to go to the bank and take over when I have no clue what is going on. It's not fair to everyone and not fair to me. How can I talk intelligently if I don't know what I'm talking about? It is not right. It will not make any sense and the employees will know it and they will talk behind my back. No, it is not going to happen. I want to know everything about banking."

"That was smart of you. What did Father think of the idea?"

"He and Alistair were flabbergasted but I insisted so I start Monday from the bottom. I'll join the rank and file."

"Good for you. I wish I could work but I have to finish college first. I have another year and then I will join the work force," Emma said.

Before the Nineteenth Amendment took effect, women were still considered second-class citizens, denied the right to vote and largely confined to careers as wife and mother. After the Nineteenth Amendment was ratified on August 18, 1920, they not only joined men in the voting booth, but with their emancipation, women would overnight set startling new standards in fashion and behavior. Their styles changed from clothes that went all the way down to their ankles, and long hair all pinned up, to short skirts and short "bobbed" haircuts.

"You do not have to work. You'll have plenty of money," Spencer said.

"That is not the point. I want to work. Women have to be independent."

Spencer whistled. "You'll be independently wealthy after the probate. Since when did this transformation come about?" he asked.

"The whole world is changing. Women are making contributions and I want to be a part of it. I don't intend to be a trophy lady sitting at home waiting for my man to give me everything I need. That is not for me."

Spencer looked at his sister with admiration. "Wow! You're someone to reckon with. I do admire your courage."

"Thank you."

Spencer finished his drink and got up from the settee.

"Anyway, I'm going riding. Would you care to join me or are you too tired from your trip?"

"Oh no. Give me half an hour to change and I'll go with you. We can race to the playhouse."

"You're incorrigible." Spencer laughed. His sister had not changed one bit, always challenging him. "OK, half an hour. I'll go change too. See you at the stable."

Emma ran upstairs and Spencer rang the house bell. Mr. Yates appeared.

"Yates, I'm going riding with Miss Emma. Can you tell the groom to get our horses ready in half an hour?"

"Yes, Mr. Spencer. Right away."

"Thank you, Yates."

"You're welcome, sir." Mr. Yates went towards the servant's quarter in the back and Spencer went upstairs to change.

The following day, Mr. Yates packed some clothes for Spencer to go to the city and stay at their Fifth Avenue place since he would now be working at Wentworth Bank. He could always go back to Long Island on weekends if he wanted to. His parents would be staying at *Wentworth Hall* till the end of September as usual unless they were traveling. They would move back to the city from the first of October to the end of March.

His work week would be a long day since he intended to learn everything he could as he plunged ahead and so staying in the city made more sense. It would be a totally different lifestyle for him from now on, a sudden change from the carefree life he was engaged in while abroad. Now he had the big responsibility. For a young man who was not even thirty, he was faced with the big realization that he had to work harder than most men his age. Not that he needed to but he had to even with his vast wealth. More so now because of his legacy. He could certainly leave everything to his father's employees and let them run the whole thing but he believed that was not what his grandfather wanted. He wanted a young heir to perpetuate his legacy and if his grandfather believed in his ability, he had every intention to prove that his grandfather was right.

He had to honor and protect the legacy that his grandfather handed to him. He had a duty to work diligently and protect his wealth. It came with a big responsibility that would weigh on his shoulder all his life. It had been on his mind since the night he was told he inherited the vast fortune from his grandfather. It kept him awake all night, thinking what he wanted to do and how to tackle this responsibility head on. Nothing prepared him for this unexpected turn of events. His carefree life abroad certainly did not. He had a lot of learning to do. Can he do it? He would try his best to prove to himself that he could. Not just to his parents, but more important to himself.

Smartly clad in his Savile Row suit that he bought in and brought from England, a starched white shirt and regimental tie, Spencer went to see George at the executive office of

Wentworth Bank on Monday morning, his first day at work. His Savile Row suit was stylishly cut and handmade with perfect tailoring. They betrayed who he was, a wealthy young man. He was the quintessence of sartorial elegance. He disliked anything shoddy and his weakness for fine clothes was one of his few indulgences that he cultivated while abroad. That he could not change nor wanted to change. It defined who he was. He always believed that a good impression made a vast difference on how his future employees would perceive him. Clothes always make a man and one can always tell who you are by your clothes.

They rode down the elevator to see Tom Cartwright, the branch manager of the Fifth Avenue branch. Tom Cartwright saw them as they entered the bank. Tom was not expecting them and he was wondering why a sudden visit from George Wentworth, the bank president, and who was this tall, young, good-looking fellow with him? Tom ushered them into his office. It was a small office with just the essential furniture, two chairs for clients, a desk and a chair for Tom, a bookcase and a console table.

As soon as they entered the office, Tom closed the door. "What can I do for both of you?" Tom said and looked at Spencer. George read his mind and introduced Spencer.

"Tom, meet my son. His name is Spencer," George said. Tom was taken aback and didn't know what to say. George turned to Spencer. "Spencer, I want you to meet Tom Cartwright, our branch manager."

Spencer smiled and extended his hand. "Hello, Mr. Cartwright. Glad to meet you."

"Nice to meet you too, Spencer." Tom noticed the firm handshake, a good sign. This kid was brought up properly, he thought. He didn't know George had a son but then he was fairly new to the bank, only been there for two years. He had never seen him before nor could he remember an instance when George ever mentioned a son.

"I didn't know you had a son. Where was he hiding all this time?" Tom jokingly said to George.

"He was abroad."

"I see."

Tom motioned to the chairs. "Have a seat." George and Spencer both sat in the leather arm chair in front of Tom's desk. Tom waited. He still was not sure what this was all about. The kid probably wanted his job. Although he was too young to take his place. He hoped not but you would never know. He began to wonder. After all, he was the son and heir to the boss.

"You are probably wondering why we are here," George interrupted Tom's trend of thoughts. "Spencer just came back from Europe a week ago and I have decided to put him to work. I thought I could find a place for him in the bank." He paused and waited for Tom's reaction.

"Welcome aboard," Tom said. He presumed Spencer would be working at the corporate office and he probably had to report to him.

George glanced at Spencer who smiled. Spencer did not say a word. George continued, "He does not want to work at the corporate office."

Tom was suddenly curious. "No? Why not? Where does he want to work?"

"Here," George said and turned to Spencer. "You tell him."

Spencer nodded. "Mr. Cartwright, I want to start at the bottom. I have no experience in banking or anywhere else for that matter. I need some kind of experience. I want to thoroughly understand how the bank works. I want to be a teller."

Tom's jaw dropped. He could not help staring at Spencer. "Holy smoke! Why? Why would you want to do that? Most young man wanted to start at the top. You want to start at the bottom?"

"You might think I'm crazy. But I need to start somewhere. As I said, I don't have any experience. None whatsoever. I'm not afraid nor ashamed to start at the bottom. It's just temporary until I learn the basics," Spencer said matter-of-factly.

"I'm sure you have a college degree from one of the top colleges." Tom didn't know which Ivy League school Spencer went.

"I have. I went to Harvard." Spencer looked at his father but George let him do the talking.

"So there you are," Tom said.

"It's not that simple."

"What do they teach at Harvard?"

"They teach a lot of business theories but I still need actual business experience. I want to learn the whole banking system. There is something to be said about hands-on experience. No books can duplicate that. I have to start somewhere and the most practical thing is to start from scratch. Like a kid learning to read, you learn your ABCs first and that's what I want to do."

Tom scratched his head. He did not know what to make of this young man. From how he looks, he could be the president of this company right now or just sit on the board and no one would question it. After all he was the grandson of the founder of the bank and the heir to the president. But here he was in front of him, applying for a teller's job. He was totally dumbfounded. This was unheard of.

"Are you sure you want to do this?" Tom asked Spencer, then looked at George.

"I said the same thing. Our attorney said the same thing. He was adamant," George said.

"Really, sir, I want to do this. It's rather unorthodox but here's what I propose. I'll work as a teller for a month. Maybe a month and a half. Then I can move to the next step which I told my father. I can go to the loan department next and be a loan officer. That way I can learn all the rules and workings of giving out a loan. Once I figure everything, I can move to the accounting department and see how that department works. This way, I can see the whole process and then I can figure out what works and what does not work. I can observe and make the necessary recommendations."

"I see your point. I understand what you want to accomplish. If you feel comfortable doing the work of a teller, more power to you. I'm more than happy to put you on the floor. I give you a lot of credit." Tom turned to George and said, "You have raised a fine young man."

"Thank you. I'm sure the set-up will work fine for us and for him," George said. He stood, shook hands with Tom and left to go to the executive office upstairs and let Tom handle Spencer.

And so it began. Tom took Spencer to the floor. All eyes were on Spencer and he felt a bit uncomfortable. He did not know what to expect. Tom introduced him to the head teller, David Brennan. David, a red-haired son of an Irish immigrant, was a year younger than Spencer and had been with the bank for a couple of years. Tom hired him after he started as branch manager.

"David, I want you to meet Spencer Wentworth," Tom said.

David knotted his brow. "Wentworth? Any relation to the bank?" David asked.

"Yes, he is the son of George Wentworth, our president," Tom said.

"Oh my! Glad to meet you," David said and offered his hand.

"Nice meeting you too," Spencer said and shook hands.

"What can I do for you, Spencer?" David asked.

Spencer looked at Tom who said, "He will start working with us starting today."

David's jaw dropped. "You mean here, not upstairs."

Spencer nodded. Tom said, "He wants to be a teller."

"A teller?" David gave Spencer a questioning look. "I'll be darned."

"Never mind that. Just show him how things work here and see that he learns everything," Tom said.

"OK, boss. No problem." Tom left them and went back to his office.

"Follow me," David said and they went to the back office where there was a working table. David picked up a deposit ticket and showed Spencer how to handle the deposit, then he showed his new student how to count the money, how to reconcile the receipt at the end of the day and how to talk to a customer. Spencer took few notes, listened carefully and paid close attention while David Brennan explained everything on what had to be done from the time you start the day until you close at night.

"Any questions," David asked after the lecture.

"I'm sure I can handle it. Easy enough. I just have to practice to count the bill faster. Is there a trick to that?" Spencer asked.

"Yes, make sure everything is in the same direction. It's easier that way."

"Good to know. Thank you very much," Spencer said.

"You're welcome. By the way, can I ask you a stupid question if you don't mind?" David said.

"Shoot."

"Why are you doing this? Your father is the president of the bank. You can just work with him, not here," David said.

"I have my reason and people will never understand it but I have no business experience whatsoever and I want to learn everything there is to learn about the banking industry. From soup to nuts. Does that make sense?" Spencer said.

David thought about it for a moment and nodded his head. "I guess so."

"I want a feel of the place so I can make recommendations to my father," Spencer said.

"Well, if you need anything, just let me know. Welcome aboard. I'm happy to have you around."

"Thanks. I do appreciate it," Spencer said. He likes David.

"Shall we go on the floor? I want you to watch me all morning and then you can officially be on the window this afternoon. How's that?"

"Good idea."

They went to the floor and Spencer stationed himself behind David while David was taking customer's deposit and in the afternoon, he began his job as a teller. The day went by quickly and by the end of the day, he was confident enough to process the day's transactions. By the end of the week, he was observing what was going on the floor and taking notes mentally to report to his father by the weekend.

Spencer took to the job like fish to water. Most of all, he got along very well with everyone on the floor with his easy-going ways but he did not want to be too familiar with everyone. He learned fast and was a great role model for his co-employees. He was hardworking and wanted to know everything. He was affable and polite and greeted the customers with that winning smile which won the heart of their customers. He was very friendly with everyone but there was a social divide between him and most of the employees. His co-employees knew who he was and they respected him. They treated him the same way as everyone yet they knew he was different from everyone else on the floor. The ways and habits of the people below his social strata were so different than the way he was brought up but he tried to take it in stride. He realized that someday he would take the helm of the company and so he had to keep his distance but still remained friendly to gain their respect.

Having a Wentworth on the tellers' floor was unheard of and the employees loved it. The customers loved it. Spencer was a sensation. With his good looks and easy smile, he gained the confidence of the customers and female customers flocked to the bank when they heard about the new teller. Wives of owners of small businesses urged their husbands to transfer their accounts to Wentworth Bank. George was very pleased and so was Tom Cartwright.

Spencer did not just learn the job. He observed and made notes on where they could improve. He saw there was only two tellers at one time and the line was getting longer.

"We have to install more tellers to service the customers," he told his father one day.

"But that would cost the bank more money to hire more employees," George said.

"But look at what it would create. Better service for the customer and less wait on line. When people spread the excellent service we provide, they will tell their friends. Word will spread out and we will gain more business. We shall also have someone greet our customer when they enter the bank and answer questions."

"Let me bring this up with Tom. I see the merit of your suggestions. I'm sure he'll agree with me."

By the time he left the floor and moved to the loan department, Tom had hired two more tellers and a receptionist to sit near the front door to greet customers. Tom was very pleased with the improvement because as Spencer predicted, the business improved greatly with word of mouth spreading the great service Wentworth Bank was providing their customers. When it was time for him to leave the branch, his co-workers on the floor were sad to see him go when he transferred to the loan department.

Spencer worked as a teller for just over a month. Then he transferred to the Loan Department under Albert Johnson, the Loan Department head. He was given a desk, not a private office. It was a little disturbing for some of the loan processors to have a son of the president of the bank working with them. But Spencer proved to be a good addition to the department.

"I advise you to come to training with us," Albert Johnson told Spencer the following day after he started at the Loan Department.

"Absolutely. I'd love to go."

"We'll have it at the conference room every morning the next three days. We'll go over the various forms and different guidelines."

"That would be wonderful. I'll be there. Will they teach us how to fill up the various forms?"

"Yes."

"That's great."

So he went to training with the other loan officers the following day. He asked questions when he thought he did not understand something. He practiced filling up forms following all the guidelines. He learned about all kinds of fees and loan to assets ratios and interest rates and different kinds of loans. It was like going to class in Finance 101 but this was hands-on. He found every aspect of loan processing very interesting, from the time they received the application form to the final approval by the loan officer. He also found out that it took a couple of weeks to get a loan approved. That should not be the case. He observed why it was taking so long to process a loan. It should be done in a week. He made notes and submitted it to his father.

"There should be a checklist of what the bank needs when someone applies for a loan. This way, when we get the paperwork, it was just a matter of checking them and running the numbers. The process should move from the application to the underwriting and final approval in a week," Spencer told his father.

"So why do you think it took so long?" George asked.

"There were so much time wasted between each process. All application received in the morning should be processed by the end of the day and go to the next process the next day. I saw some applications sitting on the loan processor's desk for several days. It should not be that way."

"There must be a reason why it was sitting there for so long," George said.

"I don't see any except employees spending too much time socializing. I've been observing everyone each day."

"Do you think that's a good idea? You, watching every move they take."

"If we have to make money, we have to be efficient."

"Maybe the volume of loan applications has increased." George tried to reason out. He was uncomfortable to make drastic changes in the department.

"If that's the case, we have to hire more people to handle the increase in the volume of loan applications or let the loan department personnel stay late."

Spencer wondered why it took so long for the underwriters to process the loan. So while he was there, he timed himself and knew it could be done. He then reported his findings to his father at their next meeting.

A month later, he started calling some new businesses and asked them if he could help them with their new endeavors. He would explain the advantage of having enough capital to get their business going. Then he started taking in big commercial accounts. He spent three months in the loan department. As he grew accustomed to his work, he gave reports to his father once a week. George was very pleased with his progress. The bank was doing a brisk business since he came on board.

By late August, Spencer decided he would take a break and go to Long Island at the end of the month and enjoy the end of the summer. He had been with the loan department for three months and working very hard. He needed a break. He called his mother and told her he would be home at the end of the month. He was looking forward to being in the country after the oppressive summer heat in the city and go riding. Within minutes after he hung up the phone, he got a call from his father.

"Can you come to my office at your lunch break?" George said.

"Sure. I'll be over." He hung up the phone and wondered what his father wanted to talk about.

At about noon, he took the elevator to the executive office. As soon as he approached the desk of Mrs. Perkins, George's secretary, she said, "Mr. Wentworth is expecting you. You may just knock and go in."

He knocked softly at the door and walked in. George motioned him to sit down.

"Thanks. What's up?" Spencer asked.

"Your mother just called and said you are going to *Wentworth Hall* at the end of the month. I'm glad to hear that you are taking a break," George said.

"I want to take advantage of what little is left of the summer. I miss riding and it will do me some good to get some exercise."

"Of course. You've been working hard. Do you think you are ready for the next move?" George asked.

Spencer looked at his father, knowing his father could not wait to get him to the executive office and said, "I believe I am. I enjoyed working for the loan department and I believe I have absorbed a lot of knowledge there. Yes, I'm now ready to go to the Finance Department."

"Excellent. I'll take you to see William Storms, our Controller, next week and you can work in the Accounting Department in September."

"I would like to start at the Account Payable section if you don't mind and see how all the expenses are treated. I think it is very important to know how we spent the company's money."

"That's excellent. We are always interested in our income but we also should manage our expenses prudently," George said.

"I had that in mind."

"Perfect," George said.

Spencer was about to get up when George asked, "What are you doing for lunch?"

"As usual. I'll eat at the cafeteria."

"How about going out with me to lunch for a change?" George asked.

"That would be great. Let me tell Albert I'll be a little late coming back," Spencer said.

"No need to. I'll let Mrs. Perkins do that for you," George said and picked up the phone.

"Mrs. Perkins, can you call Albert Johnson and tell him I'm having a lunch meeting with Spencer and he will be gone for a couple of hours?"

"Sure. Anything else, sir?"

"That's it. Thank you, Mrs. Perkins."

"You're welcome."

"We're going to the Knickerbocker by the way," George said and hung up.

## Chapter 7

The weekend promised to be sunny with temperature in the 60s. It would be a great time to enjoy the mild weather outdoors before the weather turned really cold. The leaves started to turn colors. The outdoors seemed the perfect place to be and enjoy the majestic colors ranging from golden yellow to flaming red. Margaret was glad to have both Spencer and Emma for the long weekend. Spencer came Friday night on a late train. Emma was still home and was due back at Vassar College the following week. Emma was excited to have her brother around. She had not seen much of him since he came back from England. He was much too busy at work.

Margaret and George were having their breakfast of eggs, bacon, sausages and toast with orange marmalade and lemon curd when they heard the front doorbell ringing. Mr. Yates went to answer the bell. A boy handed him what looked like an invitation. He put it on the silver tray on the front hall and went into the breakfast room, a small room adjoining the dining room where the family had their breakfast. It was a bright room facing east with a connecting door to the pantry into the kitchen. There was a fireplace next to the door to the pantry. A collection of blue and white Delft porcelain was housed in a niche next to the fireplace.

Mr. Yates handed George the silver tray.

"Thank you, Yates," George said, taking the envelope off the silver tray. Mr. Yates stepped back and left the room. George slit it open and saw a beautiful invitation to a dinner party at "Overlook", the home of Michael and Cice Cook in Glen Cove.

"What is it?" Margaret asked, sipping on her coffee.

"A dinner invitation for Sunday night."

"From whom?"

"The Cooks."

Michael Cook, a very successful entrepreneur in the food business, and his wife, Cice were one of his big depositors at Wentworth bank. Michael and Cice, as they were now known lived in "Overlook", an enormous mansion overlooking the Long Island Sound. Cook was not their real name but given the success of their business, they were right to have changed their names years ago from Mikolajek and Zuzana Kurcharnewski to Michael and Cice Cook. If you think Kurcharnewski's name was hard to pronoun, let alone remember it, Cice's maiden name was even harder to pronounce. It was Wojciechowski which nobody could pronounce nor be able to spell. Changing their names were part of their success in business, so they thought. It was easy for everyone to remember and since they were in the food industry, Cook seemed quite appropriate in their estimation. In spite of their Polish origin, they were able to assimilate successfully in their new homeland and with their hard work, they became very successful in the food business. They were what you called the American success story. They worked so hard in the beginning and saved and started a small grocery store and little by little added more stores until they became a big entrepreneur. The Cooks were not really in the same social strata as the Wentworths but they have plenty of money deposited at Wentworth Bank from their grocery stores and from their food and kitchen emporium. They were self-made millionaires, the "nouveau riches" as the old money would say.

    Spencer walked in the breakfast room and went directly to get his breakfast from the sideboard. "Good Morning," he greeted his parents.
    "Good Morning, Spencer," his father said, looking up from the invitation.
    "Good Morning, Darling. Did you get enough sleep?" his mother asked knowing he was late coming home last night.
    "Plenty, Mother." Spencer saw his father reading the invitation. "What is that you're reading, coming in so early?"
    "Oh, an invitation to dinner."
    "Where?" Spencer took a bite of a piece of bacon and then sat next to his mother.
    "At the Cooks at 'Overlook' in Glen Cove."
    "Cook's? Is that the green grocer who I heard was Kurcharnewski before they made the big time?" Spencer asked.
    "Spencer!" His mother was horrified at his description. "Watch what you're saying."

"But, Mother, it is true." He turned to his father looking for confirmation. "Is it not? Everyone knows that."

"It is true they made their money from the food business but you don't call them green grocer." He chastised his son though he could not help smile himself.

"See, I am right. Well, in England they call those people green grocers." He continued eating his breakfast. "So are you going?" he asked his father.

"Going where?" Emma just walked in the breakfast room and heard the conversation.

"To the green grocer's party," Spencer said and continued eating.

"Who?" Emma stopped, raised an eyebrow. "Green grocer's Party? Who are they? Do I know them?" Emma asked and went straight to the sideboard to get her breakfast.

"Mr. & Mrs. Michael Cook," George said.

Emma turned to her brother and asked laughing, "Spencer, did you call them green grocers?"

"Yes, I did. They are the green grocers. That's what they call them in England."

"Do they really? I heard they are filthy rich."

"People have to eat and they are in the food business and they are doing quite well. Look at their house," George said.

"I heard. So are you going?" Emma asked Spencer as she sat opposite her brother.

"I was not invited. They are." He pointed toward his parents.

"Yes, you are now," his mother said.

"No, I'm not. I don't want to go." He took a sip of his coffee and looked at his father wishing he would say no. "Don't tell me I have to go?" Spencer tried to get out of going to the Cook's dinner party.

"They are one of our big depositors. You don't want to lose their account by being a snob? Do you?" George asked Spencer.

Spencer frowned. "No. I guess not. But do I really have to go?"

"I think it is a good idea if you go. If you are to become the President of Wentworth Bank someday, it's best to get acquainted with your depositors especially those with big accounts. It will be a great public relation," his father said.

"I can pretend I'm not here."

"But you are here and everyone knows you are here," his father argued.

"You might as well get used to it. There are things called obligation and this is one of them. So relax and have fun," his mother said.

"I guess I have no choice. I'll try my best." Spencer agreed grudgingly. He looked at Emma. "Why don't you come with us? You'll be my partner. In case I get bored, I have someone to talk to."

"That's not a bad idea," Emma said. She loved parties and this one was something she would like to see knowing how rich the Cooks were. She was interested in how they do things. She turned to her father. "May I go?"

George looked at Margaret who nodded. "Of course, you may," George said.

"Great. I would love to see their house. I have never been there. I heard it's gorgeous," Emma said.

Spencer beamed at his sister. "I'm glad you are coming," he said.

"So am I."

"Now that it's settled, I will write to Mrs. Cook and tell her we are all coming," Margaret said.

Emma turned to Spencer, changed the subject abruptly and asked, "What are you up to today?"

"I thought I'd spend some time in the library and check those loan applications I brought home."

"Loan applications?" Emma rolled her eyes in disgust. "Do you have time for anything else these days besides your job? Why don't you and I go riding this morning? You are supposed to take a break and I would like to spend some time with my brother to catch up on things." She looked at her father as if asking for permission.

"Good idea. Emma has not seen you much these days. You can work at those loan applications later in the afternoon," George suggested.

"Thank you, Father. He is working too hard," Emma said frowning.

"I am not. I just want to finish those loan applications that were on my desk before I start working in the accounting department," Spencer said.

"Yes, you are working too hard. The bank got along very well without you for three years. It would stay in business for as long as Father is there," Emma said.

"Emma, you're absolutely right. Spencer is working too hard but it is good for him and the bank. It's also for his own good that he takes a break once in a while." George then turned to Spencer and said, "Go spend some time with your sister. Take her riding."

"All right. We'll go riding after breakfast. How is that? You talked me into it."

"Great! About time."

Margaret could not help smile at the banter of her two children. They sounded like little kids but definitely showed great affection for each other. She looked at George who was also amused.

Saturday came and Spencer went to the party with his parents. George and Spencer wore formal white tie and tails and Margaret was in a long maroon evening gown and Emma was in a mid-calf length silver gray Chantilly lace gown with boa feather, a new craze in fashion. Emma looked ravishing in her outfit with a couple of long strands of pearls around her neck and matching silver gray headband with beads wrapped around her blond bobbed hair. Spencer could not help admire his little sister. She would break a few hearts. She would. No doubt about that. She was tall, lithe and slender and walked gracefully. He guessed all those lessons in deportment paid off. She had grown into a beautiful young lady. Spencer could not believe the change in her appearance since he left home three years ago.

Paul Conley, the Wentworth's chauffeur, drove them in a Silver Rolls Royce to "Overlook", an imposing marble structure overlooking Long Island Sound. The white marble shone in the bright lights illuminating the whole building. Balustrades and columns grace the perimeter of the building surrounded with boxwood lining the path to the entrance steps like sentinels standing guard to protect the big monstrosity of a building. Scattered around the lawn near the house were evergreen topiaries of various sizes and shapes with some blue spruce trees all lit up here and there. There were more boxwoods on huge stone pots with classic designs.

The building spoke volume as if saying "I have arrived" and this was probably the message it was trying to convey. A couple of matching curved stairways converging into a single stairway on the first landing lead to the main portico as you ascended the marble steps. There was a wide covered veranda supported by two sets of double ionic columns flanking the portico. A balustrade passageway on each side of the portico has two curved windows with a keystone on top. This passageway contained a ladies' and men's cloakrooms which led to the round gazebo-like structure on both ends below a balustrade terrace with potted trees and shrubs on the second floor. Palladian windows shed lights to the second floor's central rooms while the two wings on each side had rectangular mullioned windows. The third floor rooms which house the staff had rectangular windows. More terraces can be seen on the third and fourth floors with a pergola and a garden on the fourth floor terrace. The fourth floor can only be accessed by an elevator from the second floor and was used as another entertaining room during the summer months for intimate gathering. To the left of the building, a connecting hallway with Palladian windows connects to the expansive ballroom. The whole place was lit up like a big white cake.

Paul Conley parked the Silver Rolls Royce in front of the portico. He opened the car door in back of him and let George and Margaret and Emma step out of the car. Spencer was seated in front and let himself out. They walked quickly past the topiary greenery in huge pots silhouetted against the edge of the pebbled courtyard like a sentinels from a bygone era. They went up the stairways while Paul parked the car and joined the other chauffeurs in the chauffeur's cottage.

Margaret and Emma went to the Ladies Cloakroom on the east part of the passageway while George and Spencer went to the Gentlemen's Cloakroom in the opposite direction on the west part of the passageway. In the Gentlemen's Cloakroom, white envelopes were arranged on a silver tray, with a gentleman's name on each envelope. Inside was a card with a lady's name on it – the lady he was to take into the dining room. That way, a lady never knew which gentleman would escort her. George took his and saw he had to take Cice Cook, their hostess. Spencer however had Anna's name, the Cooks' daughter which he had not met yet. Then they proceeded to the front hall and waited for Margaret and Emma who came back in no time. They were then ushered inside to meet the host and hostess.

Just outside the door to the main salon, Michael stood in formal white tie and tails with Cice Cook in a velvet dark blue evening gown greeting their guests. After shaking hands with their host and hostess, all four of them proceeded to the main salon, a cavernous room full of Italian furniture. There were several paintings hanging on the wall, mostly religious paintings. A huge Steinway piano was positioned on one side of the room.

A manservant came with a tray of glasses filled with champagne and handed one to each guest. Spencer took one and gave it to Emma and took another one for him. A maid followed with a tray of canapés – one piece for everyone. No one got a second drink or a second canapé. The Cooks were known to only serve one drink but Michael Cook liked Champagne and so that was what was served. George and Margaret were handed their drinks and they left Spencer and Emma and wandered to the other side of the room where older guests were converging. Spencer looked around and saw a couple coming in their direction. The couple stopped in front of them, smiled and introduced themselves. The lady was about 5-ft tall, heavily made up with her brunette hair pulled up in a chignon hairdo and wearing a black beaded gown. The gentleman was about 5'6" tall, black sleek hair in a black tie.

"I am Anna and this is my husband, Victor Winiarski. I'm Michael's and Cice's daughter."

"Glad to meet you." Spencer shook Anna's hand and then Victor's. They were both looking at Emma.

"I want you to meet my sister, Emma," Spencer said. Anna was staring at Emma as Emma shook hands with Victor. Emma smiled and then extended her hand to Anna.

"I thought she was your date," Anna said to Spencer.

"Yes, she is. I invited her," Spencer said.

"I thought . . . Never mind," Anna said.

Spencer did not miss what Anna was implying. He began to laugh. Emma pinched him on his arm.

"You're not the first one who thinks the same thing. She could be my girlfriend but she is not. She's my little sister."

Spencer wrapped his right arm around Emma's waist who blushed and they all laughed. They exchanged few pleasantries and then Anna took Victor's arm and they moved on to the other guests.

"Did you notice Victor was staring at you?" Spencer told Emma.

"What?"

"You better be careful. I think Anna noticed it too. I could see daggers in her eyes."

"Don't be ridiculous. Didn't she say they were childhood sweethearts. They must be in love for eons of years," Emma said.

"So what? People fall out of love sometimes."

"Where did you learn all this? Listen to you, my worldly brother."

"I'm just saying be careful."

"Besides being married, he is Polish and a Jew." Emma tried to reason out.

"That would not go very well with a WASP. Would it?" Spencer asked. WASP stands for White Anglo-Saxon Protestant.

"No, it wouldn't but let's not get carried away. You're imagining things. Let's go circulate." Emma saw the manservant with the silver tray and deposited her glass on it, hooked her left arm around Spencer right arm and they moved across the room. Their parents were talking to Alistair and Lilly Prescott. Standing next to them was a red-headed young man. Alistair saw them coming.

"Hello, Spencer. Hello, Emma. Are you two enjoying yourself?" Alistair greeted them.

"Splendid." Spencer looked at the young fellow. "I don't think we have met before." He extended his hand.

"No, we have not. I'm just visiting my uncle." The young fellow looked at Alistair. "I'm from the West Coast. San Francisco. California."

"Well, how do you like Long Island?"

"Very well."

Emma coughed. She wanted to know who was this good looking young man with wavy red hair, a high forehead, excited and friendly eyes set wide apart, tall and well-dressed. The two young men then realized that she was standing there being ignored. They both smiled.

"Oh, I'm sorry. How rude of me. I want you to meet my sister, Emma," Spencer said.

"Glad to meet you." Emma shook hands with the new fellow. She found him very attractive.

"My pleasure. Name is Todd Prescott."

"How long will you be staying?" Spencer asked.

"I don't know. It depends. My uncle wants me to work at his law firm. I haven't made up my mind yet. We'll see."

"That's great. Hope you decide to stay," Spencer said.

"I hope so too," Emma echoed right away. She hoped she did not sound too anxious.

Todd was looking at Emma intently, then said, "I just might do that."

Dinner was served with a big fanfare in the huge dining room. The men started looking for their partner. There was another couple who was introduced earlier as Olga & Sergei Kuminsky, a family friend. Michael Cook escorted Olga Kuminsky. George Wentworth escorted Cice Cook, Sergei Kuminsky escorted Lilly Prescott. Spencer Wentworth escorted Anna Winiarski, Victor Winiarski escorted Emma Wentworth, Alistair Prescott escorted Margaret Wentworth. Todd Prescott was left with no partner. Todd just followed everyone as they walked in the dining room and looked for their place cards. The older people sat on one end and the young people sat on the other end. Michael at the head of the table next to his wife, Cice on his right and Olga on his left next to Alistair who sat next to Margaret. George sat between Cice and Lilly. To Lilly's right is Sergei who sat next to Spencer. To Spencer's right is Anna with Victor at the head of the table. Emma was seated to the right of Victor and Todd sat to the right of Emma.

Michael Cook was animated during dinner. He talked about his business. George and Alistair listened attentively. George being his banker and Alistair his attorney, the two men had to know what Michael was up to. On the other side of the table, the conversation was a bit different. Victor said very few words while his wife chattered away about innocuous things looking left to Spencer and right to Victor. Spencer was getting bored with all this nonsense talk so he tried to talk to Sergei instead. Spencer was having a tough time understanding Sergei with his thick Russian accent. Emma was not paying much attention to Anna's chatter. Instead, she talked to Todd who she found fascinating with his story about San Francisco and its grande dames.

Todd was talking about a Mrs. Sheldon Snowden. She was tall and imposing woman, he said, who would roar at a good joke and slapped her knee loudly.

*"Somehow my mother would be horrified at that,"* Emma thought but said nothing. She could not see her mother's reaction since Todd was next to Margaret.

Todd continued, "There is a saying in San Francisco that it takes three generations of education and breeding to rub the rough edges off first generation's money. Mrs. Snowden also liked to entertain guests in her bedroom. Coming home from a busy day, she would remove her stockings, talking full-steam to her visitors all the while. She also entertained in one of her twenty-five bathrooms. She made a game of trying to shock people, and judged people by their reactions to some of her more startling actions. She was fond of asking casual acquaintance over for a swim in her covered pool, and then adding, "Of course I swim in the raw. Hope you don't mind."

By this time, the other side of the table heard the last sentence and Michael said, "Is that true? I would love to see that."

George and Alistair were laughing but Margaret and Lilly were not amused and remained silent. The young people could not help but smile.

"I heard she was descended from a titled French family who emigrated to Denmark many generations ago. She was impoverished by the time her branch of the family joined the California Gold Rush but found very little gold. As a young woman, she used to walk two miles a day to save a five-cent streetcar fare. That was before she met her husband," Todd continued his story.

"What a woman!" George said.

"She is a disgrace," Margaret finally said. She felt that someone so rich should act with more decorum.

"I don't subscribe to that kind of behavior but she must have a strong character and the confidence in herself enough to do such things," Michael said.

"She must be. She could not care less about what people think," Todd said.

"There's got to be one everywhere," George said. "I understand Mrs. Robert Homans of Boston was of the same nature. She did a daring move once and she came from a distinguished family. She was the former Abigail Adams, a descendant of two United States Presidents and the present dowager of the Adams family. Mrs. Homans possessed the audacity and the ability to plunge into situations that would surely daunt lesser mortals. Once, when Beacon Street had become impassable in a blizzard, Mrs. Homans ordered her taxi to stop in front of her husband's club, the august Somerset Club, and demanded a room for the night. Somerset Club had a rule against giving rooms to unescorted women. She was politely told of the rule. She could not be deterred by it. Mrs. Homans said, 'Very well. In that case, I'll go out and get my taxi driver.' She got her room."

"Woman after my own heart," Todd said.

"That was daring," Anna said. "I don't think I could do that."

"I might consider it given the circumstance," Emma said much to the dismay of her mother who glanced at her with a piercing look.

Todd smiled and nodded. He's beginning to like this girl next to him.

"You sure would," Spencer said and smiled at his sister. He knew his sister well enough to believe that she would do such a thing.

Just then, Michael informed everyone that the dessert was on its way. At that, the butler came with a trolley full of Viennese pastries and passed around the table.

## Chapter 8

The weather was gloriously sunny as Paul Conley drove Spencer back to New York City. He would drop Spencer at his office and then proceed to the house to bring home Spencer's valise. Spencer would stay in the city till Christmas vacation. He was now faced with a new challenge. He would be moving to a new department as he planned to do.

As soon as he got to the office, he met with Albert Johnson. They went through all the loan applications that he finished over the weekend. After cleaning his desk, he went to the Accounting Department and presented himself to William Storms, the Controller who took him to see Esther Potts, the Accounts Payable Supervisor. Esther showed him a box of bills for payment and a chart of accounts. It was like he was back in a classroom and doing Accounting 101. He remembered the things he learned in college and told Esther after the lecture that he should be able to figure things out as soon as he familiarized himself with the account numbers.

He spent the whole month of September at the Accounts Payable section, paying bills, taking notes of what was spent and for what. Then he moved on to the Controller's Department. He learned all aspects of the bank's finances. He checked the accounting books, asked questions about journal entries, general ledger and trial balance. Since he took accounting classes in college, he had a little knowledge of how the double-entry accounting system works. He had no problem understanding what was going on. He learned to read Balance Sheet and Profit and Loss Statement and Working Capital. It was a crash course in advanced accounting.

Spencer was smart enough to learn fast and grasp things. He listened attentively to whatever William was telling him and asked questions when he did not understand what William was saying. He would question William about why certain expenses had big variances from month to month, why certain expenses were charged to certain accounts as he saw while he was at the Accounts Payable Department. He asked what was included in the miscellaneous account and analyzed each item thoroughly, why fixed assets were depreciated a certain number of years, what was in the reserve account. He was very curious about the financial health of the bank.

He would stay late and brought home financial statements and studied them. George was extremely pleased at Spencer's interest in the bank. By Christmas, Spencer was totally absorbed in his job at the Accounting Department. He'd been working at Wentworth Bank for eight months now and had learned all accounting and banking terms.

By mid-December, 1927, George felt comfortable that Spencer was ready to take on a management position at the bank. He would soon promote him to an executive positon. He decided to make him Vice President – Operation. He had proven himself that he was capable of understanding the banking system. Tom Cartwright, Albert Johnson and William Storms would now report to Spencer. Tom Cartwright and Albert Johnson were not surprised and were glad to see him get the title. They thought he would be a great addition to the bank and had a very high regards for their new boss.

William Storms was not particularly happy with the set-up but since he knew Spencer was the son of the owner of the bank, he thought it would be wise to go along with the decision. It was an awkward situation since William felt he had to train him before and now he had to report to him but he could not do anything about it. William also wanted a Vice President's title for himself and was working hard to get it. However, he realized Spencer seemed a fast learner and he was amazed at how fast he could grasp the financial aspect of the bank. Spencer might not do the legwork but his analytical mind was incredible. William finally resigned to the fact that it might not be a bad idea. If he played his cards right, Spencer might even help him climb the corporate ladder someday. He also knew that eventually, Spencer would be President of the bank and he could be in a better position than anyone else.

At the office Christmas Party, there was a lot of merriment. After the teller window closes at 3 PM, some employees decorated the conference room. By 5 PM when the other departments finished work, they started streaming to the conference room and had their drinks. No liquor was served since it was illegal but non-alcoholic beverages and hors d'oeuvres were plentiful. Everyone was having a great time. In the middle of the celebration, George called the group to attention. There will be an announcement to be made. Everyone stopped the conversation and listened to what George had to say.

"Ladies and Gentlemen," George began. "I want you to know that the bank did a wonderful business this year. We have seen a lot of improvements on how we do things at the bank. Thanks to some innovative ideas of our new employee, my son, Spencer." Everyone applauded. George paused for a few moments and then continued, "The management is very happy with the outcome of this new initiative. Spencer has proven himself to be a great employee since he started as a teller last spring. It was unheard of that a son of the owner would work as a teller but to tell you the truth, it was what he wanted to do. His promotion went very fast." George laughed and everyone cheered.

"I know some of you appreciated what he did and now I'm happy to announce that he is again promoted and will now be part of the executive team. Starting in January, he will be Vice-President, in charge of operations. He will be a great asset to the company."

It was received with great joy since Spencer had proven himself worth the promotion. Everyone knew the story that he started from the bottom and had been a great employee since he started as a teller. His co-employees appreciated what he did and were more than happy to see him be a part of the management team. They felt he was one of them. He was well-liked and his working habit was commendable and they had a great respect and admiration for him. He was a great role model for all of them.

They raised their glasses and someone started singing and everyone joined in . . .

"For he is jolly good fellow,
For he is a jolly good fellow,
For he is a jolly good fellow,
Which nobody can deny."

Spencer found his way to be next to his father and said to the crowd, "Thank you very much. I enjoyed my short stint on the teller floor, at the Loan Department and the Accounting Department. I learned a lot, thanks to Tom Cartwright, David Brennan, Albert Johnson, Esther Potts and William Storms. Now, I'm ready for the new adventure. In the meantime, let's enjoy and celebrate today."

The party continued for another hour. Before they left for home, the payroll clerk handed everyone their Christmas bonus. George and Spencer wished everyone "Merry Christmas" as they headed out the door of the bank.

"Merry Christmas, Mr. Wentworth," they said to George.

"Merry Christmas, Spencer," they said to Spencer.

Between Christmas and New Year, Spencer took time off and headed for *Wentworth Hall* before he started his new job as Vice President-Operation at the beginning of next year. It was a time of celebration, his first Christmas at home since he came home from England.

In spite of heavy snow forecast for Christmas, Margaret Wentworth decided to have Christmas at *Wentworth Hall*. It would be a special occasion since Spencer was home for the first time after a long absence. Emma invited a friend, Lorna Beckett to spend Christmas with them since her friend could not make it home to Pittsburgh because of the heavy snowstorm. Lorna was adamant and would rather stay in New York alone but Emma persuaded her to come along. They took the train and came to Long Island a day early. Paul Conley met them at the train station in Oyster Bay. Spencer followed the day after on

Christmas Eve. He was wrapping things up at the bank before he went on vacation till the end of the year. He was looking forward to the holidays ahead of him. George and Margaret were back in residence for the duration of the holiday and then would move back to the city afterwards.

*Wentworth Hall* looked festive for the holiday. There were huge Christmas trees which were gaily decorated in the hall, in the drawing room, in the library and the ballroom. There was a cheerful log fire burning in the fireplace. There were presents under the Christmas tree in the ballroom for the family and the staff. The whole house was decked with garlands and branches of evergreens and mistletoe tied and decorated with red ribbons, tinsels and pine cones. Crystal compotes held miniature pyramids of fruit and pine cones and nuts and had been trimmed with red bows. There were masses of white candles in silver candelabras everywhere. Even the library which was so dim and gloomy at times was aglow with lights coming from the burning embers in the fireplace and the candle lights from the Christmas tree. A few bright red poinsettia plants were displayed at strategic places around the house. Outside there was a huge wreath of balsam pine with a red bow adorning the massive front door. The house had never looked so lovely.

Spencer decided to take the train instead of Paul Conley driving to New York to pick him up. The train station was crowded with people going home for the holiday. He was buying his ticket at Penn Station when he saw Todd Prescott among the crowd.

"Hi, Todd."

"Well, fancy meeting you here. I thought you were home already. I understand Emma went home early," Todd said.

"She did. I had so much work to do before I go on vacation," Spencer said.

"So you'll be home the rest of the holiday?" Todd asked.

"Yes. Any plan for tomorrow?" Spencer asked Todd.

"I think we are going to your house for dinner," Todd said.

"Oh, I didn't know that. I never know what Mother does. But that's great," Spencer said as the ticket clerk handed him his ticket.

"Thank you," Spencer told the clerk and got off the line.

"Maybe we can do something while you're on holiday. I also took time off," Todd said as they walked to the platform.

"That's fantastic." Suddenly, an idea sparked on Spencer's head. "Why don't you bring a few change of clothes when you come to dinner and then stay with us for a few days. Emma is bringing a friend from college so you can keep me company."

Todd nodded his head. "Great. That's a splendid idea."

Christmas Day started with a trip to Christ Church in Oyster Bay where the Wentworths worshipped when they were in the country. All their friends in the same social circle worshipped there with a few exceptions who went across the street at the First Presbyterian Church. Most of the staff from the estates close by went to St. Dominic Church. All three churches are within a few yards of each other.

Some families celebrated Christmas dinner either on the afternoon or at night with few Italians having their Christmas dinner on Christmas Eve. At *Wentworth Hall*, it was on the night of Christmas. George and Margaret Wentworth all dressed up for the evening festivities. Spencer was in white tie and tails as well. Emma and her friend, Lorna came down the stairs dramatically in their evening gowns from The House of Worth. Emma was radiant in her ankle-length velvet blue gown with several strings of pearls. Her friend, Lorna, a little taller than Emma, was a little bit shy and demure, also in an ankle-length silvery evening gown and a single strand of pearls. It was the new fashion. Spencer thought he had seen the silver gown before that Lorna was wearing. Maybe Emma lent it to her friend that evening but it suited Lorna fine. Spencer was awestruck by what he saw which somehow escaped him the day before when he arrived home. He must be so tired, it skipped his attention. Now that she was all dressed up, he noticed the transformation. Lorna was slender and tall, almost his height. He knew she was not from a rich family but from the middle class, yet her face was that of an upper class, for it contained breeding and refinement. It was these aspects that combined to create that indefinable quality he had detected as she came down the stairs with Emma.

Spencer could not call Lorna beautiful, if he was to measure her by the popular picture-perfect standard of the day. She was not the Gibson Glamour Girl in some beauty magazine but she was pretty, arresting and there was something in her poise that captured his imagination and made him catch his breath as he studied her. Her face was a perfect oval, with high prominent cheekbones, a straight and slender nose, and a delicately curved mouth that dimpled at the corners when she smiled. Her teeth were very white between her pale pink lips. Her blue eyes were the color of the ocean, set below the exquisitely shaped brows that were sweeping golden-brown arcs above her wide-set eyes with thick and curling golden-brown lashes. Her skin was like pale cream silk and as smooth, and without blemish. Her golden blond hair in a bob cut which was the latest craze was adorned with headband of pearls and beads. He could not keep his eyes off her. She noticed it and felt uncomfortable.

They were all gathered in the drawing room when Mr. Yates announced that the Prescotts had arrived. Todd had handed his valise to Mr. Yates who gave it to Frank who took it up to one of the guest rooms upstairs. George and Margaret met them by the door to the drawing room. Todd gravitated to the young group. He shook hands with Spencer and gave Emma a kiss on her cheeks. Emma introduced Lorna to Todd.

"Todd, meet my friend, Lorna," Emma said.

Todd extended his hands. "Nice to meet you," Todd said to Lorna.

"Nice to meet you too," Lorna said and shook Todd's hands.

"So you are spending Christmas here?" Todd asked Lorna.

She nodded and said, "I have no choice. I can't go home to Pittsburgh because of the snowstorm and Emma insisted I join her and her family here."

"I don't want her to spend Christmas alone in New York," Emma said.

"That is very sensible," Todd said.

"I agree," Spencer said smiling.

Mr. Yates served them their cocktails with the help of Frank and John, the footmen. While George, Margaret, Alistair and Lilly sat on the sofa, Spencer, Todd, Emma and Lorna remained standing on the other end of the room. Emma found Todd irresistible and was very interested in his stories about San Francisco. Lorna seemed so quiet and shy and Spencer was wondering how his sister and Lorna got along so well together when his sister was just the opposite of Lorna. Emma who he thought was wild at times and here was Lorna so tame compared to his sister. He found it so intriguing. Mysterious at best. What was it that he found so attractive in her? Was it the unknown that he found as a challenge? When he was in England, the ladies seemed to be seeking him. Here, Lorna did not seem to care. She was not flirting with him at all. She was nice and pleasant, very proper and seemed at ease though he understood she did not come from a wealthy family like his. But something in her exuded confidence. He was beginning to like her, like her at lot and he just met her the day before.

In fifteen minutes, dinner was announced. It was exactly 7 PM. They left their unfinished drinks in the drawing room. No one would think of carrying an unfinished cocktail to the dinner table. The table was perfectly set. At the table were printed place cards and menus, outlining the courses through the appetizer, soup, fish, meat, salad, cheese, fruit, dessert, and coffee. Fine silverware and gleaming china and crystals were placed in perfect precision along with two silver candelabra. In the center of the table was a fresh arrangement of evergreens with red and white carnations from the greenhouse.

Dinner was started with soup. Sherry was served with the soup. As the soup bowl and sherry glass were taken out, a fish dish followed. Conversation was animated. There was talk about the Standard Oil refinery in Tientsin which caught fire the day before during a battle between opposing forces in China. Both George and Alistair were worried because of their clients' and friends' vast holdings at Standard Oil. However, they knew the United States Marines were sent there early in the year to protect American interests so they were hoping they would protect the refinery.

Mr. Yates was hovering by the door with the two footmen, Frank and John. The footmen were waiting for Mr. Yates' signal to clear the fish course. A sherbet course came in next to wash off the fish taste. Dishes after dishes followed with an abundance of dessert of Christmas yule log and various cakes and fruit. After dessert, a bowl with water was placed on everyone salver. Todd who was not used to this kind of affair was wondering what to do with the bowl. There was nothing on it except water. Was he supposed to drink it, he wondered. He waited for everyone on what they would do. He saw Emma put her hand on it. Everyone seemed to do the same. So he decided to follow suit. Dinner lasted at least two hours. How they managed to eat so much, nobody knew. It was a day of gracious living. It was an era so accustomed to lavish and unruffled entertaining.

After dinner, instead of going for cigars, the men stayed with the ladies. George led everybody to the ballroom and they had some entertainment there. The ballroom was seldom used and only for special occasions. It was decorated beautifully with a huge Christmas tree at the far end of the room. There was a grand Steinway piano on the other end. A fire was burning in the marble fireplace. The elders went to sit by the fireplace. Todd approached the grand piano and started playing Liszt's "Liebestraum". Spencer leaned on the piano.

"I didn't know you played the piano," Spencer said to Todd.

"I started piano lessons when I was young but I just play for my own enjoyment. It relaxes me after reading all those legal briefs," Todd said. "Do you play a musical instrument?" he asked Spencer.

"I was never interested in learning a musical instrument but I do enjoy listening to music. I began going to the opera while I was in Milan. Then when I toured Austria, I visited the Opera House in Vienna and I just fell in love listening to classical music. Emma took piano lessons when we were young and is quite proficient in it."

As Todd was getting more and more into the music, Emma and Lorna joined them by the piano. They listened quietly and when Todd finished, Spencer looked at Emma with that mischievous smile on his face.

"How about you and Emma do a duet?" Spencer suggested.

"That a great idea." He heard his mother say from across the room.

"Oh no." Emma was embarrassed. She was listening to Todd and knew he played very well. She could not match his proficiency but Spencer was persistent.

"Come on, Emma. Be a sport." Spencer nudged his sister.

"Go on, Emma. We want to hear you too," Lorna said.

Todd moved a little bit on the bench to give Emma room. He looked at Emma, stood up and waved his hand signaling Emma to sit down.

Finally Emma acquiesced. "All right."

Emma sat on the piano bench with Todd on her left. Todd started playing a few bars from Schumann's "Träumerei" and Emma picked it up. They played nicely together. Spencer and Lorna looked at each other and leaned on the piano enjoying the music. Then Emma stood up and motioned Todd to stand up. She lifted the piano bench. Todd shifted through the music pieces and pulled out Rachmaninoff's "Rhapsody in Blue." He sat back on the bench and started playing the piano while Emma stood next to Todd and helped turn the pages of the music piece as Todd played the piano. It was a beautiful piece. Everyone was mesmerized. Spencer stole a fleeting glance at Lorna. He wondered what she was thinking.

After Todd finished his beautiful rendition, they all clapped. Then Todd played a couple of Chopin's Polonaises - "Polonaise No.2 in E-Flat Minor" and Polonaise No. 6 in A–Flat ending with Chopin's Nocturne No. 2 in E-Flat, Op. 9. He stood from the bench and bowed as if he was on stage. Everyone stood up and cheered and gave him a thunderous applause.

George decided to break the merriment and announced that he'd give out the presents under the tree. Mr. Yates summoned all the staff to come upstairs and they all lined up on one side as George handed everyone their presents. Everyone was having a great time. Todd went back to the piano and started playing "Silent Night." Everyone started singing.

Afterwards, the staff went back to the kitchen with their presents. In a few minutes, Alistair and Lilly Prescott took their leave without Todd. He was staying for a few days.

## Chapter 9

The next day, Spencer was up early. He looked out his bedroom window and saw the whole surrounding was blanketed in white. It looked wonderful outside. The tree branches were lined up with snow. He could see the undulating contour of the landscape with the snow glistening in the morning sun. It was a winter wonderland. The snow must have fallen all night after they had gone to bed. It looked like the snow was tapering off now. There were still little flurries but the heavy snowfall was gone. It was immaculately beautiful outside.

He got dressed and then headed downstairs. He was looking forward to see Lorna this morning. He could not forget how she looked the night before. It kept him awake most of the night. Maybe she would want to go sledding today. They could pick a spot where there was an incline and it would be fun to spend the day outside.

He went to the breakfast room and saw Mr. Yates had already put the breakfast food on the sideboard. He helped himself to some ham, bacon, eggs and toast. He poured his coffee and placed his food and his coffee on the table. As he took his seat, his father entered the breakfast room.

"Good morning, Spencer. You're up early," George greeted his son.

"I could not sleep anymore so I decided I might as well get up. I saw the snow finally arrived."

"Yes, that means we will just have a quiet day today."

"Quiet? It should be a fun day to be outside in the snow." Just then he saw Todd coming toward them. "Here comes Todd."

"Good morning," Todd said as he entered the breakfast room.

"Good morning," Spencer and George said. Spencer pointed him to the sideboard and Todd helped himself. After he got his breakfast, he brought his plate to the table and sat across from Spencer.

"So what are you two up today?" George asked Todd and Spencer.

"That depends on what Spencer wants to do," Todd said and looked at Spencer. He looked around looking for the ladies. "Where are Emma and Lorna?"

"Still asleep I presume," Spencer said. Then they heard footsteps coming down the hallway.

"I think they are here," Todd said. The two ladies entered the breakfast room, both dressed casually in sweaters and mid-calves skirts.

After breakfast, Todd and Spencer headed outside to the terrace. It was a bit chilly so they went back in and got their parkas. They saw Emma and Lorna heading toward the library.
Spencer called, "Emma."
Emma turned around. "Yes, Spencer."
"Why don't you two join us and we can go for a walk? Todd was already putting his snow shoes on."
Emma asked Lorna, "Would you care if we join them?"
"I'd rather stay in and read."
"Come on. It should be fun and we can get some fresh air." Spencer was almost begging for Lorna to go. Lorna felt she could not possibly say no to him. He was quite irresistible and she did not want to disappoint him.
"Spencer was right. I can also show you the ground. Come on Lorna. Let's go," Emma said.
Lorna did not want to disappoint Emma either so she said, "All right. I'll go."
So the four of them bundled up in a down parka and put on their snow shoes. They took their ski poles from the rack and headed down the steps toward the ground. They trekked around the huge property. The ground was lovely with rolling hills all covered with snow, glistening under a bright sunny day. It was magical. Spencer and Todd were leading them and Emma and Lorna followed. It looked easy at first but when they got to the hilly part of the property, it was a challenge. Lorna was having trouble keeping up with everyone. She was not used to this kind of exercise. She wished she had stayed in the library but it would be more difficult to go back now than it was to continue with their outing. She continued trying to catch up with the group. She could see the undulating slope farther ahead and the snow

hanging from the trees. It was a magnificent sight. She began to enjoy herself. She kept on walking as in a daydream. It was then as they were walking up an incline, her snow shoes got caught on some branches of brambles laying on the ground and she tripped. She landed awkwardly on her knee, her right leg stretched out behind her. Snow flying around her and she was sprawled on the thick layer of snow with her hands spread to steady herself. She lost her ski poles as she went down.

"Ouch!" She cried out and felt a stabbing pain on her left foot. Emma heard her gasp of pain. She turned around and saw Lorna sprawled on the snowbank. She hurried to her friend's side.

"Are you all right," Emma asked, concern written on her face.

"Ouch!" Lorna grimaced with pain.

Emma called, "Spencer. Help."

Spencer turned around and saw Lorna on the ground. He ran back, his snow shoes digging in the ground as fast as he could, followed by Todd.

"Are you all right?" Spencer asked Lorna with a tinge of concern in his voice as he approached her.

"I think so. I felt so clumsy." She felt so embarrassed, red-flushed on her cheek. She had trouble getting herself up so Spencer lifted her up. She leaned on him.

"Nonsense. You were doing fine. I'm sorry, we should have stayed with you and Emma instead of walking way ahead."

"Yes, we should have." Todd felt contrite too.

"Can we rest a little bit?" Lorna asked pointing to a tree nearby.

"Sure. Let me help you," Spencer said.

They walked to the tree with Lorna's one hand resting on Spencer's shoulder and the other hand on Todd's shoulder. They walked slowly to the tree. Lorna limped a little bit. Her left foot began to hurt badly. She leaned against the tree in agony.

Emma looked concerned about her friend. "Shall I go back to the house and get the sled," she asked Spencer.

"Yes, please do. That's a great idea."

Lorna was feeling awkward with all the fuss but Emma insisted it better for her to go on the sled.

"I'll go with you," Todd said.

Lorna leaned on the tree and felt a throbbing pain on her foot. She closed her eyes not wanting to show Spencer how she felt. Spencer noticed it and knew she was in pain but trying to be brave. He knelt down.

"What are you doing?" Lorna asked.

"Let me take a look at your ankle." Lorna was about to protest but he was already pulling her boot out of the snow shoes. He unlaced her boots, pulled it out and lowered her sock and saw her ankle was red. He touched her ankle and Lorna cried.

"I'm sorry." He raised back her sock and put back her boots and strapped it to her snow shoes. "You cannot put weight on that foot otherwise it would aggravate it," Spencer said.

"I realized that."

Emma and Todd walked back to the house. It was quite a distance. They didn't realize they had walked that far. They got to the house and Mr. Yates intercepted them at the door. "What happened? Where is Mr. Spencer and Miss Lorna?"

"We need help. Lorna tripped and she's limping. Spencer is with her. We need the sled." Mr. Yates ordered Frank to get the sled and to tell Sarah, the upstairs maid to run the hot water in the bath for Lorna to soak her feet when she gets there.

It didn't take long for Frank to return with the sled. "Do you need help?" Frank asked Todd.

"No. Thanks. We'll be fine. Spencer and I can tow her back in."

Todd went back pulling the sled. Emma stayed behind. As Todd got near them, he saw Lorna being carried by Spencer. He could not help smile at the sight of them.

"How romantic," Todd teased them. Spencer ignored him.

Lorna started blushing and wanted to get down. Spencer tightened his grip. "Don't you dare?" he whispered to Lorna and she felt something she never felt before. She closed her eyes for a brief moment afraid to look at him.

"How bad is it?" Todd asked Spencer. "Did you check it?"

Spencer nodded. "It's all red. She wanted to walk but I won't allow it. She should not walk on it otherwise it will get worse."

"OK then. Spencer and I will pull you home," Todd told Laura with a smile.

"I think I can walk back," Lorna insisted as Spencer put her down gently.

"No, you're not. Don't be a martyr. You do not want to aggravate your foot in case you twisted it," Spencer said sternly.

Lorna looked at Spencer. She did not like the tone in his voice but there was also concern in it so she went along with them. There was nothing else she could do. Too bad, her foot was hurting badly otherwise she would show him what a brute he was and she did not need his help and commanding tone. But then, he might be right. It would be better if she went along with what he was saying. There was no point arguing with him. She felt foolish though.

She thought it would be fun to see these two men pulling her back home. She was beginning to enjoy the attention. She quietly got on the sled with their help and the two men started to pull her back to the house. Spencer and Todd were enjoying themselves and she was enjoying the ride. With the wavy contour of the landscape, it was not easy to maneuver the sled but Spencer who knew the place was alert and directed Todd to avoid all the bumps on the terrain. As for Lorna, she could not help admiring the men exerting so much energy as they pulled her back to the house and saw they were enjoying themselves as much as she did.

She felt she was a child again on a snowy day in Pittsburgh. Her father was pulling her on her sled. Her father, who she adored very much, always took her outing on snowy day. They would go sledding or ice skating. Sometimes, he would bring the toboggan and they would find a hilly place and go tobogganing. She enjoyed those outings very much. Then one day, he was gone. He became totally estranged from her mother. She had not seen him for years. She could remember the scene when he stormed out of the house and never came back. It tormented her heart to see her parent fight. They never seemed happy. She wondered if it has something to do with their background. For what she knew, her mother married her father in a hurry because her mother was pregnant with her. Her mother married beneath her station and they were both regretful. Lorna grew up wishing things were different. After her father left them, she and her mother moved back to her grandparents' house and lived there until she went to college. Then her mother got very sick and she passed on while she was in college. She remained with her grandmother who adored her and paid for her college tuition. It was at Vassar that she met Emma and they became fast friends. Emma never mentioned her brother to her. It was a shock to find out that Spencer existed. He seemed fun to be with but something is contradictory in his nature. That little incident before she got on the sled bothered her. He could be very bossy.

Lorna was deep in her reverie when she heard the commotion. They were near the house and Mr. Yates and Emma were at the terrace waiting for them. They reached the house and Todd and Spencer helped her out of the sled and up the terrace steps. By this time, Margaret and George came out of the house and were concerned too. After taking off their winter gears, Margaret told Lorna, "You should soak your foot in hot water with Epsom salts. Sarah has started the water in your bathtub."

"Yes, ma'am." Lorna said and slowly limped toward the stairway. Spencer was at her side and was about to lift her up.

"It's all right. I can manage," Lorna began to protest but Emma convinced her to let him carry her up the stairs. Emma followed behind them as Spencer carried Lorna upstairs. Todd stayed downstairs with Margaret and George and went to the library. Todd stayed at the library warming up by the fireplace.

After depositing Lorna in the bathroom, Spencer left and Emma helped Lorna into the bathtub. Spencer joined Todd and his parents in the library. He rubbed his hands together near the fire. They heard a quiet tap on the door and Mr. Yates walked in with a tray of hot chocolate.

"I thought you can use this since it is too early for cocktail," Mr. Yates said.

"Thank you, Yates," Margaret said.

Mr. Yates put the tray on the coffee table. "Anything else, ma'am."

"That would be fine. Thank you."

Mr. Yates left the room and quietly shut the door behind him. Todd and Spencer took a cup and sip the hot chocolate. It felt good as the chocolate started warming them up.

"I hope Lorna is not hurt badly. We should not have walked too far ahead of the girls," Spencer said to Todd as Emma entered the room. George looked at Margaret and they both smiled.

"Yes, you should not," Emma said.

"How is she?" Margaret asked.

"Is she all right?" Spencer asked with concern written all over his face which did not escape Emma and her parents.

"She'll be fine. She felt wretched for ruining the day. I told her she did not. I also said we should not walk that fast and it was our fault. She was not used to this kind of activity, she told me."

"Bloody thing! I should have known that," Spencer said suddenly feeling guilty. Margaret and George exchanged glances.

But we didn't know that, did we?" Todd asked.

"No we didn't. Basically I was the one who insisted we go with you guys," Emma said.

"Still we should stay together," Spencer said.

"So what exactly happened?" George was curious to know.

"We were walking leisurely," Spencer said.

"No, we were not walking leisurely. At least the two of you." Emma looked at Todd who nodded his head, then at Spencer. "We were trying to catch up with them. I was a bit ahead of Lorna. Then I heard her cry. I turned around and she was sprawled on the ground. Her snow shoes got caught with some brambles on the ground."

"Emma, you should not have gone too far from her," Spencer said.

"I know." Emma felt awful.

Spencer finished his chocolate and then excused himself and went upstairs. Todd and Emma stayed at the library. Spencer stopped in front of Lorna's bedroom. He was wondering whether to knock at the door or just walked in. He wanted to see how she was doing. He was worried about her. Finally he knocked softly. Lorna heard the soft tap at the door.

"Who is it?" Lorna asked.

"It's me. Spencer. May I come in?"

"Yes. The door is open."

Spencer walked in. Lorna was now sitting on her bed with her left foot raised on a pillow.

He stood close to the bed. "How's your foot?"

"It's not bad. That bath soak helps a lot," Lorna said.

"May I take a look?" Spencer asked, sat on the foot of the bed before Lorna could say something. He bent down and checked her foot. At the touch of his hand, Lorna felt like an electric shock hit her. She felt some kind of sensation she could not understand.

"It's still swollen. Are you sure you're all right?" Spencer asked. "Shall we call a doctor?"

"Oh no! Really I am fine. I'll be as good as new by tomorrow." Lorna reassured him, ignoring the strange feeling.

"We'll take it easy this afternoon. Maybe we can play backgammon or a card game instead of venturing out again. We can bring a card table here so you don't have to come down. How is that?" Spencer suggested.

"That's a wonderful idea but you should not be put out because of me," Lorna said. He looked at her and their eyes locked. For a few second, there was something unspoken there.

Spencer quickly recovered and said, "Nonsense." He stood up and walked toward the door.

He stopped at the doorway, glanced back at her and said, "We'll see you later." He then quietly left the room. Lorna stared at the door wondering what was happening.

## Chapter 10

Lorna stayed in bed all day while resting her foot. She felt bad for being confined in bed but Spencer insisted she rest her foot. Margaret told Mr. Yates to have her lunch brought up to her room and Emma agreed. Spencer told Mr. Yates to also set up a card table at Lorna's bedroom in case they wanted to join her in the room later for a card game. Maybe she might want to play a card game or just the four of them be together. He did not want her to feel left out.

After lunch, Emma took her brother and Todd to play card games in Lorna's room. They moved the card table next to the bed so Lorna did not have to get up. They played a couple of games and then left Lorna to take a nap. Spencer and Todd went outside and took another trek through the snow. Emma stayed indoor at the library and read.

Lorna was feeling better the next day. The pain had subsided and her foot was less swollen. Sarah brought her a breakfast tray and she ate her breakfast in bed. She felt terrible not to be able to join the family at breakfast but Spencer was in to see her early and insisted she stay in bed and would let the maid bring her a breakfast tray. Before he left, he also said that she should take her lunch in her room so as not to aggravate or do damage to her foot and he would join her for lunch. Before she could protest, he was out of the door already. So that was it. Emma popped in her room a little later after breakfast and was glad to know that Spencer was taking interest in her friend.

"He most likely feels guilty you got hurt. As the host, he felt responsible to the guests," Emma said.

Lorna knotted her brow and gave her a quizzical look. "I don't understand. Did you say he is the host? What about your parents?" Lorna asked.

"As the owner of *Wentworth Hall*, Spencer is your host."

Lorna's jaw dropped. "Spencer owns this place? Now I'm really confused."

"Oh, I guess you don't know about that."

"What are you talking about?"

"You see, when our grandfather died, Spencer inherited this place, lock, stock and barrel."

Lorna's eyes popped up. "Are you kidding me?"

"No. It's the truth. We can stay here for the rest of our life but Spencer owns *Wentworth Hall*, not our parents."

"I'll be darned. Is it common knowledge?" Lorna asked.

"Aside from us and the lawyer and the servants, I don't think anyone knows. Todd probably knows since he works for Alistair Prescott, our family lawyer."

Lorna was quiet for a while. Now she realized why he was so concerned about her. She was a guest at his house and she should feel comfortable and taken good care of. That would explain why he was so concerned about her. Still, he was going beyond the call of duty. *There was something strange the way he was acting. Was I imagining things or what?*

After Emma's visit, Sarah helped Lorna to her bath and then she stayed in bed to rest her foot. She tried to read a little till lunchtime when a table was set up next to her bed and food was brought in. A tray of food for her and another was laid on the table for Spencer. Spencer came and ate at the table next to her. Spencer was animated while he ate. Lorna was feeling awkward at first but soon felt relaxed. Spencer had a way about him which made her feel comfortable. Lorna asked about his sojourn abroad and he told her some of the places he went to and things which he thought would be interesting to her. Lorna enjoyed her lunch and was sad when it was over. But then Spencer said maybe later if she was up to it, she could come down and join them downstairs. She was glad to do that.

"OK, I'll come up and get you then. Say around 4 o'clock."

"That would be lovely. I feel terrible for ruining your holiday," she said.

"Don't be silly. You're no bother. The whole family loves to have you this week. I was just glad Emma invited you," he said giving her a warm smile.

"Thank you. Then I'll see you later."

"I'll be back," he said and quietly went out of the room.

Later, Lorna came downstairs in the arms of Spencer who carried her downstairs. They went to the ballroom and listened to music while Todd played the piano. Sometimes Emma played by herself or she and Todd did a duet.

The following day was nice and sunny. It was still chilly but the glistening snow was tempting so they ventured outside. Lorna was feeling much better. Todd and Spencer made their way to the lawn and made a snowman and threw snow at each other. Todd was enjoying his first winter on the East Coast with plenty of snow. Emma and Lorna stood by the railing on the terrace and watched Todd and Spencer. They seemed to be having a great time being a kid again. Afterwards, they headed back to the library with the roaring fire and played backgammon. It was the happiest Spencer had been since he could remember. He could not remember when he was happy and relaxed during the holiday in England. He was glad he was home again and with the company of his new friend, his sister's friend and his family, he could not ask for more. He was sorry his holidays would end so soon.

Todd stayed for four days and the four of them had the loveliest of time. Then Todd went back to his uncle's house. Emma and Lorna went back to the city at the same time. Spencer stayed behind at *Wentworth Hall* with his parents. While Todd, Emma and Lorna were around, he hardly opened his briefcase. He was enjoying Todd's company and beginning to take notice of his sister's friend. After they left, he suddenly felt alone. There was so much merriment when his sister was around, he forgot that he brought some work home. He never opened his briefcase, never thought of looking at the paperwork but then he was supposed to take a much needed vacation. Now, he was feeling bored with no one to talk to except his parents. The house seemed so quiet and empty.

For the first time since he got home on Christmas Eve, he went to the library and sat at his grandfather desk. He opened his briefcase and pulled out some papers. The year end was closing in and he had to study the balance sheet and profit and loss from last month and see how the bank stood. He had a preliminary report from William Storms for the month of December. Nothing could happen much the rest of the year so he had all the tools he needed to plan for next year.

He saw the deposits were down tremendously compared to last year. In spite of some new customers that he brought in, the amount of money deposited was not as much as the previous year. There were also plenty of withdrawals. Something was going on. Is the economy going downhill and affecting the bank? He started taking notes and would talk to his father who was still running the bank. Maybe he had more insights into this situation than he could see since he was just starting to know the business. He was also away for too long and had no idea how the economy was doing in the States during his absence. He was not paying much attention to the economy since his own bank account was always full while he was abroad.

He stood up. He had been working all afternoon. He needed some fresh air. He walked toward the French door to the terrace. As he opened the door, a cold air swept through the door. He breathed in the fresh cold air. He stepped outside and let the cold breeze enveloped him. He looked around him and as far as he could see, the whole place was blanketed with snow. The sun was starting to go down and the shadows made a lovely impression on the snow. He remembered just few days ago, he was out there with his new friend, Todd, Emma and her friend, Lorna, having a wonderful time just walking and enjoying the scenery. He thought of Lorna and how she looked so fragile after she fell down. He had been watching her quietly since that fall. There was something about her that fascinated him. She was very quiet, always deep in thought it seemed. Unlike his sister who was always full of energy, Lorna had a quiet demeanor. He wondered how Lorna and her sister became fast friends. They seemed to be of opposite temperament. He wondered what they talked about when they were alone. Is she as quiet with Emma or just around us since she did not know us? She never talked about her family. He wanted to ask Emma about it but he knew what she would think. Better to keep it to himself for a while. He would find out about it sooner or later. Maybe when he got back to the city, he would find a way to see her again.

Then in an instant, he made a quick decision. He changed his plan and would go back to the city earlier than planned and spend New Year's Eve in the city. He was certain Emma and Lorna were planning something to celebrate New Year's Eve together and he could find a way to see her. He rubbed his arms feeling the cold air and decided to go back inside. It was getting close to cocktail time. He better got back in and dress for dinner. He went up the stairs in a hurry taking two steps at a time. He changed to his dinner jacket quickly and went back downstairs in a hurry. He saw his parents already in the drawing room having cocktails. He went straight to the console where the silver ice bucket and glasses were. He opened the cabinet and took a bottle of scotch. He poured himself a drink and joined his parents.

"Cheers!" he said. Both his parents raised their glasses.

George greeted his son, "How was your day? Did you accomplish much? I understand you were at the library all afternoon."

Spencer took a sip of his drink. "Yes, I was. I was reading the preliminary reports from William Storms. There are some financial data that worry me and I want to discuss them with you tomorrow. I don't like to bore Mother with the details tonight."

"We can do it sometime tomorrow afternoon."

"That would be great since I'm planning to go back to the city the next day," Spencer said.

His mother raised an eyebrow. She looked at George who was also astounded with the change in plan. "So soon? I thought you are staying here till after the New Year," his mother said.

"Something came up and I would like to go to the city earlier," Spencer answered and walked toward the bar to get more ice for his drink. He was trying to avoid the look from his parents.

His father looked at his mother but said nothing.

"I thought you said you need a vacation and that's why you took a week off from the bank," his mother said sounding disappointed.

Spencer walked back toward them and stood by the fireplace with the drink in his hand. "Well, I am not going to the bank. I'll still be on vacation. I just thought it might be fun to spend New Year's Eve in the city. I have been out of circulation for a long time and maybe Emma can take me to meet some friends of hers. You never know with her. She seemed to know a ton of people. She might even need an escort to some fancy balls and I could be very handy if I were around."

"You don't really mean to escort Emma. More likely, you want to see someone and I think I know who." His father could not help himself. Spencer looked at his father sheepishly but ignored the comment.

Margaret looked at George and then at Spencer. "Who?"

"I really want to see Emma," Spencer lied but his father knew. Nothing could fool him. He saw the attraction there when Lorna spent the few days with them. Lorna might not know it but he knew. He was observing Spencer who was very solicitous of her especially after the accident. He also noticed the look on his son's face while talking to her. She was a lovely girl but they did not know much about her. All they knew was she came from Pittsburgh and Emma and Lorna had been great friends in college.

Spencer then sat next to his mother, afraid if he sat across, she could read his eyes. Mr. Yates knocked at the door announcing dinner was served. Spencer breathed a sigh of relief. He was not yet ready to answer any questions from his mother in case she suspected something.

The next morning, he dressed up with his riding clothes and decided to take a ride around the property. The groom saddled Sultan and handed him the reins and he took off. He galloped through the meadows, then slowed down to a canter into the woods. After an hour outside in the fresh air, he felt exhilarated. Then he trotted the last mile of his ride. Back to the stable, he reined in the horse. Alighting from it, he handed the rein to the groom and walked briskly toward the house. Mr. Yates was at the front door to take his coat. He proceeded to the library and warmed himself by the fire. He then picked up his briefcase and took out folders and started pouring over the financial statements again. He was trying to figure out how he could reverse the trend the bank was heading in. He started taking notes. He really had to talk to his father thoroughly about this. Something was happening and he wanted to find out.

Before the New Year of 1928, Spencer found himself riding the train back to Manhattan. The train was packed with people from Long Island wanting to be in the city for the New Year's Eve celebration. It was not on his original plan but he was anxious to be in the city. He knew he was not expected to be in the city at all. He did not intend to go to the office. Everyone knew he was on vacation in Long Island but he wanted to see Lorna. She had been on his mind all his waking hours. He could not concentrate. *What will Emma say when I walk in the house? I better think of a good excuse to tell Emma when I walk in the door.*

Emma heard the door opened. She was not expecting anyone. She ran to the top of the stairway and saw Spencer walk in. She came running downstairs and greeted her brother.

"What are you doing here? I was not expecting you but I'm glad to see you. I thought you were staying at *Wentworth Hall* for the rest of your holiday." Emma gave his brother a big hug. Spencer gave his sister a peck on her cheek.

After he released her, he said, "I was getting bored so I thought maybe I'd be better off here in the city. Maybe we can go to the theater or something. Would you like to do that?"

"Splendid." They saw the butler hovering about them. Spencer turned to Mr. Clarkson and said, "Clarkson, you can take my stuff to my room."

"Yes, sir," Mr. Clarkson said and picked up his bag.

"And Clarkson," Emma said.

"Yes, Miss Emma."

"Tell Nelly that Mr. Spencer will join me for dinner tonight."

"Yes, ma'am." Mr. Clarkson disappeared with the bag and Spencer and Emma went to the library. Spencer went near the fireplace where a blazing fire was going on. He placed his hands near it to warm them up.

"I do not believe you are spending the rest of your vacation in the city," Emma said.

"Well, this is my first winter back here. There must be some fabulous things going on in the city." He kept staring at the fire trying to avoid Emma's eyes.

Emma seated herself on the sofa and eyeing his brother curiously. "Yes, as a matter of fact. *Show Boat,* a musical play by Jerome Kern and Oscar Hammerstein II just opened up on Broadway a few days ago. It is based on Edna Ferber's novel and produced by Florenz Ziegfeld."

"Where is it shown? Is it any good?" Spencer asked.

"The show opened on Broadway at the Ziegfeld Theatre on Dec. 27. The critics were immediately enthusiastic, loved it and the show was a great success. I would love to see it," Emma said.

"Great. Maybe we can go see it," Spencer suggested.

Emma stood up and went to the table at the far end of the room and picked up the New York Times. "Brooks Atkinson of the New York Times gave the opening night a rave review." She said and gave the paper to Spencer.

The paper read: *"The book's adaptation was intelligently made, the production one of unimpeachable skill and taste, Norma Terris as Magnolia Hawks a revelation, Charles Winninger as Cap'n Andy Hawks extraordinarily persuasive and convincing, and Jules Bledsoe playing the character of Joe who sings Ol' Man River is remarkably effective."*

"I'm impressed. We really have to go and see the show. Would you like me to treat you to the show?" Spencer asked.

Emma was ecstatic. "I'd love that," Emma said. She gave his brother a kiss on his cheek. "Thank you."

"We can go tomorrow night and then we can go somewhere and celebrate New Year's Eve. How is that?" He was hoping Emma would take the hint and she did not disappoint him.

Her face brightened up and she blurted out, "I got a better idea. Why don't I invite Lorna to join us?"

"She might be going somewhere. It's such a short notice," Spencer said trying not to sound too anxious. He did not want his sister to suspect something.

"Don't be silly. I'll call her right now." She went straight to the phone and dialed Lorna's number.

Spencer watched his sister getting giddy with excitement as she talked Lorna into joining them at the theater.

"OK, Spencer will pick you up at 5 PM and we can have a quick dinner here and then head to the theater. Then we can go to the Stork Club to celebrate New Year's Eve," he heard Emma say. Before Lorna could protest, Emma hung up.

"There. It's settled. You'll pick Lorna up at 5 PM."

"What? That was not part of the deal."

"Sorry. It's done. Be a sport."

"OK." He walked towards her and it was his turn to give her a peck on her cheek. "You're incorrigible but I love you dearly."

"Well, fetch me a drink already."

"Aren't we getting dressed for dinner?"

"You're fine. It's just you and me so we don't have to bother."

"I think we should. We don't want to shock the servants."

"OK. Whatever you say. I could just have Clarkson bring me a tray to my room."

"Now you are being silly. I'm going up to my room and I'll see you back here in half an hour for cocktails." Spencer walked towards the door to go upstairs.

"I can be ready in fifteen minutes," Emma said.

"Half an hour," he said and ran upstairs.

Spencer knocked at the door of a house in Chelsea. Emma gave him the address and their chauffeur drove him there. A butler opened the door and let him in. He was ushered into the drawing room. The room had the Victorian look with flowered wallpaper and Belcher furniture with velvet maroon upholstery. He stood by the fireplace. There was a beautiful portrait of a pretty young girl above the mantelpiece. He looked at it intently, a smile on his face. Then he looked around and saw a small photo on the side table next to a small vase with a nosegay. The young girl seemed happy riding on a sled with a handsome man. He wondered if he was Lorna's father.

He heard footsteps coming down the stairs. He remained standing by the fireplace trying to gather his nerve. All of a sudden he felt an eagerness to see her but his stomach fluttered nervously. He had not seen Lorna since she left *Wentworth Hall* a few days ago and he had been longing to see her again.

Lorna tapped quietly at the door and walked in. Spencer turned around and what he saw was a different Lorna. She was dressed in an exquisite lavender gown looking radiant. What he saw at *Wentworth Hall* was a simple girl. She looked more grown up today, sophisticated and very beautiful.

"You're staring at me," Lorna said with a smile.

"You're a sight for sore eyes. You look beautiful. At first, I thought it was not you," Spencer said in admiration.

She started to blush. "We are not in the country anymore. It's good of you to take Emma and me to celebrate the New Year's Eve so I decided to dress up for the occasion."

"How is your foot? Is it still bothering you?" Spencer said for nothing better to say. He was still gathering his nerve.

"It's fine now."

"Great. Shall we go?"

"Sure. I'm ready."

"By the way, who is that lady on the picture above the fireplace?"

"Oh that. She's my mother."

"She's very pretty. And the girl on the small photograph?"

"That's me with my father."

"Your father?"

"Yes, my father. Shall we go?"

"Yes."

Spencer noticed she did not want to say anything more so he did not press the subject. He wondered why she did not want to talk about her parents.

They walked out of the drawing room and the butler was out on the hallway ready with Lorna's mink coat. Spencer took it and helped Lorna put it on.

"Don't wait for me, Menton. I'll let myself in when I get home."

"Very well ma'am," Mr. Menton opened the front door and Spencer and Lorna stepped out into the cold. Spencer's chauffeur opened the car door. Lorna stepped in and Spencer followed. The chauffeur then drove them to Wentworth place.

Inside the car, they were both very quiet. Spencer suddenly went tongue-tied. Lorna could not speak either afraid to break the silence. They both stared ahead of them looking out at the scenery ahead of the car. Finally Spencer took the courage to speak.

"I hope this invitation was not so sudden. I just got here yesterday and Emma insisted we all go out."

"Oh no. I was glad she called. I had no plans for today."

"Good. How about next week?" Spencer said without thinking.

Lorna looked at him surprised. She did not know what to say or what to make of what he was asking. "Are you asking me what my plan is for next week?"

"Yes," he said with a smile. "I would like to have dinner with you next week if it is okay." He paused, then added "Without Emma, of course."

"Are you asking me for a date?"

"Precisely." He looked her in the eyes. She looked down trying to avoid his gaze.

"Spencer, I have known you for just a few days last week. I don't know what this means."

"Lorna, I want to know you better. Can I take you out to dinner next Friday? I will be tied up at work all week but I'm sure I can get away Friday night."

She remained silent for a while, thinking what the implication of this sudden invitation.

"So what do you say?" Spencer asked.

"I guess there is no harm to it."

"Does that mean yes?"

She nodded her head. She did not know if it is the right thing to do but she agreed.

"Great, I'll pick you up at 7 PM."

"I'll be ready."

They reached the Wentworth house at Fifth Avenue. Spencer stepped out of the car and helped Lorna alight from the car.

"Thank you," he told his chauffeur. "We'll take a cab to the theater later so you can retire for the night."

"Very well, sir. Thank you and have a great time. Happy New Year."

"Happy New Year too."

They walked up the steps to the house. Emma was waiting in the drawing room. She walked to the entrance hall and greeted her friend.

"Lorna, you look ravishing! Doesn't she?" Emma looked at Spencer for approval.

"She is! I didn't recognize her at first." He gave his sister a broad smile.

"Come in the drawing room. Dinner will be served shortly and then we can head to the theater. Did Spencer give you trouble?"

"Why would I do that?" Spencer asked smiling.

"No. He was a perfect gentleman."

Emma glanced at her brother and saw that glint in his eyes. She thought she detected something but she ignored it.

## Chapter 11

The night was cold but lovely with the streetlights all aglow. The snow was still piled high on the sidewalk and the trees along the perimeter of Central Park were glistening with mist from the cold air but the revelers were not deterred. Plenty of young people were out on the street and getting ready to celebrate the New Year. As they walked out the door of the Wentworth's house, they felt the cold air. Lorna and Emma stood side by side on the sidewalk with their gloved hands and mink coat ignoring the cold air. Empty taxicabs seemed at a premium so they decided to walk to the corner of Fifth Avenue and 59th Street where there was a better chance to get one. Just as they reached the corner, Spencer saw a taxicab stop and deliver a passenger so he ran for it and was able to get it. They all hopped in. Traffic was more than usual as on an ordinary night. It seemed everyone was out on the town.

They made it to the theatre with enough time to spare. They joined a long line of people buying tickets and Spencer bought three tickets and they proceeded inside. The ushers took them to their seats. Emma went in first. Spencer motioned Lorna to get in next and he sat at the end of their row next to Lorna. They had a good view of the stage.

The show opened up with a big fanfare. Everyone was excited about the show since the review was outstanding.

As Gaylord Ravenel, the leading man and Magnolia, the leading lady and the daughter of the owner, Cap'n Andy Hawks, of the show boat *Cotton Blossom* kissed for the first time, Spencer could not help thinking what would it be like to kiss Lorna the first time. He now realized he was beginning to fall in love with his sister's friend just like Ravenel falling in love with Magnolia. He wondered if Lorna felt the same way about him. Then when Ravenel proposed to Magnolia and she accepted and they happily sang "You are Love", he took a glance at Lorna and saw her mesmerized at what she was watching on the stage. Lorna sensed he was looking at her but pretended she was busy watching the show. Spencer wondered if she was thinking the same thing. Little did he know that she was thinking the same thing.

In Act II, when Ravenel and Magnolia sang "Why do I love you?" Spencer saw Lorna looked at him briefly. He saw her glance and he smiled at her. She felt embarrassed. She felt blood rushing to her face. She was thankful the place was dark. She hoped Spencer did not see her face reddened. But it did not escape Spencer. He reached for her hand and squeezed it lightly. She looked at him and smiled. There was plenty of emotion crowding Lorna's head. *Am I falling in love with him? I just met him a week ago. I didn't even know he existed before that. What is happening? I don't know him at all and yet there is this strong attraction. I remember when I saw him the first time, when he came home and Emma introduced him to me. He was rather cold and arrogant but at Christmas dinner, he seemed friendlier. I could not believe the change in his attitude. Then when I fell, he was so solicitous. Why?*

All these thoughts came rushing in and she could not concentrate on the show. Emma was oblivious to what was going on. She was too engrossed in the show.

When the show was over, they joined a throng of late-night revelers coming out of the theatres amid the din of car horns and subway rambles. Spencer hailed another taxicab and headed toward the east end. There was already a multitude of revelers crowding the streets near Broadway. They got off at Columbus Circle and decided to walk the rest of the way. They reached the Stork Club owned by Sherman Billingsley and Spencer told the maître d' that they had a reservation. The waiter ushered them to a table near the corner. They were just seated when a gentleman with red hair walked towards their direction. Spencer was seated facing the door and saw him coming. He got up.

Lorna and Emma looked up at him. "What's wrong? Who are you looking at?" Emma asked.

"Guess who is here?" Spencer said.

"Who?" Emma and Lorna asked in unison. They turned around and saw Todd Prescott coming up in their direction.

"Hello, Todd," Spencer said. "What are you doing here?"

Lorna and Emma looked at each other.

"Hello, Spencer. I'm looking for you." He shook hands with Spencer. He raised his hand and waved to the ladies who remained seated. "Happy New Year," he said to all three.

"Happy New Year," Emma said. "How did you get here?" she asked Todd as he approached their table.

"I walked," he said smiling.

"I mean how did you know we were here?" Emma asked unbelieving to see Todd there.

"I called your house to see if you wanted to do anything tonight and I was told by Mr. Clarkson that Spencer was taking you and Lorna to the theatre to see the *Show Boat* and will be at the Stork Club afterwards. So here I am. Do you mind if I join you?"

"No. Not at all," Spencer said.

Todd turned to the table next to them and pulled out a chair and brought it to their table. Spencer sat down. Todd did the same after getting his chair.

"Glad you are joining us," Emma said.

"I should have called you. Why didn't I think of that?" Spencer apologized.

"Don't worry about it? You probably thought I would be in Long Island," Todd said.

"As a matter of fact, I did," Spencer said.

"Well, I called *Wentworth Hall* and Mr. Yates said you left for the city yesterday. So I decided to surprise you all," Todd said.

"Are you going back to Long Island tonight?" Emma asked.

"No. I'm staying at the Plaza tonight. Why don't we all go to the Plaza later?" Todd suggested.

"Splendid idea," Spencer said.

The waiter came and they ordered their drink.

"This place is great. Don't you think?" Todd said.

"It's the only place in town where you can get a decent drink," Spencer said.

Todd looked around. It seemed all the big names in town were there. He wondered how it was possible for them to get liquor when it was illegal. As an attorney, he felt he should not be there. He was uncomfortable. But then big politicians were there so it could not possibly be that bad. No law enforcement officers would dare to do an arrest tonight, not on New Year's Eve with all the big names there.

They had a couple of drinks and left. They strolled toward the Plaza. The night was clear and it was a pleasant walk. There were plenty of revelers walking and enjoying themselves. Emma walked with Todd and Lorna behind them with Spencer. They passed some stores with Christmas display and they stopped and gawked.

They reached the Plaza and joined another crowd of well-dressed partygoers. The place was beautifully decorated for the holiday. Poinsettias and silver tinsel were everywhere. There was a gay mood in the air. They went in the ballroom where Lester Lanin's orchestra was playing. The noise was in high decibel and you could barely hear yourself. As the night progressed, the conversation got louder, competing with the sound coming from the music playing. Everyone was in a joyous mood.

Before the strike of midnight, Spencer looked at Lorna and asked, "Shall we dance?"

Lorna smiled, stood up and Spencer took her to the dance floor. As Spencer put his hand behind her waist, Lorna felt an electric wave enveloped her. It was the same feeling she felt when Spencer touched her feet at his house. She looked up at him and he was smiling and his eyes was a pool of emotion. He pressed his hands tight on hers. She smiled and leaned on his shoulders.

"I'm glad I met you. This is the best New Year's Eve I have ever had," he whispered in her ears. Lorna looked him in the eyes and they understood. She did not have to say anything. She was just as happy as Spencer.

Todd stood up and motioned to Emma and they went to the dance floor too. Todd took Emma a distance away from Spencer and Lorna. He wanted Spencer to have a private moment with Lorna. He sensed they wanted to be alone and so did he with Emma.

Everyone was getting giddy with excitement. Confetti was flying on the dance floor and the crowd was now wild with excitement. At the stroke of midnight, the band played *Auld Lang Syne* and the noise got louder. Todd gave Emma a light kiss on her lips. Spencer looked Lorna in the eyes and kissed her too on the lips. Just the touch of their lips sent another electric wave on Lorna. She became conscious on what was going on inside her. Spencer felt the same way but he tried to control himself. He wanted to kiss her more passionately but not in front of too many people. Besides, his sister was close by and he would never hear the end of it.

He pulled back and said smiling, "Happy New Year, Lorna."

"Happy New Year, Spencer."

He kissed her again. This time with more passion and he did not care who was watching. Lorna responded and brought her arms around his neck.

After a while, they looked around and did not see Todd and Emma. "Where are Emma and Todd? Where did they go?" Lorna asked.

"Let's look for them," Spencer suggested.

"Let's and wish them Happy New Year."

They walked across the ballroom floor holding hands and looking for Todd and Emma. They both seemed very happy.

## Chapter 12

The week seemed to drag on forever. Spencer could not wait for Friday so he could see Lorna again. He came back to work after New Year and got very busy at work but when he got home late at night, all he could think of was Lorna.

By Friday, he was home earlier than usual. He showered and got ready to go out. He knocked at Emma's bedroom door.

"Who is it?"

"Me." Emma heard Spencer's voice. "Can I come in?"

"Yes." He opened the door. Emma was standing before her looking glass trying on a new gown with Sarah, her maid, behind her. Sarah stepped back and left the room.

"I just want to tell you I will not be joining you for dinner," he said.

Emma turned around and gave him a quizzical look. "Where may I ask are you going? You look like you're going someplace special."

"Yes, I am. I'm taking Lorna to dinner and the opera afterwards," Spencer said sheepishly.

"Oh, I see," Emma said smiling. "Tell me, when did this thing happen?"

"What do you mean, 'happen'?" Spencer said pretending to be innocent.

Emma started laughing. "I was not born yesterday you know. Besides, she's my friend, remember?"

"Nothing has happened yet. You're very nosey?" Spencer said.

"Spencer, Lorna is my best friend. I'm warning you. If you hurt her, I'll never forgive you. Ever."

"Don't worry. I'll behave myself."

"You better."

Spencer kissed his sister on her forehead. "OK, I better be going. I don't want her to keep waiting."

"Enjoy your night while I stay home bored to tears."

"You? Bored? That will be the day. You'll find something to do, I know you well enough."

"All right now. Kiss Lorna for me," she said then realized she said the wrong thing.

"Will do. Anytime," Spencer laughed.

"You're a brute, you know that. Just say hello for me, will you?"

"I will. Bye." He closed the door humming to himself.

Emma shook her head. "Men."

After their first date, Spencer tried to have dinner with Lorna as often as his schedule at the bank allowed him to. They were happy together and found easy company with each other. All through winter break from college, Spencer took Lorna to the theater, to the opera and to dinner as often as he could. Sometimes, Emma would join them. They were having such a great time and he knew he was falling in love with Lorna and so did she.

Then college resumed and Lorna left for Vassar with Emma. Spencer was busy at the bank. He called her during the weekend when he was home. Hearing her voice on the other end of the line gave him much pleasure. He knew she wanted to finish her studies and he was proud of her. He looked forward to rare occasions when Lorna came home. Spencer found excuses to take off from work early and take her out to dinner. He wished he could see her more often.

Since Lorna was out of town, he kept himself busy working late at night. His social life was nil. He was too exhausted anyway to go out after work. Besides, he did not want to see anyone else. He knew he had found the girl he wanted to marry. He went straight home with more work to do. His father was very pleased at the way he was working hard at the bank.

Emma and Lorna graduated from college in late April and went back to New York. Emma could not make up her mind whether to look for a job or joined the League of Women Voters. Lorna found a temporary job as a secretary in a public relation office. She and Spencer saw each other more often now that she was back in New York.

As spring turned into summer, things were not doing well at the bank. As Spencer worked more late hours at the bank, he saw Lorna less and less. He was getting depressed. He wanted to see her more often but his job needed more of his attention.

The financial situation at work was beginning to deteriorate. The Depression was beginning to be felt at home as well. Spencer was getting worried about how the bank would survive. It was beginning to take its toll on his relationship with Lorna. He could not see her more often and he did not want to make any permanent commitment to Lorna.

For the Labor Day weekend, Emma invited Lorna to spend some time with her at *Wentworth Hall* unbeknownst to Spencer. Lorna just finished her temporary assignment at the public relation office where she was working. Lorna agreed to come to *Wentworth Hall*. Spencer also planned to spend the Labor Day weekend in Long Island to take advantage of the last weekend of the summer. Margaret and George were away on vacation at the French Riviera so they had the house to themselves.

The day after they arrived, Lorna told Emma she wanted to talk to Spencer alone and can she give her an hour to be with him alone.

"Is something wrong?" Emma asked.

"I don't know."

Emma did not pursue the subject. She agreed to let Lorna alone in the house with Spencer. Then she went to the library knowing Spencer would be there and told Spencer she had to do some errands in town.

"Is Lorna going with you?"

"No. She does not want to," she said not wanting to tell him that it was Lorna's idea.

"OK. I'll keep her company."

"I know you would," Emma said and smiled broadly.

"Where is she now?"

"I left her in the drawing room reading."

"OK. I'll join her in a while."

As soon as Emma went to see Spencer, Lorna went out to the terrace thinking how to approach the subject. She was staring at the landscape beyond. The leaves were beginning to turn colors. She was trying to gather her courage on how to tell Spencer what she was thinking. She knew he would not be happy but it had to be done. It was bothering her for too long. She stood poised at the edge of the terrace, gazing down the long green stretch of lawn, yet not really seeing it, an abstracted expression on her face. She was thinking in the last month or so, Spencer was preoccupied. Something was bothering him. She had asked him about it several times but he would not open up. She wanted to reach out to him but he refused to share what was bothering him. He was getting obtuse and she was losing her patience. They had a few arguments about it and that's when she decided to go to Bar Harbor and give their relationship a needed break. She also wanted to know what's holding him up. She wanted to marry him if only he would say the word but he was stalling. Why? There's got to be a reason. There was something he was not telling her. It could not go on forever like this. On the outside Spencer seemed happy but he refused to commit. She could not understand what he was waiting for. She decided maybe it was time to cool off their relationship and really sort out their feelings. She would tell Spencer about her plan.

She heard the French door open and Spencer joined her at the terrace.

"So you're here. I was looking for you. Emma said you were in the drawing room. Penny for your thought," he said.

"Hi," she said quietly without looking at him and kept staring at the landscape.

"What's wrong?" Spencer asked.

"Spencer, my temporary job just finished and before I look for another job, I want to go away and give our relationship a necessary break. Maybe it is better for both of us. This way, we can sort out our feelings."

Spencer was stunned. He was not expecting it. "Lorna, please don't do that. I want you near me. I love you and you know that," Spencer said almost pleading.

"I love you too but something is bothering you and you don't want to tell me. Something is holding you up and you don't want me to know the reason. Why?"

"I just want you to wait a while. Right now, I cannot afford to lavish you with things you deserve."

"I don't want anything. I just want you to love me as I love you."

"Maybe things will turn around soon."

"That's what I mean, Spencer. We cannot go on like this forever. What's holding you up? You have to tell me and trust me. If you love me, you have to let me share what's bothering you."

"I can't. I wish I could. We just have to wait." Spencer refused to tell her his financial worries.

"In that case, there is no point in arguing. I think it is better for both of us to take a break. I'll go away for a while."

"No. Don't say that. I don't want you to go," Spencer begged her.

Lorna shook her head and was almost in tears but she controlled herself. Seeing her so upset, Spencer asked, "Where are you going and when?"

"I'm staying at my grandmother's place in Bar Harbor. She has a small cottage there overlooking the ocean. It would be very peaceful. I'm going tomorrow after I leave from here."

"So soon? I did not know your grandmother has a place there."

"She's had it for a long time. She used to have a cottage in Newport but with the influx of the nouveau riche as she called them, Grandma moved out of Newport northward to Bar Harbor on Mount Desert Island in Maine."

Newport, often considered the queen of American resort cities became fashionable as early as the late eighteenth century. Wealthy entrepreneurs from South Carolina, Georgia and Philadelphia spent their excess money in the pursuit of expensive recreation in the refreshing northern climate. Life in Newport in those days was decorous and restrained. In addition to the heavy schedule of balls in the evening, there were days spent in sport, in eating large meals, and in exposure to the healthy salt air. Newport's "cottages", though large were really cottages. It was not until the Civil War that the age of the gilt-and-marble Newport palace began, and vulgarity was introduced by such "new" wealthy people as the Vanderbilts contributing "The Breakers," certainly the most famous, if not the largest, of Newport's mansions lining up Bellevue Avenue. Newport had become too grand and ostentatious. Older people of "refinement, wealth, and fashion" took a horrified look at what was happening, and began moving quietly away to a more sedate place like Saunderstown, Rhode Island across Narragansett Bay or Bar Harbor hoping to capture the old Newport, rustic and athletic.

Lorna left the next day and headed straight to her grandmother's place in Bar Harbor. Spencer was not too happy about it but neither was she but she was determined to do it just to make sure about their feelings. Maybe it was not meant to be. For the first few days at Bar Harbor, she missed Spencer and was miserable. She tried to keep herself busy. She played tennis, went hiking, tried to climb as many of the island's hills as possible in the morning, and then sat down for picnic lunch under the trees with her grandmother.

By the end of the first week, she was getting attuned to her surroundings and there was one place in the property where she found peace. The garden was a magical place for her and therapeutic as well. She still missed Spencer and wanted to contact him but pride was in the way. She struggled hard not to call him. She wanted him to call her but he never did. Maybe he was busy at work but even on weekends, the call never came. She was beginning to wonder if his love for her was real. She buried herself with things she enjoyed just to forget her misery. The garden never failed to give her a sense of accomplishment and satisfaction. Whenever she began to garden, whether large or small, she gave free rein to her imagination, and every plot of ground that fell into her talented hands was miraculously transformed, became a breathtaking testament to her instinctive understanding of nature. She was now contented and trying to forget Spencer but there were times that she could not. He was still in her mind no matter what.

Lorna was an inspired gardener. Flowers, plants, trees, and shrubs were woven into a tapestry of living color and design by her, one that stunned the eye with its compelling beauty. Yet despite her careful planning, none of her gardens ever looked in the least contrived. Indeed, there was a genuine old-world charm about them, for she planted them with wild abandon. It was a typical English garden with old-fashioned flowers, plenty of roses and shrubs with colors complementing each other. She could not wait for spring when all the spring bulbs she planted would be coming up. She looked at her garden and in spite of her effort to forget Spencer, the garden reminded her of the garden at *Wentworth Hall*. There were days when all she could think of was Spencer and she felt depressed. She wondered if he missed her.

Spencer was miserable after Lorna left for Bar Harbor. He wanted to marry her but at this time, he was worried about the bank. He thought of going up to Bar Harbor but he could not take a day off. He was torn between seeing Lorna or staying at home and keeping an eye on what was happening to the economy. If the economy did not recover, the bank could lose a lot of money and his portfolio could suffer a big hit. He could not marry now with his financial situation in limbo. What if the stock market collapsed? There were rumors going around Wall Street and it looked like it was inevitable. If he went broke, he could lose everything including *Wentworth Hall*. He had to find a solution to his dilemma. Much as he loved Lorna, what kind of future could he give her if he had no money. He would not have anything to offer her.

His first priority was to find a way to save *Wentworth Hall*, his legacy. That was his duty, to preserve his inheritance. It was expected of him. He could not disappoint his parents and the trust that his grandfather left him. It was a big order which took priority over his own happiness.

## Chapter 13

October weather was perfect. The summer heat was gone and the cool air was invigorating with the autumn leaves turning such majestic colors. Spencer decided he would spend a few days at *Wentworth Hall* to unwind. Nothing like riding with the wind blowing around his face to lift his spirits. He looked forward to riding around the property with Sultan. He was in need of some rest and relaxation. He had been having too much stress lately. His breakup with Lorna and his work were too much for him. Maybe a respite from the city would do him some good. He was looking forward to a quiet time at home at *Wentworth Hall*. He always found solace and peace there. He missed Lorna.

Emma decided to join her brother at *Wentworth Hall*. Paul Conley drove them to Long Island early Friday afternoon.

Emma knew what happened between him and Lorna. Lorna told her before she left for Bar Harbor. She could not do anything about it. She was mad at her brother for causing the breakup. She just hoped they would be reconciled soon.

There was a polo match that Saturday and Emma wanted to go see the polo match at the Meadow Brook Country Club. She asked Spencer to go with her. He did not really want to go. He would rather stay home and go riding as he intended to do. Emma was persistent. To please his sister, he finally agreed and took her.

At half time, Spencer walked to the hospitality tent to get some refreshment. Emma stayed at their table talking with some friends. As he approached the hospitality tent, Spencer saw a familiar face, an old classmate from Harvard, Richard Savage from South Carolina.

"Hello, Richard. Fancy meeting you here."

"Hello, Spencer. You look great."

"What's up with you? What are you doing up North?"

"I decided to see how my horse is doing? One of those horses playing came from my farm in Aiken."

"Really? Who is riding it?"

"That fellow, Sinclair from Mill Neck."

"I don't think I know him."

"You should. They have plenty of dough. I heard you are running a bank now."

"Just started last year. I was abroad for three years."

"Good for you. I never made it out of the country. Dad wanted me to manage the horse farm after graduation so I got stuck in South Carolina."

"So when are you going back?"

"In a day or so." At that moment, a beautiful blonde lady walked into the tent. She looked about twenty-three years old.

"Oh, there you are. Your wife is looking for you," she told Richard.

Richard turned to Spencer. "I want you to meet my hostess, Sally Sinclair. We are staying at her parents' house." He turned to Sally. "This is Spencer Wentworth, an old buddy from Harvard."

"Nice meeting you, Mr. Wentworth." They shook hands.

"My pleasure, Miss Sinclair," Spencer said.

"Call me Sally," she said.

"Spencer then."

"OK." She gave him a broad smile. She looked rather pretty, Spencer thought.

Richard excused himself and went looking for his wife. Spencer did the same and went back to Emma with a couple of drinks.

"What took you so long?" Emma said.

"Where are your friends?" Spencer said handing her a glass of ginger ale.

"They went back to their table. I was getting bored here waiting for you to come back. The game is about to begin again."

"Sorry. I met an old friend from Harvard."

"Who?" Emma took a sip of her drink and looked at him quizzically.

"Richard Savage. Remember him?"

"Vaguely. Is that the guy from Charleston?"

"Well, not exactly. He is from Aiken, South Carolina."

"Same thing. What's he doing here?"

"One of the horses playing came from his horse farm and he wanted to see him play. Sinclair is riding him."

"They played very well together."

"Yes, they did so far. We'll see."

The following day, Spencer got an invitation for a dinner party at the Sinclair House that night. People of the horse crowd would be gathered to honor Richard Savage and his wife whose horse just won the day before. It would be their last night in New York. They were leaving the next day for South Carolina.

Spencer wanted to see his old Harvard buddy again. He sent a reply that he would be coming. He was looking forward to seeing Richard one more time before he went back to South Carolina. He did not know when he would see him again.

Paul Conley drove him to Mill Neck that night. He told Paul to pick him up after three hours. They passed through an iron grilled gate then along a winding road to a big white painted colonial home on top of a hill. The house was lit brightly. Paul went around the circular courtyard with a three-tiered fountain. He stopped the car and opened the door for Spencer to come out.

"Thank you, Paul. See you in three hours," Spencer said.

"OK, Mr. Spencer. I'll be on time," Paul said. Spencer climbed the couple of steps to the portico and knocked at the door. Paul drove off.

The large front doors opened before him and a servant let him in. He took Spencer's card and led him through the long corridor lined with horse pictures and hunting scenes to the drawing room where the reception had already begun.

The room was magnificent. Scattered columns and pilasters stretching up to the coffered painted ceiling gave it an illusion of even greater height. It was lit by two massive, dazzling chandeliers hanging on chains that glistened like gold, though of course they weren't. An Aubusson rug was on the floor. There were two marble fireplaces at each end of the room.

As he entered the room, he saw Sally come to the door with her parents. She was wearing a light yellow chiffon ankle length dress which accentuated her blond hair. Mrs. Sinclair was in a navy blue evening dress and Mr. Sinclair was in a white tie and tails.

After the formal introduction to her parents, Sally ushered Spencer inside to join the horsey crowd. Within minutes, they were surrounded by a swirl of color and voices, muted laughter, and the clink of glasses. The conversation was polite and most of it meaningless, simply a way for everyone to take stock of one another while not seeming to do so. Spencer appeared perfectly at ease as they spoke to one group, then another. Sally watched him with admiration as he smiled at everyone even people he did not know, showed interest and passed subtle compliments. There was an art to it that she was not yet quite ready to do. She was afraid she would end up looking as if she was trying too hard to copy those born into this social station, and they would never forgot such a slip. Someone spoke to Spencer casually. He could not remember the man's name, but he listened as if he were interested. Someone else joined in and the discussion became more serious. He made the odd remark as he took a glass of champagne from a passing footman.

Spencer glanced around and saw his friend. Sally turned to the direction where he was looking and saw Richard. They excused themselves and moved on and made their way toward Richard.

Richard introduced Spencer to his wife, Marilyn, a Southern beauty. Richard and Spencer tried to catch up on the news. Spencer filled him up with his travel experience in Europe. Sally was fascinated with all the stories.

When the dinner was announced, Spencer found that he was to sit between Sally to his right and Marilyn to his left. He really wanted to be near Richard so they could talk more freely. But the Sinclairs had a different agenda in mind.

Sally's father was a self-made millionaire who just moved in the neighborhood from New Jersey. Her parents wanted her to marry up to improve their social status in the community and what a better way than to marry their daughter to one from old money who also belongs to more exclusive clubs in Long Island. With her beauty and fat bankroll, her parents knew they could find a suitable husband for their daughter. They thought they found one in Spencer. A good looking fellow from old money, prominent banking family, well-educated, just a perfect match for their daughter.

Sally was supposed to charm Spencer. Her parents found out all about Spencer and his family from Richard Savage. Richard told them all what he knew about Spencer when they were roommates at Elliot House at Harvard. As far as Richard knew, his parents were of the old money. His grandfather was quite wealthy and well known in the business community. After hearing all that, Mr. and Mrs. Sinclair knew that Spencer would be a good catch for their daughter. They could match money for money except the Wentworths got the old money and the Sinclairs got the new money.

The Sinclairs went all out to be nice to Spencer and all Spencer wanted to do was talk to Richard. Spencer not wanting to be rude, played a perfect guest but he was not too happy.

"Spencer, what do you do with your spare time," Sally asked while they were having dessert.

"I barely have any spare time these days. We are extremely busy at the bank and they constantly need my attention."

She knotted her eyebrows.

"But since you own the bank, you can always take off, can't you?"

"I don't own the bank, not yet anyway. But it is not that easy. I have a duty to work harder than anyone else."

"That's nonsense."

I'm afraid it is true."

By the time Spencer left the party, Sally had talked him into taking her out to the opera. He did not quite know how she was able to wiggle that out of him. But she did somehow.

And so the following weekend, he told Emma he was taking out Sally Sinclair to the Metropolitan Opera. Emma did not like the idea.

"Why are doing this?" Emma asked Spencer.

"Doing what?"

"Taking Sally to the opera. She might not like opera."

"She asked me to take her. I could not refuse without being rude."

"Don't you know what she was trying to do?"

"I know. So what?"

"Spencer. I always thought you're very much in love with Lorna. Apparently I was wrong," Emma sat on the couch looking sad and felt sorry for her friend.

"She broke off with me. Remember? I did not. What do you want me to do? Be a hermit."

"That's what I mean. You're still vulnerable. You're upset and you are doing this on the rebound."

"I am not. Besides, Sally is beautiful and has tons of money."

"Spencer, how can you talk that way? It's not like you. Since when did money become important to you? When did this change happen?" Emma was suddenly sorry for her brother.

"Leave me alone. I know what I'm doing. I don't want to talk about it anymore. OK? I'm going to take her out and no one can stop me," he said and stormed out of the room.

Emma stared at his back and shook her head. She was mortified. She was always close to her brother and they never fought like this before. Something was terribly wrong.

Spencer walked for a couple of blocks to clear his head before he hailed a taxicab to take him to East 50th Street and First Avenue where Sally was in residence at her parent's co-op overlooking the East River. He was so upset of what transpired between him and his sister. They never fought like this before. What has gotten into him? He was in a lot of stress with what was going on in the economy and his break-up with Lorna was not helping a bit. Both his business worries and his personal life had gotten worse. Maybe this outing with Sally will ease his pain a bit about his break-up with Lorna.

The ride did not take too long. He entered the building and approached the concierge desk.

"May I help you, sir?" the clerk said.

"My name is Spencer Wentworth. I'm looking for Room 725, Sinclair." Spencer said.

"Yes, sir. Just take the elevator to your left."

"Thanks," Spencer said and proceeded to the elevator. The elevator man took him upstairs. He got off on the seventh floor and followed the rooms' sign. He knocked at the door and Sally opened it. She was dressed in a beautiful coral shift with multiple strands of pearl hanging from her neck. Her hair was cut short and bobbed adorned with a band of silvery fabric with glittering stones.

"You look fabulous," he said.

"Thank you. Do you want to have a drink before we go?" she said demurely. It was tempting. He really needed a drink but decided not to.

"I better not. We don't want to miss the starting aria."

"OK then. I'm ready," she said. She took her wrap and they went down by the elevator. The elevator man said as they alighted on the first floor. "Good night, Miss Sinclair. Have a great time."

"Thank you. I will," she said.

Spencer smiled.

"Good night, sir," he said to Spencer.

"Goodnight."

## Chapter 14

It was a lovely autumn evening. The air was crisp coming from the East River. Spencer and Sally decided to walk to the corner a few steps from the entrance to the building. Sally was in a happy mood and Spencer tried to be as cheerful as he could be. The scene with Emma still bothered him. He did not know why he acted the way he did. He tried to shake it off his mind. He saw a taxicab coming their way and he hailed it. The taxicab abruptly stopped in front of them. He opened the door for her to get in. He sat beside her on the back seat. "Metropolitan Opera please," he told the driver.

"Yes, sir," the driver said as he started the taxicab across town and down Broadway.

"What opera are we seeing?" Sally asked Spencer as she leaned back on her seat.

"Didn't I tell you? I'm sorry. It's called Norma by Vincenzo Bellini," Spencer said.

*Norma* is an opera in two acts by Vincenzo Bellini with libretto by Felice Romani after *Norma* by Alexandre Soumet. It was first produced at La Scala in Milan on December 26, 1831. The opera is regarded as a leading example of the *bel canto* genre and a major soprano aria, *Casta diva*, in act 1, is one of the most famous arias of the nineteenth century. Richard Wagner wrote that *Norma* was "indisputably Bellini's most successful composition". In this opera, Bellini has undoubtedly risen to the greatest heights of his talent.

"I have never been to an opera," Sally said.

"You haven't? Why?" He wondered if it was a mistake taking Sally to the opera but it's too late now. Besides she was the one who suggested it.

"Nobody asked me before," she said lamely. "Basically, I don't know anyone who likes opera." She thought maybe asking Spencer to take her to one would impress him.

Spencer felt sorry for her. He knew most of his family's friends go to the opera. A lot of them had a theater box. His family had theirs. "You'll love it. I started seeing them while I was in Europe and I started to like them," Spencer said. "Rosa Ponselle is singing the title role."

"Who is she? I've never heard of her," Sally said.

"She is an American operatic soprano with the most beautiful voice, considered one of the greatest sopranos of the century for the opulence of tone, breadth of range and perfection of technique," Spencer said.

"She must be very talented," Sally said in awe.

"She is. The title role is one of the most difficult and wide-ranging parts in the entire repertoire. It calls for great vocal control of range, flexibility, and dynamics as well as containing a wide range of emotions: conflict of personal and public life, romantic life, maternal love, friendship, jealousy, murderous intent, and resignation. Rosa Ponselle did it all effortlessly."

"I can't wait to hear her. Who is conducting?" Sally asked.

"Most likely it will be Tullio Serafin. Artur Bodanzky usually does the German repertory," he said. The whole thing went over Sally's head but she could not let Spencer know that.

The taxicab stopped in front of an industrial looking building at 1411 Broadway between West 39th Street and West 40th. Because of its outside façade, people nicknamed the Metropolitan Opera House "The Yellow Brick Brewery".

"Here we are," Spencer said. He paid the cab driver and opened the door. He got out of the cab and held the door open and helped Sally out of the cab.

Patrons were already pouring in to the theater. Ladies in exquisite gowns with glittering jewelry and gentlemen in black tie were crowding in to get inside. As soon as they walked in the building, they joined in the crowd of several patrons going to their respective boxes. Spencer led Sally to the Wentworth's box on the right side of the hall on the first tier of boxes from the "Golden Horseshoe" of the opera house, a showplace for New York society. They had a nice view of the orchestra pit and the distance from their seat to the stage was just perfect. They could see the performers closely. Sally was very impressed. She wanted to be with this class of people, not the group of people her parents associated with.

The Metropolitan Opera Company was founded in 1880 and was designed by J. Cleaveland Cady to create an alternative to New York's old established Academy of Music opera house. The subscribers to the Academy's limited number of private boxes represented the highest stratum in New York society. It was the opera season that made the Academy the mainstay of social life for New York's "uppertens". Upper Ten Thousand, or simply, *The Upper Ten*, is a phrase coined in 1852 by American poet Nathaniel Parker Willis to describe the upper circles of New York, and hence of other major cities. The oldest and most prominent families owned seats in the theater's boxes. This emblem of social prominence was passed down from generation to generation. Spencer's family was one of them.

By 1880, these "old money" families would not admit New York's newly minted industrialists into their long-established social circle. The inability of New York's wealthy industrial and mercantile families, including the Vanderbilts, Goulds and Morgans, to gain access to this closed society inspired the creation of the new Metropolitan Opera Association in 1880. Frustrated with being excluded, the Metropolitan Opera's founding subscribers determined to build a new opera house that would outshine the old Academy in every way. A group of men assembled at Delmonico's restaurant on April 28, 1880. They elected officers and established subscriptions for ownership in the new company. The first Met subscribers included members of the Morgan, Roosevelt, and Vanderbilt families, all of whom had been excluded from the Academy.

The trustees of the Academy belatedly attempted to head off the competition by offering to add 26 new boxes to the 18 the Academy already had, to accommodate the Vanderbilts, Morgans, Rockefellers who were behind the planned new venue, but it was too late to fend them off.

The Metropolitan Opera opened its doors for the first time on October 22, 1883 at 39th and Broadway with a performance of *Faust*. It was twice the size of the Academy. The building was financed by wealthy New Yorkers, among them the Vanderbilts and Astors, and it was no accident that special seating was provided for this elite group in 122 very visible boxes called the "Golden Horseshoe." The building contained three tiers of private elegant boxes in which the scions of New York's powerful new Industrial families could display their wealth and establish their social prominence. The new opera house was an instant success with New York society and music lovers alike, and the Academy of Music's opera season folded just three years after the Met opened.

After a fire gutted the interior of the building in the summer of 1892, the theater was immediately rebuilt, reopening in the fall of 1893. Boxes were reduced to seventy, divided between two tiers. The damage from the 1892 fire was estimated at $300,000 at a time when the building was insured for only $60,000. However, even with the renovations the Metropolitan Opera always had physical inadequacies: continued poor sight lines, a small stage and backstage, and very little storage space. Rehearsals took place on the main stage; the chorus sought out any unoccupied room (usually the smoking room or the ladies' parlor) and the ballet rehearsed in what later became Sherry's Restaurant. Costumes, sets, wigs, props, and accessories were all brought to the House as needed for each performance.

A major renovation was completed in 1903. The interior of the opera house was extensively redesigned by the architects, Carrère and Hastings. The familiar golden auditorium with its sunburst chandelier, and curved proscenium, the area of a theatre surrounding the stage opening, inscribed with the names of six composers (Gluck, Mozart, Beethoven, Wagner, Gounod and Verdi), dates from this time. The first of the Met's signature gold damask stage curtains was installed in 1906, completing the look that the old Metropolitan Opera House maintained until its closing in 1966.

The theater was noted for its elegant interior and excellent acoustics, providing a glamorous home for the company. However, as early as the 1900s the backstage facilities were deemed to be severely inadequate for a large opera company. The Met's scenery and sets were a regular sight leaning against the building outside on 39th Street where they had to be shifted between performances. It was inevitable that the Company would seek a new home. Various plans were put forward over the years to build a new home and designs for new opera houses were created by various architects including Joseph Urban. Proposed new locations included Columbus Circle but none of these plans came to fruition. In the 1920s John D. Rockefeller included a new home for the Metropolitan Opera in the plans for Rockefeller Center making it the centerpiece of Rockefeller Center but by the 1930s the idea was shelved due to the Depression. Only with the development of Lincoln Center on New York's Upper West Side did the Met finally have the opportunity to build a modern opera house.

The orchestra started playing the overture and all eyes strained toward the proscenium. The curtain rose.

*Oroveso leads the procession of the druids in the forest to pray for victory against the invading Romans. The Druids pray that Norma will come and have the courage to break the peace with the Romans. Pollione and Flavio enter. Although Norma has secretly broken her vows in order to love him and has borne him two children, Pollione tells Flavio that he no longer loves her, having fallen in love with the priestess Adalgisa. But he expresses some remorse, describing his dream in which Adalgisa was beside him at the altar of Venus and a huge storm arose.*

They hear the trumpets sounding to announce Norma's arrival.

*All kneel as she approaches. "The time is not ripe for our revenge", she declares, stating that Rome will perish one day by being worn down. Then, with the mistletoe in hand, she approaches the altar with a plea to the "Chaste Goddess".*

Rosa Ponzelle sang the most beautiful aria "Casta diva".

*Norma calls for all to complete the rites and then clear the uninitiated from the grove. To herself, she declares that she cannot hurt Pollione, but desires that things return to where they used to be. The assembled crowd accepts her cautious approach, and all leave the grove.*

The opera continued . . .

*With Adalgisa and Pollione at the Temple of Irminsul in the grove, Pollione sang an aria called "Va crudele" and then Adalgisa and Pollione did a duet called Vieni in Roma. At Norma's residence, Norma appears to be upset and orders her maid, Clotilde, to take the two children away from her, expressing very conflicted feelings about them. She tells Clotilde that Pollione has been recalled to Rome, but does not know if he will take her or how he feels about leaving his children. As Adalgisa approaches, the children are taken away. Adalgisa tells Norma she has fallen in love with a Roman whom she does not name. When Norma asks to describe the man whom she loves, Pollione enters the room. As Norma furiously turns to confront Pollione, Adalgisa is confused. Then a trio was sung beginning with Norma, then Adalgisa, then the two women together, followed by Pollione alone. After which all three repeat their part, singing at first singly, then together. After angry exchanges, then a brief duet of Adalgisa and Pollione and a trio. Then the sound of the Druids calling Norma to the temple. Pollione storms out.*

In Act 2, after orchestral introduction . . .

*The scene started at Norma's dwelling with Norma considering to kill her children but changed her mind. She demands to see Adalgisa and instructs her to take her kids to*

Rome to be with their father and she became Pollione's wife. Instead, Adalgisa renounces Pollione. In Scene 2, the Druid warriors gather and prepare themselves to attack the Romans. Oroveso enters with the news that the time has not arrived to strike.

Norma enters the temple and found out that Adalgisa has failed to persuade Pollione to return but Adalgisa is returning and wishes to take her vows at the altar and that the Roman has sworn to abduct her from the temple. In anger, Norma strikes a gong-like shield as a summons to war. Trumpets sound and Oroveso and the Druids all rush in, demanding to know what is happening. They hear Norma's answer and the soldiers take up the refrain: "Guerra, guerra!" / War, war!, while Norma proclaims "Blood, blood! Revenge!"

In order for Norma to complete the rites to authorize going to war, Oroveso demands to know who will be the sacrificial victim. At that moment, Clotilde rushes in to announce that a Roman has desecrated the temple, but that he has been apprehended. It is Pollione who is led in, and Norma is urged to take the sacrificial knife to stab him, but upon approaching him, she is unable to perform the deed. The assembled crowd demands to know why, but she dismisses them, stating that she needs to question her victim.

The crowd departs and Norma and Pollione sang a duet. Norma demands that he forever shun Adalgisa; only then will she release him and never see him again. He refuses, and she vents her anger by telling him that she will then kill her children. "Strike me instead", he demands, "so that only I alone will die", but she quickly rounds on him with the announcement that not only will all the Romans die, but so will Adalgisa, who has broken her vows as a priestess. This prompts him to plead for her life. When Pollione demands the knife, she calls the priests to assemble. Norma announces that it would be better to sacrifice a priestess who has broken her *vows, and orders the pyre to be lit. Oroveso demands to know who is to be sacrificed while Pollione demands that she keep silent, but Norma then reveals that it is she who is to be the victim because she is the guilty one, a high Priestess who has broken her vows, has become involved with the enemy, and has borne his children.*

*In the concerted finale, Norma pleads with Oroveso to spare her children. As she prepares to leap into the flames, the re-enamoured Pollione joins her, declaring "your pyre is mine as well. There, a holier and everlasting love will begin".*

All through the opera, all Spencer could think was Lorna, how he, like Pollione was unfaithful to her. He missed Lorna and he realized how wrong it was for him to shift his attention to Sally. Lorna was his true love and no other woman could replace her in his heart. Sally was a mere diversion. He wondered why Emma had not even mentioned Lorna to him. He was sure they were communicating with each other. He somehow had to find out how she was.

The opera was a roaring success. Sally was mesmerized at some points. She could not believe that she would love it but she did.

"Thank you for taking me," she told Spencer as they sat down to dinner at Lüchow's.

"Did you like it?" he asked.

"Immensely. I never thought I would but the music was fabulous and the singers were magnificent. What a voice that Rosa Ponzell has," she said.

"I'm glad you enjoy it," Spencer said.

That first outing lead to another and whenever he could get out of the bank, Sally never stopped asking him to take her somewhere. Spencer tried to resist at first but with constant invitation, Spencer finally gave up and started enjoying her company. He still missed Lorna and she occupied much of his mind. But since Lorna was too far away, he could not do much. He was busy at the bank and could not go to see her in Bar Harbor, he reasoned out. His conscience was still nagging him that he was doing it wrong. He should not be involved with anyone else whom he did not intend to marry. But he could not shake out his old habits. He was a playboy in Europe so why could he not be here at home. Maybe he could marry someone who had plenty of money and then he could save *Wentworth Hall*. It was the only way he could think of saving his skin. Marry someone rich like Sally with her money and then his problem would be solved. Sounded like a brilliant idea.

He knew his parents would not approve of Sally. They wanted him to marry someone else in their social circle. However, there was only one person he wanted to marry and that was Lorna but she did not have any money. By marrying Sally he would save *Wentworth Hall*. The Sinclairs wanted their social status and he wanted their money. Not a bad exchange, he thought.

By early November 1928, Spencer decided he would ask Sally to marry him. He had not heard from Lorna and he imagined their relationship was finished. Gone forever and he had to move on.

Spencer went to see Sally the day after Thanksgiving. After dinner with her family, they wandered into the conservatory. Sally was showing him her mother's collection of orchids when Spencer suddenly went on his knees and held Sally's hand. He looked up to her who seemed to be surprised.

"Sally, will you marry me?"

Sally could not believe it. "Are you asking me to marry you?"

"Yes, will you say yes?"

Without thinking, she said, "Yes, I will."

Spencer pulled out a robin egg blue box from his pocket. "Open it," he said.

She untied the ribbon and opened the box and saw a ring of beautiful sapphire surrounded by diamonds. Spencer got off his knees and helped her put it on. Then he kissed her lightly on her lips. Sally could not be happier.

They went back in the drawing room where her family was gathered and made the announcement.

"We just got engaged," she said beaming broadly.

"Yes, we did," Spencer said smiling.

Everyone got off their chairs and congratulated the newly betrothed. Her parents were thrilled. They were not expecting it to happen so soon. Their daughter must have done a pretty good job to hook up one of the most eligible bachelors in town. Now they had something to look forward to. They would now be included in the inner circle of the old-moneyed class.

The next few days were hectic at the Sinclair's house. Mrs. Sinclair started making a guest list after putting the announcement in the papers. Plans for the wedding went into full force. The date was picked for next spring. They intended to show the old money that their daughter was worth it. They would do everything to impress Spencer's friends and relatives.

The Wentworths were not too keen by the engagement but they went along with Spencer's decision. His parents thought he was old enough to know what he was doing. Emma was livid but she loved her brother too much and did not want to alienate him so she went along with it too. Spencer seemed happy on the surface but deep down he was not. His heart belonged to someone else and it would always be. There were times when he questioned himself if he was doing the right thing. It did not bode well with his conscience but he wanted to save his legacy and with the bank on the brink of bankruptcy, he could not think of any other solution. Maybe he would learn to love Sally in the future. He would try his best. He would put Lorna out of his mind though difficult it might be. Since he had not heard anything from her, he knew they were finished.

While Spencer found a solution to his personal problem, his business problem was another matter. The business atmosphere was getting worse.

## Chapter 15

As Spencer walked up Wall Street after seeing his stockbroker, his mind was in turmoil like the market was in turmoil. People on Wall Street were panicking all over. Everyone was selling. The stock market was in its downward spiral and nobody knew what would happen next. It was a scary situation. Unemployment was high. There was a long line at the soup kitchen. There was uncertainty in the economy and people were beginning to panic.

Spencer walked aimlessly toward uptown. He paused at the corner of Broadway and Wall Street in front of the Trinity Church with its high steeple.

The Trinity Church had been part of the downtown landscape since it was built in 1696. New York Episcopalians had attended this handsome edifice made of brown hewn stone and commanded a formidable view of the Hudson River. Trinity Church opened its doors during a church-building boom on Manhattan when Quaker meetinghouse, a Huguenot church, Presbyterians church, Baptists church and Dutch Reformed church joined them. North American's first synagogue opened in a private home off Broadway on Beaver Street in 1691. Worshippers would not get a free-standing temple until 1730. The Act of Toleration, passed by Parliament in 1689, guaranteed the right of all to public worship, as did legislation adopted by the New York Assembly two years later. Trinity Church expanded twice before 1737 to accommodate a burgeoning congregation that consisted not only of English colonists but also Huguenots and Dutch recruits.

As if some magnet was directing him, Spencer entered the church. He sat down in one of the pews near the back and started to pray. It was not like him to do it. He was not a religious man. This time, he had the urge of asking for Providence's assistance. His financial situation was in dire need of divine intervention if nothing else.

He looked up and saw the single stained glass window at the east end, all the other windows were plain and bathed the interior of the church in a soft light. The walls were wood-paneled like that of a library. It reminded Spencer of the library at *Wentworth Hall*, his beloved home that he wanted to save desperately.

Trinity was a fine church, he thought. It was also rich and it had used its money wisely. The church still owned much of the area since its land endowments back in the seventeenth century by Lord Cornbury. The church had been an integral part of New York City, having founded numerous other churches during the early part of the city's history and provided the funds to educate the Negro population at a time when many churches disapproved. Yet the church in its simplicity remains a sanctuary for a lost soul like Spencer. The church had managed its wealth over the years and yet here he is, about to lose everything he had.

He tried to think about what had gone wrong. He should have been more conservative. His grandfather was and so was his father. They depended on fees paid by their clients to manage their money. It was the banker's way. Since they had big clientele and with their political connection, they were able to get some government funds to be placed in their custody and the fee they collected amounted to a fortune. But he was not satisfied with that.

He wanted to make it big and he gambled. He started with his own money but it was not going anywhere so he started borrowing from his rich depositors. He lost some money here and there but as long as he was able to string them along, no one knew he was losing their money. So he borrowed more, recouped some and borrowed more. He figured he could borrow half a million, make ten percent, return the money with a little interest and still he would be able to make nearly fifty thousand dollars. But all the transactions he made, the complete bets he placed on the future of this and that, the hedging of positions, and everything else came down to the fundamental facts that he was placing his bets with someone's else's money and if something went wrong, he would not be able to pay them back.

Now, he realized he could not pay. He had done the numbers. His liabilities exceeded his assets and panic gripped him to his core. Everyone would want their money soon and he was wiped out. He would not be able to pay.

He sat at the pew for quite sometimes and tried to think. He had never been in this difficult situation before. When he was abroad, money seemed to flow freely. His allowance was constantly coming in from his grandfather. How could he be such a fool? His father was very conservative too and managed the bank very efficiently. He thought he could make a big difference by doing what everyone was doing. The market was booming and he decided to play the stock market. He thought the rise in equity would go on forever. Why didn't he see the signs? His stockbroker should have advised him but he kept on pushing him to invest more. He was too busy at the bank to pay much attention on what was going on with his portfolio. That's why he got a financial adviser to advise him but apparently the financial adviser did not do his job. Now he was about to lose everything and he was sick with worries.

After a few minutes, he went outside the church and walked down Wall Street toward the battery. He sat on one of the benches next to a fellow reading the Wall Street Journal. He glanced at the paper and the headline was the same like most days. The market was tumbling down. Everyone was panicking and selling. Something had to be done. The government should do something about it before it got worse.

He stood up and walked uptown. He reached Chelsea. He thought of Lorna. He wanted to see her but he knew she was not home. She was still in Bar Harbor or God knows where. He had not heard from her for a long time. His heart ached. Here he was, engaged to be married to Sally but longing to see someone else. He thought he could talk to Lorna if only she was here. She knew how to cheer him up. But he was engaged now. It made matters worse. He needed Sally's money. He could not back out now. Sally was his only hope for survival. He blamed himself for his stupidity. If he was not greedy, he would not be in this situation. He realized now more than ever that he could not gamble with everyone's money. But it was too late and he had to suffer the consequences. Maybe he could end it all like most people. But that was cowardice. He could not do that to his family. He decided to see Alistair Prescott and get some legal advice. He walked toward Alistair's office.

"I would like to see Mr. Alistair Prescott," he told the receptionist when he got to Alistair's office.

"I'm sorry, Mr. Wentworth. But he is out of town. Do you have an appointment with him? I don't see your name on his appointment book," the receptionist asked because he was not registered on the list of appointments.

"Unhappily no. But it is an emergency."

"Do you want to talk to Mr. Todd Prescott? I'm sure he can help you," the receptionist suggested.

"That would be wonderful."

"He was just finishing up with another client. Can you wait?"

"Certainly." He picked up the newspaper lying on the table. The news was grim. The unemployment rate was going up. Talk of a great depression was imminent. He dropped the paper, disgusted on what he was reading. A man walked out the door of Todd's office. The receptionist picked up the phone and dialed Todd.

"Mr. Spencer Wentworth is here to see you, sir," she said.

"Thanks. I'll come out," Todd said on the other end of the line.

"Mr. Wentworth, he'll be out in a minute," she told Spencer.

"Thank you."

In a few minutes, Todd walked in the reception hall.

"Hi, Spencer. Nice seeing you. This is a surprise. Come on in." Todd shook hands with Spencer who gave him a cursory smile. They walked into Todd's office and Todd closed the door.

"What's up? You don't look happy. Is something the matter?" Todd asked.

"Everything," Spencer said as he sat on the chair opposite Todd.

"So tell me. I'm listening."

"I don't know where to begin."

"Just tell me. Is this something to do with the bank?"

"Not entirely."

"Whew. Personal matters?"

"Sort of."

"OK. In that case, I'm not charging you for this one. As a friend, do tell me your problem."

"I'm in a big mess. I got engaged to Sally Sinclair for the wrong reason. I'm going bankrupt and I need her money to save me from financial ruin."

Todd was shocked at the revelation. Of all people, he did not think Spencer would do such a thing. He was so much in love with Lorna. He sat silent for a while trying to digest the news. He looked at Spencer who looked troubled like a lion trapped in a cave not knowing how to get out.

"First what happened with you and Lorna?" Todd asked.

"We broke off before she went to Bar Harbor."

"Is that the reason why she left for Maine?"

"Yes."

"But why? You were so much in love. I always thought that."

"It was my fault. I could not make up my mind on when to get married. She said she needed a break to sort out her feeling. I haven't heard from her since she left."

"Did you try to write or call her?" Todd asked.

"No, why should I? Besides, I'm so busy," Spencer said lamely.

"Pride, my boy. Pride." Todd started laughing.

"What's so funny?"

"Obviously you are still in love with Lorna and you are miserable. Does Sally know about Lorna?"

"I don't think so."

"Well, at least that part is good. You are not telling her about you and Lorna. Are you?"

"No. Absolutely not."

"That could be a problem later. So are you really proceeding with this crazy plan of yours to marry Sally?" Todd asked.

"I have to. I had no choice if I want to save my skin. I just went to my stockbroker and he told me I'm broke."

Todd felt sorry for his friend. "Maybe you'll learn to love Sally once you are married."

"Maybe." Spencer said although he had his doubts. He stood up. "Thanks for listening. I better get back to work."

Todd stood up. He pat Spencer on the shoulder. "I hate to tell you this but this is my advice to you as a friend. You have to follow your heart or you'll never be happy. Does Emma approve of your engagement to Sally?"

"Not really. We had a fight about that. But you know, Lorna is her best friend so she is prejudiced. She has the opinion that I am making a big mistake."

"I'm afraid I feel the same way but you have to do what you have to do," Todd said.

"Thanks, my friend. What a mess! What have I done?" He walked toward the door. Then he stopped and turned around.

"Why don't you join us for dinner next week?" Spencer asked.

"Splendid idea."

"This weekend is shot. Is Saturday next week good? It's just Emma and me. I'll ask Sally to join us," Spencer said.

"That's fine. I'll put it on my calendar. I have not seen Emma for a while. I've been so busy here too and when I get home, I still have all those briefs to read. I'll see you next week then."

"Great and thanks for listening."

"That's what a friend is for."

## Chapter 16

A couple of weeks after Thanksgiving, Emma got a phone call from Lorna who had gone back to Pittsburgh with her grandmother after two months in Bar Harbor. Lorna told her that her grandmother had a heart attack and passed away. Emma was totally shocked and offered her sincerest condolences. She felt she should go and be with her friend in Pittsburgh since now Lorna was all alone. Emma told her to expect her the next day. When Spencer got home from work, Emma told him.

"I'm leaving tomorrow for Pittsburgh," Emma said.

"Pittsburgh? What for?" Spencer knew Lorna was from Pittsburgh but he thought she was in Bar Harbor vacationing.

"I presume you have not heard the news," Emma said.

"What news?" Spencer suddenly felt worried. He hoped nothing bad had happened to Lorna.

"I thought so. Lorna's grandmother passed away in Pittsburgh. I want to be with her. She's all alone and she needs a friend," she simply said.

Spencer was speechless. He started pacing the floor. Emma watched him in discomfort. She had an idea of what was going on his head. He just got engaged to Sally a couple of weeks ago and now this. He knew Lorna was very close to her grandmother and Emma was her best friend. Emma ought to be with her to comfort her. Deep down he wanted to be with her too and share her grief. But he was now engaged to Sally. How would that look? It could create complications especially if Sally found out about his relationship with Lorna before. He could not possibly be in Pittsburgh.

"I agree. You better go see her. She needs you," he finally said. He bit his lips and aimed toward the door, not wanting his sister to know how he felt.

"Spencer, is that all you have to say?"

He turned around. "What do you want me to say?" he asked angrily.

"I don't understand you," Emma said.

"OK. Give her my sympathy. Are you happy?" Spencer stormed out. He went straight to his room. He paused in front of his desk. He took a picture out of the drawer. It was Lorna's picture taken at Christmas at the house the first time he met her.

"Lorna, why is this happening to us? Why? If you only knew how much you meant to me. I'm a fool getting engaged to someone I don't love. It's not fair." He put the picture back in the drawer. He placed his hands on his head. He was angry at himself. He went towards the window. He looked at the landscape ahead of him. It reminded him of the day he fell in love with her. There at the crest of the little hill where she fell. That was the beginning of it all. From then on, she had been on his mind all the time. He had loved her ever since and wanted to live the rest of his life with her. His financial worries were in the way of his happiness. He wanted her but he also wanted to save his inheritance. It seemed his obligations to his grandfather was winning.

He went to the library, closed the door behind him. He walked toward the fireplace and stood in front of it. He put his hand on the mantle and looked up at the picture above the fireplace, his grandfather's portrait.

"Grandfather, why did you do it? Why did you give me *Wentworth Hall*? I don't deserve it." He stared at his grandfather intently. "How can I save the place? How?" He banged his fist on the mantelpiece.

As if his grandfather was listening, he heard a voice in his head saying. "Everything will be all right. Trust me."

"It's not all right. I know it's not all right." He went to the couch and slumped on it. He put his hand through his hair agonizing on what was happening. He glanced at the picture once more. He stared at it for a long time. He kept on hearing his grandfather's voice in his head. "It will be all right. It will be all right. Trust me. Follow your heart."

"I can't. Sally is my only salvation."

After the funeral, Emma stayed with Lorna for a few days. They had a quiet time together. Emma helped her sort things at the house. Lorna did not know what to do with all the stuff there. Someday, she had to sell most of it. Maybe even the house. She'd rather live in Bar Harbor. She loved the place there near the ocean.

A thought suddenly entered Emma's mind.

"Why don't you spend some time with us at *Wentworth Hall* over the Christmas holidays. It would be good for you to get away. It would be like old times," Emma said. She did not like her friend to be all alone during the holiday.

"Are you sure your parents won't mind?" Lorna asked.

"Are you kidding? They would love to see you," Emma said.

"How about Spencer?" Lorna was adamant because she was afraid to see Spencer again. They had not communicated since they broke off. She knew he was now engaged. Emma told her. It would be awkward to say the least. But Emma was persistent.

Emma did not approve of Spencer's engagement to Sally one bit and she would try to get Lorna and Spencer back together and hoped her plan would work. She would not tell Spencer that Lorna would spend her Christmas with them.

"We'll give him the biggest surprise of his life. I want to see his reaction when he sees you. I don't like that girl, Sally."

It hurts to hear Sally's name. Lorna found out about Sally from Emma who told her everything. Lorna did not like the idea at all of seeing Spencer again. It would open old wounds that she was trying to forget but Emma won't take no for an answer so Lorna finally said, "Yes, I'll go."

"Fantastic. You can take the train and I'll pick you up in Oyster Bay," Emma said with a twinkle in her eyes.

The day before Christmas Spencer came home to find Lorna was staying at *Wentworth Hall* for the Christmas holiday. He was surprised to see her but was told Emma invited her. He was happy to see her but he was in a big dilemma because he invited Sally to have Christmas dinner with the family. He hoped it would not cause any problem with either of the ladies.

Dinner was a disaster as could be expected. Emma made sure Spencer sat next to Lorna and across Sally. Sally was not too happy with the seating arrangement and acted badly. Spencer was animated and paid more attention to Lorna. Sally did not know about Spencer's past relationship with Lorna but she sensed something was going on. Sally sat between Margaret on her left and Emma on her right. Margaret tried hard to talk more to Sally since Spencer was too busy talking to Lorna. Sally became very jealous of Lorna and looked very annoyed all through dinner. Emma was pleased and knew her plan was working.

When Spencer took Sally home to Mill Neck, Sally was in a terrible mood. Spencer noticed her aloofness.

"What is wrong?" he asked.

She did not answer him. She kept on pouting. Spencer asked her once more, "What is the matter with you? Didn't you enjoy the dinner with my family? You might as well get used to it. What did I do?"

"You know exactly what you did," Sally answered.

"What?"

"You ignored me completely at dinner. You are more interested with that girl, Lorna. Who is she?"

"She is Emma's roommate in college," he said.

"You seemed very friendly with her."

"What do you mean exactly by that?"

"You spent all dinner talking to her."

"Did I? I did not know that."

"You did."

"And if I was, what's the difference? I haven't seen her for a while and we are catching up on things. You're jealous." He started laughing.

"I'm not jealous. Why should I be?"

"I don't know but you are. There is no reason for that. I'm engaged to you, am I not?" he reminded her.

"Yes, you are."

Spencer did not know whether he was relieved that Sally accepted what he said and left it at that. He was worried that Sally would find out the truth about him and Lorna. He had to be more careful.

When he got back home, he went straight to bed but he could not sleep. Lorna was just a few feet away in her room. He saw the light peeking out of Lorna's bedroom door as he passed her room. He paused in front of the door, was tempted to knock but decided not to. He continued walking to his bedroom. He entered his room. It was dark. He walked towards the window and opened it. He inhaled the cold air and stood by the window for a long time. He was thinking of Lorna. He wondered if she was awake and what was she thinking. He was watching her all night and he knew she still loved him. *What kind of fool am I? I should not have gotten engaged to Sally. I still love Lorna more than anything else. I cannot possibly marry Sally. It is wrong. What am I to do? I don't want to hurt Sally. I don't want to hurt Lorna either. Especially Lorna. I have to talk to Lorna and explain. Explain what?*

He shut the window. He went to his desk and pulled something from the drawer. It was Lorna's picture. He stared at the picture for a long time. Then he put it back in the drawer. In an instant, he stood up and turned towards the door. He knew what he wanted to do. He walked silently the long corridor to her room. It was very quiet. Everyone was sound asleep. He tapped Lorna's door quietly and walked in. He did not hear a thing but saw a silhouette of her sitting on the bed. She did not stir for a while until he walked toward her. She knew it was Spencer. She was expecting him if truth be known. She stood up and walked toward him. In the dark, he could see the outline of her face. There was a sad look on it. He reached for her hand. She took his hands. "I miss you," she said, her voice barely audible.

"I'm sorry," he said.

She was trying to hold her tears but she could not. Her tears glistened through the darkness. Spencer saw it. He took a handkerchief from his pocket and wiped it tenderly. The room was very quiet but they could sense the hammering of their hearts. He looked at her eyes in the dark and could see the agony in them. He kissed her lightly. She did not resist. She put her arms around his neck. He kissed her more passionately, more urgently now. She responded with the same urgent desire. He was feeling the heat all over him. He wanted her. He could no longer control himself. He wanted her and he knew she wanted him as much. He swept her in his arms and without saying a word carried her to bed.

Spencer woke up early. He was out of the house before everyone got up. He wanted to clear his head. He was with Lorna for most of the night before he returned to his bedroom. He lay down on his bed but could not sleep. He just stared at the ceiling. He could not shake off the happiness both he and Lorna felt a few hours ago. They were really meant for each other. But what about Sally? His mind was in turmoil.

*How could I do what I just did? It's not fair to Lorna. But we both wanted it. She loves me as much as I love her. Suppose she gets pregnant. I just hope she does not get pregnant. I should have more self-control. It's too late now.*

He took Sultan galloping around the property. By the time Margaret and George came to the breakfast room, he was gone already.

Emma came bouncing down the stairs and headed towards the breakfast room. "Good morning," she greeted her parents.

"Good morning," George said.

"Good morning," Margaret said.

Emma looked around and did not see her brother. "Where is Spencer? He is usually down early."

"I have not seen him this morning," Margaret said. "Go ask Yates. Maybe he knows."

"He usually comes down before I do on the day after Christmas. He took Sally home last night but I was too tired, I did not hear him come in," Emma said.

Yates was just outside the door and heard the conversation. He volunteered the information. "He was up early and said he wanted to go riding and not wait for him for breakfast."

"That was weird. That's unlike him," Emma said.

"Well, he was in so much stress lately. What with the trouble brewing on Wall Street and his impending marriage," his father said.

"Yes, his impending marriage! I'm sorry for him. I told you he should not get engaged to Sally so soon. It does not bode well if you ask me," Emma said without qualm. "Did you see how that girl looked at Lorna last night? She had dagger in her eyes. I was watching her. I bet you they quarreled when Spencer took her home."

"Emma, stop it. Lorna might hear you," her mother admonished her.

"So what? She's my friend and I think she and Spencer belong to each other. He's marrying Sally for her money to save this house."

"Emma, enough already," her father said and gave her a sharp look.

Emma heard Lorna coming down the stairs. She met her friend halfway on the entrance hall. "Have you seen Spencer this morning?" she asked Lorna.

"No. Why?" Lorna's heart started pounding.

"He went riding early. That was not like him."

"Did he say anything?"

"Yates said Spencer told him not to wait for him for breakfast. No reason. Just like that."

"I wonder why," was all Lorna could say. She could not possibly tell Emma what happened last night and he staying with her for quite some time.

"Anyway, he is out," Emma said. "Let's have breakfast. He'll come back after he gets tired. Father said he was all stressed out because of what's happening on Wall Street. Maybe he needs some fresh air."

Lorna did not think the reason was Wall Street. She was positive it had something to do with last night.

After breakfast, Emma decided to go riding with Lorna. Spencer had not returned yet. Emma knew where she could find him. *He must be at the Temple of Love. He always goes there when he's upset.*

Emma saw Yates as they went through the hallway on the way upstairs. She asked him, "Can you tell the groom that Miss Lorna and I are going riding and get two of the horses ready."

"Yes, Miss Emma."

"Thank you, Yates."

She and Lorna went back upstairs and changed into their riding habit.

A few minutes later, they both headed toward the stables. The horses were ready.

"We can go to the Temple of Love. I always wanted to show you that. It's so beautiful out there and peaceful. It overlooks a pond and you can just sit and meditate," Emma said.

"Sounds wonderful," Lorna said.

Emma and Lorna trotted leisurely. Lorna seemed to enjoy the ride. Emma noticed she seemed happy this morning, more so since her grandmother died. There was a glow on her face.

They went through the wood at a walk, then came out on a long stretch of undulating slope.

"There it is." Emma pointed out. They saw the Temple of Love at a distance. It's a beautiful structure with an elaborate domed roof on top of four magnificent columns next to a pond. Someone was there with the horse tethered not far from the Temple.

"I see someone is there. Someone had the same idea," Lorna said.

Emma looked straight ahead and saw it was Spencer. She was right. She knew she would find Spencer there. Lorna looked at Emma questioningly.

"Yes. I know I'm guilty. I had a funny feeling he would be here," Emma said and reined in the horse to stop. Lorna did the same. "Lorna, listen to me. You're my best friend. If you love Spencer and I know you do, fight for him. It's not too late yet. He is not getting married till next spring. There is still time for you to win him back."

Lorna looked at her friend. She understood what Emma was saying. She saw the logic in it and her heart was saying the same thing. "Emma, I do love him. I don't deny it but it is up to him. All he has to do is say the word. I think he's troubled. He made a commitment to Sally and he cannot break it."

"Nonsense. He does not love her," Emma said.

"If that was true, why did he ask her to marry him?"

"I hate to say this but he feels obligated to save the house and also from what I hear, the bank is in big trouble too. He is sacrificing his happiness to save his inheritance. Sally is an only child and her parents are quite wealthy. He is marrying her for her money. Her dowry will save *Wentworth Hall*."

Lorna was silent for a while. She was shocked at the revelation. "He should have told me the real reason why he is doing it."

"He is too proud to tell you. I'll tell you what. Why don't we ride to the Temple and then I can excuse myself and you stay with him?"

"Emma, you can't do that."

"Yes, I can. I'm telling you he still loves you and you have to do something about it so he does not make the biggest mistake of his life. If you love him, you'll do what I say. Let's go." Emma started toward the temple followed by Lorna in hot pursuit.

Spencer heard the horse hooves. He turned around and saw two riders coming his way. He recognized Emma immediately. There was someone behind her. Then he realized it was Lorna. He stood up just as Emma reached the temple. She alighted from her horse. Lorna was not far behind.

"What are you doing here?" Spencer asked.

"I wanted to show Lorna the Temple. I didn't know I'd find you here," Emma lied. "You were missing at breakfast."

"I needed to be alone to think," Spencer said.

"About what?" Emma said. Just then Lorna arrived. Spencer looked at Lorna. His heart started to ache. Lorna got off her horse.

"Hello, Spencer," Lorna said. "Emma, this is wonderful."

"I told you so," Emma said. 'Well, since Spencer is here, why doesn't he show you the place. I'm going to the playhouse. It's on the other side of the property. Nanny used to take us there when we were young. We used to play there all the time when we were kids. I have to check it out and maybe Spencer can show you that too. I'll ride along and I'll see you at the playhouse in a short while."

She got on her horse and left before Spencer and Lorna could protest.

For a brief moment, silence reigned. Spencer stared at a distance. Lorna was staring at him, aching to hold him and tell him everything would be all right. Finally, Spencer turned around and said, "I'm sorry about last night."

"Sorry? Why?" she asked innocently.

"We should not have done that. It was not right," Spencer solemnly said.

"It was beautiful and I don't see anything wrong with it. We were both consenting adults. I did not object. I wanted you as much as you wanted me," Lorna said.

"Even then, it was wrong." He leaned against the post and looked down at the pond.

"Why was it wrong?" she asked.

"Because I am engaged to be married to Sally," he said sadly.

It was difficult for Lorna to hear that but as Emma said, if she loves him, she has to fight for it. "Spencer, tell me something. We were very much in love before I went to Bar Harbor. I just needed a break to sort out my feeling because you were not in a hurry to get married. My feeling has not changed. I don't know about you. Why are you marrying Sally all of a sudden? The way you made love to me last night proved that you still love me and very much so. I'm sure of that."

Spencer felt trapped. He did not want to admit the truth to Lorna. "I fell in love with Sally while you were gone," he lied.

"Enough to ask her to marry you so suddenly?" she asked desperately. She moved closer to him.

"Spencer, I don't believe you. Look at me. Tell me the truth. Do you love Sally or not? It's all I want to hear," she begged.

He refused to look at her. He stayed looking at a distance. "Lorna, can't you see? I made a commitment to marry Sally and I cannot get out of it."

"But you have not answered my question. Do you love her, enough to marry her?"

"You know the darn truth, Lorna. I love you more than anyone else but I made a commitment to her."

"Commitment! That's absurd. I don't understand you. You made a commitment to her in a short time yet you did not make it with me and yet we were in love for so much longer. Why?" Lorna was trying hard not to get angry. "You'll have a miserable marriage if you marry her. I know in my heart you still love me. It's not going to work. Can't you see? Why are you doing this?"

"You're making it so difficult for me."

"Difficult? What about me? Don't you consider my feeling at all?" Lorna turned around. She was hurt beyond belief and angry at him. She was about ready to get on her horse. Spencer grabbed her arm. Lorna tried to shake him but she could not shake him. Spencer turned her around abruptly. He kissed her passionately and put his hand around her. She struggled but could not resist. Her love for him was too strong to ignore him. She went limp. He brought her hands around his neck. She looked at his eyes. She saw the intense love that she saw there last night. She closed her eyes.

"Oh, Spencer. Why do I love you so much?" she asked and slowly brushed his hair. Spencer kissed her passionately and all their pent up emotion released like a volcano erupting after its slumber for a thousand years. She wanted him and she knew she had to fight to get him back. She had to do something.

"Spencer, I love you. I love you more than anything else in this world."

"I love you too, my darling."

He could not resist. He held her tight. He could not think straight.

"Damn everything. I love you, Lorna, more than you ever know. I missed you terribly while you were in Bar Harbor."

He kissed her again passionately. He forgot everything. All it matters now was Lorna and his love for her. If they were at the house, he would have taken her to her bed but out here in the cold, he just held her tight to him.

She responded with the same passion. She thought if this is the only way she could have him back, she didn't care.

"I'm leaving tomorrow," Lorna suddenly said.

"So soon?"

"I have to get back to Pittsburgh. I have plenty of work to do about my grandmother's estate. Besides, I told Emma I'll only stay for a few days."

"Can I come to your room tonight?"

She weighed his proposition. Her heart was pounding and telling her to take the gamble if she wanted him back. She nodded her head and kissed him.

"I love you, Spencer, now and always."

"I love you too," Spencer said. He kissed her again and he forgot about his engagement to Sally.

Lorna broke off from his embrace. "We're supposed to follow Emma to the playhouse," she said.

"Yes. We're supposed to. Although I'd rather stay here and be alone with you."

"So do I but we better go."

"Remember, tonight. I'll be there," Spencer said.

"Yes."

She smiled and went to get on her horse.

## Chapter 17

January turned into February with the bitter cold winter. Spencer stayed in the city with the rest of his family. As the winter months pressed on, his affection towards Sally was still as frigid as the weather. He was making the motion but deep down his heart had not warmed up to Sally. He kept himself busy at work trying to avoid her.

Sally together with her mother was busy with planning for the wedding. No money would be spared. They planned to have this wedding, the event of the year. She and her mother ordered her gown from Bergdorf Goodman which had just moved their store from Rockefeller Center to its present location in a building with a Beaux-Arts style on the site of the demolished 43-yr old Cornelius Vanderbilt II mansion at 5th Avenue and 58th Street. All kinds of preparation were planned for the big day. The wedding would be in New York at St. Patrick's Cathedral on Fifth Avenue with reception at the Waldorf-Astoria on Park Avenue. Invitations were ordered and sent out to about 200 people. It was time to make that big impression on New York society that a daughter of the Sinclairs was marrying a scion of the "old money" banking family of New York.

Sally had managed to get Spencer to spend some time with her during the weekends. They went to the theater and dinner and some private parties given by Sally's friend. Spencer did not mind going to the theater and dinner afterwards but tried to avoid some of the parties with Sally's friends by saying he had some deadlines to meet and had to work.

Spencer had not seen nor heard from Lorna since that weekend at Wentworth Hall during Christmas. He was hoping she would call or at least write. He checked his mail every day and shuffled it twice thinking somehow the mail got lost in the pile and was disappointed every time he did not see one. He was worried about what was happening with her and it was on his mind all the time. What if she was pregnant and would not write to him? He wanted to know. He figured if she was pregnant, she would contact him. But no words were coming from her and Emma had not said anything. Surely if Lorna was pregnant, Emma would be the first to know. She and Lorna were close friends. He was sure Lorna would confide in Emma.

Still it was driving him crazy not knowing and why could he not stop thinking about her day or night, no matter how busy he was with other things. He was supposed to be thinking of Sally and the future with her but instead he could not get Lorna out of his mind. He tried to bury himself with work and was spending more time at the office. Still Lorna was always there at the back of his mind and sometimes not so far back.

Lorna.

Why? He would be crazy to marry her now. What with his impending marriage to Sally? Everything was already in place. Sally would hate him for the rest of his life if he cancelled the engagement. The embarrassment of being jilted. That would not go big with the Sinclairs. They were one of his biggest depositors. Surely they would close their account if that happens. It would be insane for him to even think of marrying Lorna. He supposed he could learn to love Sally eventually. Besides, he also needed Sally's money to save his legacy. What was he going to do? He hoped Lorna was not pregnant. It would create complications that he did not know how to deal with. *What have I done?*

It was at the end of February that Emma got a call from Lorna.

"Hello," Emma answered the phone and heard her friend's voice. She was not expecting it. She knew Lorna was busy with her grandmother's estate in Pittsburgh.

"Hello," came the answer from the other end of the line.

"Lorna, where are you? Are you still in Pittsburgh?"

"No. I'm in New York. Are you doing anything today?" Lorna asked.

"No. Why?"

"Can we meet for tea?" Lorna asked.

"Sure. I'd love to. I have not seen you for ages," Emma said.

"Yes, I know. How about at the Plaza?" Lorna said.

"Why can't you come to the house?" Emma suggested.

"I'd rather not," Lorna said, afraid she might bump into Spencer there.

"OK. What time?"

"Say three this afternoon."

"I'll be there."

"Great. See you at the Palm Court." Lorna hung up quickly before Emma could ask any questions. Emma was intrigued. *Lorna does not want to come to the house. Why? We usually meet at the house. Why at the Plaza Palm Court?*

She could not wait to see her. Too bad Spencer was at work already. She could tell him she was meeting his ex-girlfriend. He was too busy with his work, you hardly knew he was getting married in June. But then men do not do the planning for their wedding. She wondered if her brother was really happy with his betrothal. She could not tell with Spencer. Since he got engaged to Sally, she and he were not talking much about the wedding. He seemed to avoid the subject. She wondered what was going on in his head.

Emma arrived first at Palm Court. She told the waiter she was waiting for a friend and could they be seated near the corner where they could get some privacy. The waiter was obliging and seated her in the far corner of the room next to a palm tree.

The crowd started coming in. Mostly elderly ladies. The waiters were busy rolling in the cart with hot tea and trays of cakes, scones and tea sandwiches.

In no time, she saw Lorna walking toward her. She looked pale. She did not have that glow that she had during her holiday at *Wentworth Hall*. She stood up to greet her friend and they hugged each other.

Lorna sat next to Emma, spread the white napkin on her lap. The waiter approached them and asked for their order.

Emma ordered an Earl Grey and a blueberry scone and Lorna asked for an English Breakfast and watercress sandwich.

As soon as the waiter left their table, Emma asked, "What is this all about? How come you don't want to come to the house?"

"I don't want to see Spencer," Lorna said.

"Why?" Emma gave her a questioning look.

Lorna hesitated for a while. She swallowed hard and said softly, "I'm pregnant."

"What?" Emma gasped and put her hand over her mouth. She stared at Lorna for confirmation. Lorna nodded.

"How do you know?" Emma asked.

"I missed my period and I was getting nauseous in the morning. I suspected I was pregnant so I went to the doctor and he confirmed my suspicion."

Emma could not have been happier. She was ecstatic. "That's wonderful. I knew it. Something happened over Christmas holiday."

"Yes," Lorna said with a smile.

"Do you want me to tell Spencer?" Emma asked.

"No. Not yet anyway. He might think I trapped him."

"Nonsense. I don't think so. He still loves you. I'm quite certain of that."

"Let me think about it." Lorna paused. "I want to tell him myself," Lorna said.

"I wonder what Sally would think if she found out. I'm so happy for you."

"I'm scared, Emma. Supposing he does not want the baby. Supposing he does not want to marry me. He's marrying Sally in a few months. What am I going to do?"

Emma reached for Lorna's hand and assured her. "Don't worry. I bet you. He'll cancel his engagement once he hears this. I'm positive about it. You have to tell him before he gets married. You have to. You don't want him to make the biggest mistake of his life. You have to stop the wedding."

"I hope you are right. I'm really scared." Her voice quivered. She tried to hold back her tears.

"You don't have to be. Things will work out. I'm positive about that."

Emma thought of something. "I have an idea. Why don't you come to the house Saturday morning and we can go for a walk in Central Park. Let's hope Spencer is at home. We can ask him to take us to lunch."

Lorna smiled at the suggestion. "You're incorrigible. What would I do without you?"

"What are friends for? I want you to be my sister-in-law better than that frigid Sally."

Lorna could not help laughing. "Leave it to you to say such a thing."

Emma could not wait till Saturday came. Spencer was home and locked himself in his father's study working.

At 11 AM, the doorbell rang. The butler walked to the door to answer the doorbell. Emma came running downstairs as soon as she heard it.

"It's okay, Clarkson. I'll get it. I am expecting Miss Lorna."

"Very well, ma'am."

Emma opened the door. "Come in, Lorna."

Lorna came inside. Emma embraced her. "You feel like a frozen fish. Is it too cold out there?" Emma asked.

"It's mighty freezing. I don't think I want to go walking in the park."

Spencer heard the noise by the door. He thought he heard Lorna's voice. He came out of his father's study and was surprised to see Lorna.

"Hello, Lorna. Happy to see you again. What brings you here?" Spencer asked with a smile on his face. He was glad to see her. It seemed like forever that he had not seen her. She looked rather wan to him but then maybe he was imagining things. He had been worried about her but could not do much. He gave her a friendly kiss on her cheek. He wanted to take her in his arms, kiss her passionately but common sense prevailed. Emma was right in front of them and he thought it was inappropriate now that he was engaged to someone else.

"Your sister here wanted to take a walk in the park. Although I'd rather stay indoors. It's not a good day for walking."

"Emma always has this brilliant idea. Why don't you take your coat off and stay awhile?" Spencer asked smiling and helped Lorna take off her coat. Just the touch of his hand made a tingling sensation in her. She smiled at him and he smiled back.

He turned to Emma, "Take Lorna in the drawing room to warm up by the fireplace. I'll go tell Clarkson to ask Nelly to bring some hot chocolate for the three of us."

"You don't have to do that," Lorna said.

"And let you catch cold? No way." He winked at her and her heart melted away.

Emma proceeded to the drawing room and Lorna followed. Lorna went close to the fireplace and placed her hand close to the fire. Then she sat in one of the chairs next to the fireplace. Just then, Spencer walked in the door.

"Aren't you working at father's study?" Emma asked.

"Yes, I was. But I needed a break anyway. All work and no play makes you a dull boy," Spencer said.

"I say amen to that," Emma said.

Lorna watched brother and sister banter lovingly. She enjoyed watching these two people who were very dear to her.

Frank, the footman, came in with the tray of chocolate. He put the tray on the coffee table in front of them.

"Thank you, Frank," Spencer said.

Frank nodded. "Anything else, sir?"

"No. That's all, Frank."

"Very well, sir."

Frank was ready to go when Emma said, "Frank, can you tell Nelly we're eating lunch in and make it for three. Miss Lorna will be joining us."

"Yes, ma'am." Frank walked toward the door and closed it quietly.

Lorna raised her brow. "I thought . . ."

"Thought what?" Spencer asked.

Emma gave Lorna a swift glance. "Nothing," she said.

"Nothing? Look at the two of you. Always conniving," Spencer said.

"OK. I thought of asking you to take us to lunch but since it is too cold outside, eating in seemed more sensible," Emma said.

"You're right," Spencer said.

Lunch consisted of hot cream of asparagus soup, chicken pot pie and chocolate soufflé, Spencer's favorite dessert. Emma was observing Spencer intently and trying to see a sign if he knew something. He was solicitous of Lorna but he had always been when they were together. Emma was positive he did not know anything. Lorna was acting like everything was normal too. Emma could not wait to talk to Lorna alone. She was hoping Spencer would leave them alone for a while. She was glad that after lunch, Spencer excused himself and went back to his father's study.

"I better get back to work and you two can catch up on things," Spencer said. He was dying to talk to Lorna privately but did not know how to approach the subject so instead he said to Lorna, "When you decide to leave, let me know. I'll take you home."

"OK. Thank you," Lorna said.

"My pleasure." Spencer left them and headed to his father's study.

Emma and Lorna went back to the drawing room. Emma sat opposite Lorna by the fireplace. She watched her friend as she gazed toward the fire. Lorna stood up and placed her hands near the fire. She suddenly felt cold. She crossed her arms on her chest. She felt fine at lunch but now she was getting very nervous. The inevitable was at hand and she did not think she could proceed on what she wanted to do. There was a tight knot in her stomach. She was afraid what Spencer would say if he found out about the baby. He'd probably hate her.

Emma asked Lorna, "So what do you plan to do now? Are you going to tell him?"

"I'm getting cold feet. I don't know if I want to do it today. I think I'll wait," Lorna said.

"No, you're not. This is the perfect time. Nobody is here except me and Spencer and the staff and they are all in the servant's quarters. Father and Mother are in Palm Beach for another week. You could not ask for a better time."

Lorna did not know what to do. "I can't do it. I just can't. What would he say?" Lorna said. She was so terrified to do it. She was vacillating but Emma would not have it.

Emma came to her side and hugged her friend. "Come on, Lorna. He's alone there in father's study. Do it now."

Lorna looked at Emma. Emma seemed confident that it would be all right. After hesitating for a few minutes, she said, "OK. Wish me luck."

Emma gave her another hug and patted Lorna's back. "You'll be fine. It will work out. Trust me," Emma said.

"All right." Lorna swallowed hard, tried to brace herself.

Lorna left Emma in the drawing room and walked slowly down the long hall to the study. Her feet were shaking and she felt a cold sweat. Her hands were shaking too when she lightly tapped the door.

"Who is it?" she heard Spencer ask on the other side of the door.

"It's me, Lorna. May I come in?" Lorna said softly.

"Yes. The door is open," Spencer said, stood up quickly from his chair and walked towards the door.

She opened the door and peeked in. "Do you have a minute?" she asked.

"Of course. Always. Come on in." Spencer closed the door behind him. The urge to hold her in his arm was so strong but he restrained himself. Lorna stayed standing.

"Do sit down," Spencer said and pulled the chair in front of the desk. He let her sit down and then went on the other side of the table.

"What can I do for you today?" he asked like someone talking to a borrower applying for a loan.

Lorna looked at him squarely in the eyes. "I don't know how to tell you this," she said with hesitation. She was twisting her fingers. Spencer noticed she was nervous. He became alarmed.

"What's wrong? Is something the matter?" Spencer asked.

Lorna stood up. She walked towards the window. Spencer watched her. Something was definitely wrong. Something was bothering her. He wanted to know what.

"Lorna, what is it? Do you need help? Is it something to do with your grandmother's estate? Tell me." He came closer to her. She felt his eyes on her.

She turned around, shook her head. She looked him in the eye. She held her breath. There was a look of such tenderness and love on his face it was heart-stopping. She opened her mouth to speak and then closed it without uttering a word, incapable of saying anything at this moment, filled with a bewildering array of emotions.

He took her hands in his, he looked deeply into her eyes. He swallowed and asked showing deep concern, "What is it? Lorna, tell me. What is wrong?"

"I'm pregnant," she said simply and looked down.

"Oh my God!" Spencer's shock was apparent. He drew back, still holding her hands, his eyes widening as he stared at her. "Are you sure?"

"Yes, I am. I missed my period for two months so I went to see the doctor. He confirmed what I suspected. What am I going to do?" she asked.

Spencer did not answer. He withdrew his hands. He started pacing the floor, a habit he did when he was weighing things up. Lorna waited and did not know what Spencer would say or do. She was afraid Spencer would still want to marry Sally and what would happen to her and her baby. She hoped he would not suggest an abortion. She had decided she wanted to keep the baby no matter what. If Spencer did not want to marry her, at least she would have a part of him. She would be happy to do that. She did not care if she would be a social outcast. She wanted to have the baby.

Finally, Spencer stopped pacing the floor and faced her. He looked her in the eyes and held her hands. He saw the fear in them. "You'll take care of yourself and the baby. That's what you should do," she heard Spencer say to her. She could not believe what she heard. He did not want to marry her. She wanted to slap him in the face but Spencer was holding her hand. She tried to shake off his hands but he wouldn't let go.

"Of course I will take care of myself and the baby. Don't be ridiculous. I'll have this baby even if you don't want it," Lorna said angrily. Her face was getting red with rage. It was obvious she was getting upset.

"Who said I don't want it?" Spencer said with a smile on his face.

"Well, do you?" Lorna challenged him.

Spencer put his hands on her shoulders. "Of course, I do. I do want him. Or her for that matter. Very much. We'll be a family."

She stared at him and trying to comprehend what he was saying. Before Lorna could say something, he nodded and kissed her tenderly. Lorna embraced him and kissed him back. Tears rolled down her cheek. Spencer took his handkerchief and wiped her tears lovingly. She took the handkerchief from him and blew her nose.

"What about Sally?" Lorna suddenly asked.

"What about Sally?" he repeated. "Don't you worry about that? I'll break off the engagement. I'll go see her today after I take you home."

"But," she hesitated.

"But what?"

"Have you slept with her? She could be pregnant too," she said, afraid of the complications.

Spencer started to laugh.

"What's so funny?"

"Do you really think I would do that? Don't you worry about that too. I never slept with Sally. Ever. Even if we are engaged. I had no desire to."

"Oh Spencer. Do you really mean what you say? I mean about us being a family." She was so relieved but had to make sure.

"Of course I do. I love the baby already."

"Spencer, I do love you. You know that. Do you? Very much."

Spencer knelt and held her hand. "I know. Now, will you marry me?"

She did not have to think twice. "Yes, I will."

He stood up and he kissed her again with the same passion as he did the night of Christmas in her bedroom. Lorna broke off from their tender embrace. Spencer looked at her mischievously and pointed to the couch. "Afraid we might end up there?" She ignored his comment.

"Let's tell Emma," she said.

"That we are going to bed?"

"You're being silly."

"Lorna, I'm so happy I can't help it." He reached for her hand and they walked hand in hand towards the drawing room.

Emma was waiting.

## Chapter 18

It was the worst and difficult thing he had to do but he had to do it. He knew it would be tough breaking off the engagement with Sally. He dreaded the thought but he had made up his mind. He could just imagine the scene when he told her that the wedding was off. He did not love her. He was marrying her for the wrong reason and it would be a mistake. The money was not important to him now that he knew Lorna was pregnant with his child. If he lost his inheritance, so what. He would work harder and start all over again. It was important that he give his child his name. He hoped it would be a boy to carry the family's name but if it was a girl, they could try again and hope for a boy next time. He wanted to marry Lorna as soon as possible. He would talk to his parents as soon as they got back from Palm Beach. He knew in his heart they would agree with his decision. He knew they liked Lorna very much. He braced himself for a showdown with Sally.

Spencer went to see Sally the same afternoon after dropping Lorna at her place. He walked briskly from Chelsea district to midtown, embracing the cold weather. He walked Madison Avenue to East 50$^{th}$ Street, turned right and headed east to First Avenue. It was cold but he did not care. His feeling for Sally was as cold as the weather. As he walked absentmindedly, he thought of how to approach the subject with Sally. He could not think of any other way. He would tell Sally straight that he had decided to call the wedding off. Hard as he thought, he could not find any diplomatic way of doing it. He had to be frank with her. He had to deliver his message right to the point and get out of her place as quickly as he could. He knew she would not take it calmly. She was one of those persons who got everything she wanted being an only child. Why he got entangled with her, he would never know. With her beauty and her tons of money, he believed any man would fall for her. She could maneuver any man in their weakness and he would fall for it. Luckily for him, he still might be able to get out. He hoped so. He had not gone to bed with her and so his conscience was clear. In spite of her advances, he never succumbed to it even after their engagement. He did not want to. Maybe because he was not in love with her and had no desire for her.

Sally lived in one of those new buildings in the East 50s. He stopped a few feet before he reached Sally's building. He was rehearsing what to say. He resumed his walk until he got in front of Sally's building and entered it. The doorman let him in without any question since he was now a familiar face as fiancé of Sally Sinclair, the daughter of one of the owners of the co-ops in the building. Most of the owners in the building had heard the news when it was announced in the papers. They were thrilled at the upcoming wedding – a union of the new money with the old money.

Spencer took the elevator. The elevator man sitting on his chair asked, "Floor please?"

"7$^{th}$ floor, please," Spencer said.

The elevator went up to the 7$^{th}$ floor. Spencer walked off and walked to Room 725 and rang the bell. Sally answered the bell. She was happy to see him.

"Come on in. I was not expecting you." She gave Spencer a kiss on his check. He never responded. "Aren't you going to take off your coat?" she asked coquettishly. She sensed something was wrong. He was aloof and preoccupied. She began to worry.

"No, I can't stay too long. Can we go in the parlor? I want to talk to you in private," Spencer said coolly.

"No one is here," Sally said. "Mommy went out to play bridge with her friends. Daddy is out in Mill Neck. It's just you and me. Perfect."

Spencer was relieved to find her alone in the house. He ignored her comments and he walked down the hall, turned left and went in the parlor. Sally followed. As soon as Sally entered, Spencer closed the door behind him. He looked morose, Sally thought.

"What's wrong with you today?" Sally asked.

"I don't know how to tell you this. I just come to tell you something. I have given a lot of thought to our engagement and it is not right. I can't marry you," Spencer dropped the bombshell.

Sally felt as if someone knocked her on her head. She gasped.

"I'm sorry," Spencer said matter-of-factly.

Her face turned red. "Sorry? You don't know what you are talking about. You asked me to marry you a few months ago and what changed your mind now? I don't understand." She was livid.

"I can't go on with this charade. I'm not in love with you Sally. It's utterly wrong. It's not going to work. We'll have a miserable marriage and it is not fair to you."

"Not fair to me?" She was incredulous.

"Stop repeating what I said," Spencer said trying very hard to stay calm.

"What about the embarrassment? Have you considered that? We have announced the engagement in the papers. Mother and I have made all the arrangements. The invitations went out already. You can't do that to me," she started yelling at him.

"I'm truly sorry about that. I know it's my fault to think that I loved you but I don't," Spencer said.

"Why? I'm not good enough for the Wentworth family," she paused. "Oh, I know. You're in love with that Lorna girl. I knew it. The way you looked at her at the Christmas dinner at *Wentworth Hall*. I knew something was going on."

It was Spencer's turn to get mad. "She has nothing to do with this," he lied. "I can't marry you because I don't love you. Plain and simple."

She became furious at being told the truth. "What about your house? I thought you need my money to save your house as everyone kept telling me."

"I'm not that desperate, Sally. If I lost my house, so be it. I can't in all honesty marry you for your money. I have my conscience to consider. I have to love someone enough to marry her." He turned towards the door, opened it up and said, "Goodbye, Sally."

"You're a fool, Spencer Wentworth. A damned fool. I hate you," Sally yelled at him.

Spencer didn't look back and hurried toward the stairway. He did not feel like waiting for the elevator. He left Sally crying on the settee.

She grabbed hold of an expensive piece of china on the side table, picked it up and threw it toward the fireplace. "I hate you, Spencer Wentworth. I hate you." She ran upstairs, buried her face in her pillow and cried inconsolably.

Spencer hailed a taxi and went right back to Lorna's place. Lorna was waiting for him. She knew Spencer would come back and tell her what happened. She offered him a drink which he took readily.

"How did she take it?" Lorna asked.

Spencer sat down and took a sip of his drink. "Not too good, I'm afraid. Terrible as a matter of fact."

"I'm sorry." She sat next to him.

"Sorry? You amazed me. You should be ecstatic." He put his drink on the table and kissed her.

"I am ecstatic. You know I am. But I'm sorry for her."

"Lorna dear, now that that is behind us, we can plan our wedding. Where do you want to get married?"

"Anywhere you want." She looked at him and saw how happy he was. She was filled with joy to see him more relaxed and happy.

"How about in Pittsburgh?"

Lorna gave him a puzzled look. "Pittsburgh? Don't you want to have it in Long Island? At *Wentworth Hall*?" Lorna asked.

"No. Unless you want to," Spencer said.

Lorna was quiet for a while.

"What's the matter, my darling? Don't you want to get married in your hometown?" Spencer asked.

"Much as I want to, I don't have any family there anymore. Since Grandmother died, I consider New York as my home. Besides, your parents I'm sure would love to have your wedding at *Wentworth Hall*."

Spencer weighed on the matter. "OK, whatever you think is best. I'll go along with you." He kissed her on her forehead. "We'll get married at Christ Church in Oyster Bay and then a small reception at *Wentworth Hall*. How is that? I want a simple ceremony as soon as it can be arranged with just the family and few friends if it is all right with you," Spencer said.

"I want the same thing. Did you read my mind?" Lorna asked lovingly.

"Of course I do," he pulled her closer to him. "I still have to get you an engagement ring. How do you like something old from my family's jewelry box?"

"That would be fantastic."

"Are you sure? I can get you an expensive one from Tiffany."

"No. I'd rather have one of your family's jewelry. It will have a special meaning for us."

"I have to check the vault and see what you might like." He kissed her on her forehead and looked at her lovingly. "I'm sure my mother would love you to have one of the family's jewelry. She loves you very much you know."

"I have a feeling she does. She has been very kind to me whenever I visited *Wentworth Hall*."

"She's very fond of you. She will be thrilled to hear the news when they get back. I can't wait to tell them."

"About the baby?"

"No. I'll skip that part. They will figure it out eventually."

"I agree."

He looked at her eyes and saw the love and longing there. He rubbed her hair gently, lifted her face and kissed her again, this time more passionately. Lorna's hand went behind his neck and caressed it. Spencer picked her up. She clung to his neck and he carried her into the bedroom.

## Chapter 19

During the latter half of the 1920s, steel production, building construction, retail turnover, automobiles registered, even railway receipts advanced from record to record. The manufacturing and trading companies showed an increase in combined net profits. Iron and steel led the way with doubled gains. Such figures set up a crescendo of stock-exchange speculation which had led hundreds of thousands of Americans to invest heavily in the stock market. A significant number of them were borrowing money to buy more stocks. Brokers were routinely lending small investors more than two-thirds of the face value of the stocks they were buying. Billions of dollars were out on loan, more than the entire amount of currency circulating in the U.S. at the time.

The rising share prices of stocks encouraged more people including Spencer Wentworth to invest and he invested heavily. People hoped the share prices would rise further. Speculation fueled further rises and created an economic bubble. Because of margin buying, investors stood to lose large sums of money if the market turned down or even failed to advance quickly enough.

Despite the dangers of speculation, many believed that the stock market would continue to rise indefinitely. On March 25, 1929, after the Federal Reserve warned of excessive speculation, a mini crash occurred as investors started to sell stocks at a rapid pace, exposing the market's shaky foundation. Two days later, banker Charles E. Mitchell announced his company, the National City Bank, would provide $25 million in credit to stop the market's slide. Mitchell's move brought a temporary halt to the financial crisis and call money declined from twenty to eight percent. However, the American economy showed ominous signs of trouble. Steel production began to decline. Construction was sluggish. Automobile sales went down. Consumers were building up high debts because of easy credit. Spencer was getting worried but it was close to his wedding day and his mind was more in tune to his approaching wedding than the condition on Wall Street.

Early in April, on a lovely spring day, Spencer and Lorna were to get married in a simple ceremony at Christ Church, one of the oldest Anglican churches on Long Island. It used to be a wooden framed structure but was enclosed in stone in 1925 and renovation was also done inside.

The wedding ceremony was attended by a few people, - Spencer's family, close friends and some business colleagues. There was no announcement in the paper. It was what Lorna wanted. Her only attendant was Emma as the Maid of Honor and Todd acted as Best Man.

At *Wentworth Hall,* preparations went on for a few days before the wedding. It seemed the whole staff at the house was extremely busy before the big day when house guests started arriving. All the staff was busy both outside and inside the house a couple of weeks before the wedding. Workers came in to put a big tent outside by the door leading to the ballroom in case guests wanted to wander outside the ballroom. Potted plants were moved next to the tent for a beautiful setting. Tables covered in white were arranged inside the tent with garlands of white flowers hugging the posts and around the perimeter inside the tent. There were floral arrangements of white roses on the table. The ballroom was decorated with more flowers here and there. Some flowers were taken from the greenhouse to decorate the house. More flowers were brought in by floral designers who came and decorated the tent and the dining tables. Floral arrangements were placed at strategic locations around the house. In the library, tables were set up to hold wedding gifts of silver, china, porcelain pieces and *objets d'art* from friends, relatives and business associates. The whole house was beautifully decorated.

A few tables were set up in the ballroom along the side and the middle of the room was reserved for dancing with the orchestra to be staged at one end next to the grand piano.

The kitchen was abuzz with activities with the cook and an assortment of helpers making all the food preparation for the house guests before and after the wedding and for two hundred guests at the wedding reception. There was a frantic pace in the kitchen. Outside, the gardens were spruced up and the place looked wonderful with a cacophony of colors among the spring bulbs. Spring flowering trees were at their glorious best.

On the day of the wedding, Lorna put on her beautiful gown with the help of Emma who tried on the zipper. It finally glided past the waistline. Lorna was afraid it would not fit. It was made of white beaded satin with a square neckline and a high empire waistline which hid her increasing waistline.

"You look lovely," Emma said.

Lorna looked in the mirror and she really looked radiant and happy.

"The dress fits perfectly but will not in a couple of weeks," she said with a conspiratorial smile on her face.

"I agree. Hope no one will notice," Emma said.

She was beginning to show but with the current fashion, her stomach bump was hardly noticeable. Emma and Todd were the only ones privy to the secret. Besides the two of them, nobody knew and if they knew, everyone was so discreet about it and never said a thing. Her short hair was adorned with a couple of strands of pearls. Her short veil covered her face and there was a certain glow to it. Her only jewelry was a pair of diamond earring that Margaret gave her the night before the wedding. She also wore her engagement ring with a big diamond flanked by two sapphire, a Wentworth family heirloom.

She was driven to church by Paul Conley in one of the Rolls Royces with Emma by her side. Spencer went in another car earlier with Todd. Margaret and George went in another Rolls Royces driven by another driver. The other Wentworth family members who were visiting caravanned in other cars.

The church filled up with just family members and a few selected friends all dressed in formal attire. Women wore fancy hats and men wore top hats. As Lorna walked up to the altar which was simply decorated with a couple of beautiful arrangements of white calla lilies and white roses, her eyes were on Spencer's and she was glad to see him there. She was afraid he would not come and change his mind but he was there. He was there to say *I do* or *I will* or whatever it was supposed to be when the time came. He would. That he would be able to love her and the baby forever and ever. She smiled as she approached him.

How strange life was, Spencer thought. If he had not come home from abroad when that telegram came and Emma did not invite her friend because of that snowstorm over Christmas, he would never have met Lorna. If she did not fall down on that snowy slope and sprained her ankle, he might not even realize how attracted he was to her. He had never believed in fate before but fate it was that brought them together. The chances against him falling in love with her after all the women he had before in Europe and trying to avoid the marriage altar was massive but it had happened. He loved her more than he had known it possible to love.

Lorna had arrived at church and Spencer felt relaxed and excited. He was eager to begin his new life – to live happily ever after. The organ had begun to play, and the clergyman had taken his place.

When the organist started playing the music, Emma walked up the aisle, followed by Lorna on the arms of Alistair Prescott who graciously offered to give her away since she had no family. When the organ music swelled and the strains of the hymn "O Perfect Love" reverberated through the rafters, Lorna's throat tightened. Her eyes filled with tears and she ached for her parents and grandmother. But knowing she could not permit herself to break down, she took control of herself. She lifted her head higher, looked toward the altar where Spencer was waiting with Todd, his best friend. Spencer turned and stood rigidly watching her come. He could see that behind the light veil that covered her face, she was smiling. She, on the other hand, saw the love on his face which was comforting and reassuring.

Spencer waited near the altar with Todd, looking happy and beaming with pride waiting for his bride. Todd stood next to him.

Within seconds of drawing to a standstill at the altar, Alistair stepped back. Spencer took his place. His presence and the minister's kindly expression instantly dispelled the feeling of loneliness she had experienced a second before.

His family approved of the match. Margaret and George were very happy to see Spencer get married to Lorna. They thought it was a better match than Spencer and Sally. The couple seemed so much in love and very happy. When they came back from their winter vacation in Palm Beach, Spencer did not wait too long to break the news to them that he broke his engagement to Sally and was marrying Lorna instead. They were not surprised and were so relieved. They were not too keen about Sally and they were thrilled about Spencer's decision to end the engagement. They wondered though why such a rush. Spencer wanted to get married as soon as it could be arranged. They suspected something but decided not to ask. It was irrelevant at this point. They were just happy Spencer had broken his engagement to Sally.

They didn't think he was in love with Sally anyway as Emma always said so. They watched them over Christmas dinner at Wentworth Hall when both Sally and Lorna were present at the same time. They could see Spencer was still very much in love with Lorna. They were wondering then how long he would realize that what he was doing, marrying Sally was all wrong. They suspected he was marrying her for her money as Emma said. He was a grown up man and they did not want to interfere with his decision. Now it was all water under the bridge. They knew all along he loved Lorna and were overjoyed by his decision to marry Lorna instead.

A month for the banns could sometimes seem forever. But the wait was over and it was happening at last. Spencer was now inside Christ Church and he was glad to see his family and friends gather to witness his taking his marriage vows.

The organ stopped playing and the wedding service began. It was as if time slowed. Lorna listened to every word . . . for better or for worse . . . for richer or for poorer . . . in sickness and in health . . . forsaking all others. She heard every response, including her own, felt the smooth coldness of the gold as her ring slid onto her finger, sticking for just a moment at her knuckle before Spencer eased it over.

Then at last, the nuptial service was over and they were man and wife and no man was to put them asunder. She was now Mrs. Spencer Wentworth. He squeezed her hand and smiled at her, looking almost like a little school boy brimming over with excitement, and raised her veil to kiss her.

Then the register was signed and they were walking back down the aisle, smiling over to either side of them to make eye contact with as many of their relatives and friends as they could. Her arm was drawn through his and their hands were clasped tightly as the organist pumped away enthusiastically and Mendelssohn's "Wedding March", joyful, thunderous, filled the church.

Sunshine greeted them beyond the doors of the church. A hearty cheer and a deluge of confetti and rice from the small crowd gathered outside.

Spencer looked down at her.

"Well, Mrs. Spencer Wentworth. Does it sound good? Or does it sound great?" he asked her.

"Great," she said and smiled at him.

He squeezed her hand. He felt wonderful knowing he did the right thing marrying the woman he loves and the mother of his forthcoming child.

After the wedding ceremony, the reception was held at Wentworth Hall. What started as a simple wedding turned out to be a big affair. The church ceremony was simple enough as Lorna wanted. There were only fifty people in attendance at the church. However, the reception was another matter. The guest list for the reception was for two hundred guests. Margaret and Emma helped Lorna with all the wedding plans. They invited all of Spencer's family on both sides, their friends, some of his colleagues at the bank and a few people from Wall Street.

The party started at two in the afternoon with champagne flowing freely all afternoon. Lester Lanin, an American jazz and pop music bandleader, was hired to play at the reception. Emma and Todd were leading the young group in their merriment. Lorna and Spencer could not be happier.

When it was time for the newly-weds to leave, everyone lined up in the courtyard and wished them well. Spencer and Lorna stepped into one of the family's Silver Rolls Royces decorated with white crepe paper done by Paul Conley and the under-chauffeur. With Spencer at the driver seat, they drove off out of sight of their guests. They went around the property while guests went back in the ballroom and continued the celebration. As soon as they were out of sight, Spencer brought the car into the driver's cottage away from the crowd and Paul sneaked them back into the house through the service entrance and they went up the backstairs into Spencer's bedroom and locked the door.

The next day, they left early for Bar Harbor in Maine for their honeymoon. Lorna did not want to go abroad and knew Spencer would want to go back to work soon. Her grandmother's house was perfect. They would be all alone and the place was just magnificent with her garden blooming with spring flowers. She was contented and happy. Spencer was more relaxed. He forgot about Wall Street and his financial problems while on his honeymoon. All he could think of was what life would be with Lorna and their child coming into the world.

The days were filled with adventure. Spencer had never been to Bar Harbor and he loved the cottage and the beach. Lorna's grandmother's house sat close to the ocean and the view was fabulous. They would have breakfast on the terrace looking out to sea. They would sit by the rock on the beach and watched the sunset and felt the ocean breeze. They would stroll in the garden leisurely and admire the bees buzzing among the flowers. They would sometime go picnicking under the trees near the garden. Some days, they drove to town and did a little shopping or just strolled around. At night, they would sit on the porch watching the starlights. It was peaceful. All the past heartaches melted away. They looked at each other lovingly and would retire to the bedroom. Life was perfect.

After two weeks, they went back to New York and Spencer went back to work. Lorna started writing thank you letters for all the gifts they received and then organizing her grandmother's place and packing her things to move to *Wentworth Hall*. They would stay in Meadowbrook through spring and summer and move to the city after Labor Day. She called her grandmother's attorney and asked him to handle the sale of her grandmother's place in New York City which she inherited when her grandmother died. She would not need her place since she would now be living with the Wentworths in New York and also at *Wentworth Hall*. She instructed her attorney that the proceeds of the house sale should be deposited in her bank account together with her inheritance from her grandmother. She would not need the money since she would be living at the Wentworth houses and Spencer would be paying for all her expenses from now on. She would eventually put the money in trust for her baby after the baby was born.

With the weather warming up, spring at *Wentworth Hall* was glorious. The snow was beginning to melt, the trees were leafing up and the spring flowers were everywhere. Lorna was happy to be out in the country. She took a short walk in the garden every morning. She was trying to find a good place to start a cutting garden where she could cut some flower for the house every day. *Wentworth Hall* already had some themed gardens - a formal rose garden, a Japanese garden, a perennial garden and an Italian garden. She wanted something informal like her grandmother's garden in Maine, full of vibrant color during the growing season where bees and butterflies could coexist with her plants. She also needed something to keep her busy and this garden would be her own.

With the help of Lou Marconi, the head gardener, they found a nice area beyond the walled perennial garden where she could start her cutting garden. She procured her seeds and Lou and his staff started preparing the bed. Lorna told him what she wanted. She drew the plan and Lou started digging. He brought some horse manure from the stable and added it to the soil. When the ground was ready, she told the gardeners where to plant the seeds. She even planted some of the seeds herself. She was not afraid of getting her hands dirty although Spencer kept on reminding her that was what they had the gardeners for - to do that kind of work but she enjoyed doing it she would tell him.

As spring turned into summer and her stomach grew larger, she slowed down on her gardening chores. Her garden was now established and she began to enjoy it. She would stroll in the garden every day and see the progress. They had placed a wooden bench under a maple tree near the cutting garden and she would sit on it to rest when she felt tired. When Emma was in residence, she sometimes joined Lorna for a picnic near her garden. The gardeners now do the maintenance work and they cut some flowers for her every day to bring to the house. She was happy and contented. She was enjoying her stay at *Wentworth Hall* and knew someday she would be the mistress of the house. Legally, she was now the mistress of the house since Spencer owned it but as long as Margaret was in residence, she deferred to her mother-in-law, although the servants knew where she stood in the house hierarchy. They had no problems with that since they found her to be an affable person when she used to visit before her marriage to Spencer.

While Lorna waited for the baby to arrive, Emma stayed in the city. She loved the social life in New York. She saw Todd Prescott sparingly. Just like Spencer, Todd was extremely busy at his uncle's law firm. With Wall Street having big trouble, Todd found all lawyers were loaded with so much legal work. He stayed up late most nights. He had not seen Emma for quite a while. Emma kept herself busy by doing her bit for the League of Women Voters. She missed Todd a lot but knew he was extremely busy.

## Chapter 20

It was a very hot and humid day in July when Emma realized that she only had a couple of months left before Lorna would have her baby. She still had to get her sister-in-law some baby presents. She just finished her meeting at the League of Women Voters and since she had nothing else to do the rest of the day, she decided she might as well do her shopping. It was something to do while she was bored. She was already out in

Midtown anyway. As soon as she came out of the building, she realized she picked up the wrong time of day.

It was nearing 12 o'clock and people were coming out of their midtown offices going out to lunch and filling up the sidewalk up and down Fifth Avenue. There were vendors stationed on some corners of the street hawking their products which did not help the situation. The crowd was getting to her and she just wanted to get to Saks and get it over with. She walked briskly uptown on Fifth Avenue towards Saks.

In front of Charles Scribner's Sons building, a 10-story Beaux Arts-style building on Fifth Avenue and 48th Street was a man admiring the magnificent façade of the building. The building was designed by Ernest Flagg and built in 1912-13 with piers anchoring three large bays which include four medallions with busts of printers: Benjamin Franklin, William Caxton, Johann Gutenberg and Aldus Manutius. The man was fascinated with the exterior of the Scribner's Bookstore and was oblivious of the crowd.

Just as Emma rushed into the crowd in front of Scribner's Bookstore, the man turned around and Emma bumped into him.

"Excuse me, don't you watch where you are going?" the man said indignantly.

She looked at him and said apologetically, "I'm sorry."

She hurried on. The man stared at her, recognized her and followed her. Emma was walking so fast but he finally caught up to her.

"Excuse me, Miss."

"What? What do you want?" Emma was beginning to get extremely annoyed. She was hot and just wanted to get to the store. She kept on walking.

The man kept in step with her. "Are you Miss Emma Wentworth?" Victor asked.

"And if I am, what is it to you? Leave me alone," she said without looking. She kept her pace and he continued to follow her. It annoyed her that stranger had the nerve of talking to her.

"I know you," he said boldly.

"What? What are you talking about?" she glanced at him but did not recognize him. "Leave me alone or I'll call the police," she said and continued walking.

"You came to my in-laws' house at *'Overlook'* with your brother and parents for dinner a few months ago," he said.

Emma stopped dead in her track. She looked at the man. She knotted her brows. "Oh, I'm sorry. I did not recognize you."

"It's okay. How are you?" he asked.

"I'm fine and you?" Emma felt embarrassed, offered her hand and they shook hands.

"Very well. Thank you. I apologize for being rude." Victor looked at his watch. "It's almost lunch time. What are you doing for lunch?" he asked without thinking. He felt contrite for being rude to her.

"Nothing really," Emma said.

"Good, why don't I take you out to lunch?" He felt he had to offer her the olive branch.

"That would be lovely." She thought it was a nice gesture.

"We can go somewhere close by."

Just then she realized why she was in a hurry. "Oh no. I can't go. I'm sorry."

"Why not?"

"I was on my way to Saks to go shopping for a baby present," Emma said.

"Whose baby?" Victor was curious.

"My brother and his wife. She is expecting in a couple of months."

"I did not know that. I can go shopping with you and then we can go eat somewhere afterwards. Is that all right?" Victor asked.

Emma did not see any harm in it. After all, he was a family acquaintance and his in-laws were one of Wentworth Bank's rich clienteles.

"OK. If you don't mind shopping with me first."

"No. Not at all," he said.

They went to Saks. The place was jammed with people on their lunch break. They went to the Infant Department and she picked a set of layette in blue color to be sent to Lorna at the Wentworth's house on Fifth Avenue. Victor noticed the blue color.

"Why blue?" Victor asked.

"They think it will be a boy," Emma said.

"Why is it everyone wants a boy?"

"To carry the family name," she said. She noticed there was a sad look on his face. Maybe she touched a cord in him. She knew Victor had no children in spite of him being married for a long time. She wondered why.

After the sales clerk had taken the address where the merchandise was to be delivered and Emma paid for the items, they went out of the store and wound their way through the crowd in front of St. Patrick's Cathedral and then across the street to 50$^{th}$ St and walked toward Sixth Avenue. They walked a couple of blocks uptown. Victor found a nice Italian restaurant and they walked in. The place was half empty.

"Isn't this great? We practically have the place to ourselves," he said.

"Wait another half hour and this place will probably be jammed," Emma said.

"Glad we got here first," Victor said.

Emma had not been out with a Polish guy and this was such a novel idea. She knew he was married but as she remembered, his wife said they were childhood sweethearts and so she felt safe to go out with him. He talked about his childhood in a Polish neighborhood and how he and Anna met at her father's small grocery store at that time. He was very entertaining with all kinds of stories. He was so animated when he talked and Emma felt relaxed. He was different from men in her social circle. He was a novelty to her.

After lunch, Victor said, "I had a great time today. Maybe we can have lunch again. I'm in the city every Wednesday. How about next week?"

Emma being bored with not having much to do during the day since Lorna was busy packing her stuff to move with them and Todd being stuck at his office most of the time she thought it was a great idea. It was something for her to do.

"Yes, that was fun. I suppose it's all right," Emma said. She did not like him to go to her house and most Wednesday, she had a meeting with some ladies at the League of Women Voters so she added, "I can meet you in front of St. Patrick Cathedral after I get off from my club meeting. We do meet on Wednesday so that's perfect."

"OK then. I'll see you next week."

They shook hands and Emma went uptown and Victor went to Penn Station to catch the train to Long Island.

The following week, Victor was in front of St. Patrick Cathedral half an hour before Emma arrived. He wondered where to take her to lunch. He thought maybe he'll take her downtown to Greenwich Village and then show her the Caffe Reggio on MacDougal Street. To kill time, he went in to Saks and browse through the Men's Department. After 20 minutes at the store, he went back out. It did not take long and he saw Emma coming and he walked up to her.

"I was not sure if you are coming," he said.

"I said I would, didn't I?" Emma said.

"Yes, you did," he smiled and offered his hand. Emma took it and they shook hand. He held it for a longer time. Emma felt an electric shock through her. She released her hand.

"Where do you want to go?" he asked.

"Surprise me," she said.

"I know a place where you probably have not heard of nor been there before," he said.

"Where?"

"At Greenwich Village. A place called Caffe Reggio."

"No, I haven't been there before. I'd love to see the place," Emma said.

"I bet you, none of your friends had been there. It opened a couple of years ago and they have the best cappuccino."

"Sounds interesting. What's a cappuccino?" Emma asked.

"A cappuccino is an Italian coffee drink which is traditionally prepared with dark brewed coffee, hot milk and steamed milk foam. Cream may be used instead of milk and is often topped with cinnamon. The founder of Caffe Reggio, Domenico Parisi, introduced it in America."

"Sounds delicious. I would love to try it," Emma said.

"We can have lunch at Hotel Albert and then we can go to Caffe Reggio afterwards. They are both interesting places. You can see some of the best artists in both places. It's something different than what you're used to. Are you sure you want to go there?" he asked.

"Sure, I'd love to," Emma said.

Victor hailed a taxicab and they went downtown to Greenwich Village. Just as Victor said, Hotel Albert's restaurant was packed with writers. After lunch, they walked toward Caffe Reggio. The place was busy. Inside the cafe, Domenico Parisi was making cappuccino on this huge silver Espresso machine made in Italy in 1902. It was widely known that he bought it with his savings when he opened the cafe in 1927. On the wall hung some painting from an artist of The School of Caravaggio.

"This is really delicious," Emma said as she sipped her coffee with the white froth on top.

"This is the only place where you can get the best cappuccino. Others are trying to imitate it but nothing like the original," he said.

"I'm glad you took me here. I would never go here by myself and some of my friends probably won't take me," Emma said.

"I'm glad you like the place," he said.

After finishing their cappuccino, they headed back uptown. Victor wanted to take her home but Emma did not want him to. She asked to be dropped a couple of blocks from her place. They both alighted from the cab together. Emma was hoping none of her friends see her.

"Can I see you again next week?" Victor asked.

Emma did not know how to answer him. "I think . . ." She stopped in midsentence.

"You think what?"

"Victor, much as I enjoy your company, this is not a good idea. You're married and Anna might find out about this outing. I don't want to be the cause of your problem," Emma said.

Victor was quiet for just a minute, then he said. "I am not happy at home," he said simply.

"I'm sorry to hear that," Emma said. She was not happy either because Todd was too busy with his work, she had not been out with him for a long time. She missed Todd but since he was not available and Victor was, she decided it would be great to have some fun. She decided since they were both unhappy and they seemed to enjoy each other's company, she would take the little happiness she could get. She reached for his hand.

"Yes, I'll see you next week," she said. She hoped she was not making a big mistake.

Victor was dumbfounded, "Are you sure you want to do this?"

Emma nodded. "Yes, same place, same time." She turned around toward uptown. Victor stared at her back, then turned and walked toward downtown.

One date led to another and pretty soon, Emma found herself seeing Victor on a regular basis on Wednesdays for lunch.

By the middle of the summer, Victor had rented an apartment in the city. Emma was not aware of it until one day they were having lunch and Victor said, "I want to show you something."

"What?" Emma asked.

"I rented an apartment on First Avenue and 72nd Street."

"Really?" she asked.

"Yes, I told Anna in case we are in the city late and we don't feel like going home for the night, we have a place to stay."

"She agreed to that?"

"She did. Anyway, I want to show it to you today."

"I'd love to," she said.

They walked out of the restaurant and walked toward First Avenue. Emma was a little apprehensive. She suspected what he wanted. She wanted it too. Her heart was beating faster as they entered the building. Victor was quiet for a change. They went to the elevator. Victor told the elevator man, "10th floor please." They both rode the elevator in silence. They went up to the 10th floor. After they got off the elevator, Victor led Emma to the right and then took a key from his pocket. He opened the door. Emma followed him inside.

"This is it. What do you think?" Victor asked.

She walked toward the window which was facing the East River.

"Lovely. I love the view. You picked the right place," Emma said.

"It's small but it's just right for what we intended to use it for," he said. "Do you want coffee? I bought some dessert early," he said.

"That would be great."

He went to the kitchen and she followed him. He poured water in the percolator. He was getting very nervous like a young school boy on his first date. He turned to her and saw her watching him. She smiled. He put down the coffee pot, walked toward her. He looked her in the eye. Their eyes clicked. He kissed her. She was anticipating this. She responded. She found him very attractive.

# Chapter 21

Emma found solace in Victor's arms. They met every Wednesday. She did not realize how lonely she was until she met Victor again that day on Fifth Avenue. Although she found Todd a charming fellow and she enjoyed his company, nothing was said about a permanent commitment. They saw each other when he was not busy. He was committed to his job and he worked very hard at it. She wanted to marry him but it seemed that would never happen. What she could not understand was he was not going out with any other woman either and they always had fun together and at ease with each other when they were together. She wondered if he wanted to remain a bachelor all his life, not wanting any commitment.

Victor promised her that he would get a divorce from Anna. Emma did not think it would work since it was impossible for a catholic family to get a divorce. He wanted to marry Emma but Emma was having second thoughts about her affair with Victor. To her, it was just a diversion. Deep down she wanted to marry Todd Prescott. He was more of her social class and they had more things in common. Spencer and her parents were very fond of him so there would not be any problems marrying Todd Prescott if only he would say the word. With Victor, her parents would never forgive her marrying down. Besides she was not in love with Victor but she did not know how to tell Victor. She would play along as she could. Maybe Victor would get tired of her eventually. Although she had her doubts. She did not think it would happen.

At dinner one night at Victor's apartment, Emma got the courage to tell Victor what she wanted to tell him a long time ago. It was not what Victor wanted. She was quiet at dinner and Victor noticed it.

"What's the matter?" he asked.

"Victor, we cannot go on forever like this? I feel like a whore seeing you secretly all the time," she said with a steady voice.

"We always have great time together. I really want to marry you. We'll get married as soon as I can get a divorce from Anna," Victor said.

Emma shook her head. She knew Anna would not agree to that. Besides, she really wanted to end their affair but Victor was not listening.

"You and Anna are both catholic and she will not give you a divorce. I'm certain of that," Emma said.

"Just give me some time. It will work out. I promise."

"I'm not sure of that." Victor got closer to her and kissed her. She could not break from his embrace. He knew how to please a woman and she melted away. All her resolve to end their affair went out the window. Maybe she could break it off next time they met. In the meantime, she would just enjoy this evening with him.

Anna suspected something was going on with Victor but she did not know what. He was always late coming home. Most often drunk and went straight to bed. Other times, he ignored her completely. He had not taken her to bed for a long time. Anna became frustrated with his behavior and nagged him all the time. They would fight constantly and the maids heard their constant argument.

Anna was getting worried everyday with the change in Victor's attitude toward her. He was not the same man she married. He had changed lately. He was coming home later and later, always having an excuse that he was with some friends but never included her in his outings. She was stuck at the house and for nothing better to do she started drinking and taking drugs to alleviate her misery. It started with a small amount but as her problem got bigger, she had taken more and more drugs and drinking heavily too. As Victor became more involved with Emma, at home Anna took more and more drugs. That combination was lethal to anyone but she was not paying much attention. It helped ease her pain.

Anna had taken too many drugs that night. Victor had not come home yet. The house was very quiet. There was no one in the house except her. Her maid had gone to the cottage where she and her husband lived.

In the stillness of the night, Anna heard a noise. Feeling uncomfortable of being alone, all she could think of was someone was trying to break in. There was so much talk lately of burglary around town. Yes, she was positive it was a burglar wanting to break in. What was she going to do? She got scared out of her wits. She had to protect herself. But how? She suddenly thought a gun would protect her. She had to find Victor's gun. She knew it was in Victor's night table. She did not want to turn on the light. She walked in the dark not wanting the burglar to know there was someone awake. She opened the top drawer on Victor's night table. It was not there. She opened the bottom drawer. She felt the gun in the dark. She took it out and walked quietly toward the door.

She heard the footstep coming into their bedroom. Then she heard the intruder quietly open the bedroom door. She was hiding behind the door as the intruder opened it and walked in. She aimed at the shadow coming in. She steadied both her hands on the trigger and then pulled the trigger. She shot the intruder three times. The shadow slumped and dropped to the floor. She heard a silent moaning.

She turned on the light and walked to her victim. She could not believe what she saw. First it was a blur since the effect of the drugs was still on. Then her mind cleared and she saw Victor in a pool of blood, sprawled on the floor with the gunshots. She screamed. Then she remembered to call for help. She ran to the telephone. But before she could dial, she began to panic and dropped the phone. The phone just hanged by her bedside. Like a mad woman, she walked around the bedroom still with the gun in her hand. She took another glance at Victor whose eyes were opened and staring at her with a blank look. She could not take it. Horror filled her mind. She was still holding the gun. Without a second thought, she put the gun on her temple and pulled the trigger. She shot herself in the head. Blood splattered all around her. She slumped on top of Victor's body still holding the gun in her hand.

Cice, Anna's mother, usually called her in the morning. Cice could not reach her. She called several times but the phone was busy. Cice thought she could not possibly be talking this long early in the morning. She became worried. She suspected her daughter was having marital problem for a long time. She was always worried about Anna who was not herself lately. She knew she was also drinking heavily lately. The maid told her so and she was worried too.

Cice kept on calling her daughter but she could not get through. She could not take it any longer so she decided to go to her daughter's house in Mill Neck. She got to the house and knocked at the door. No one was answering the door so she used her key.

"Hello, anybody home," Cice called as she walked into the foyer. She smelled something funny. She went into the kitchen first but nobody was there. She looked in every room downstairs but nobody was there either. She noticed the cars were in the garage so they should be home. She decided to go upstairs. She went from room to room. At the end of a long corridor, she reached the master bedroom. She was greeted by a pool of blood by the door. She screamed.

The maid who lived at the cottage in back of the house heard someone screaming from the house. She ran toward the main house. She opened the backdoor and went in. She heard a sobbing sound coming from one of the rooms upstairs. She ran upstairs. She was worried about her mistress. She hoped she was all right. With her mood lately, she wondered what she was up to. As she walked through the corridor, she bumped into Cice who was still crying hysterically. Cice was out of control.

"Mrs. Cook, what's the matter? What are you doing here early in the morning?"

"Look there," Cice pointed in the direction of the master bedroom. The maid walked towards the bedroom and stopped short at the threshold. Blood was all over the place. Anna and

Victor lay in a pool of blood. Anna was still holding the revolver. She was shocked but recovered quickly. She ran out to check on Mrs. Cook. She found Cice standing like a statue next to the railing on the top of the stairway staring blankly. She took Cice downstairs and sat her in the parlor and went to the kitchen and picked up the phone and dialed the police. Then she took a bottle of brandy from the pantry. She knew where it was hidden. She poured some in a glass and brought it to Cice.

Within a few minutes, they heard the siren of police cars. The police put a police barricade by the end of the driveway and came rushing to the house.

The police saw Cice and the maid in the parlor. The maid told them to go upstairs in the master bedroom where the shooting was. Several police officers went upstairs. The police chief went upstairs quickly, saw the scene and left his deputy at the crime scene. He then went back downstairs to the parlor and tried to get a statement from Cice but she was incoherent. Then he questioned the maid. She could not tell much to the police either.

"Did you hear anything last night?" the police asked the maid.

"No. Nothing. I did not hear anything," the maid said.

"The revolver has a silencer and that's probably why you did not hear the sound," the police told the maid.

"What time did you leave for the cottage last night?" the police chief asked. His assistant started writing in earnest.

"Right after I cleaned up the kitchen after dinner. Around nine o'clock."

"How was she when you left her?"

"She was distraught when I left her last night. She was waiting for her husband to come home," the maid said.

"Is he always late?"

"Lately, yes."

"Any explanation why?"

"I have no idea. I heard he went to see some of his old friends all the time."

"Do you know who?"

"No. No idea."

"Do you know of any marital problem between them?" the cop asked.

"They were not happy lately. I heard them arguing more often."

"What about?"

"Him. He was never home most of the time and his drinking."

"Do you have any idea why?"

"Not really."

"What do you mean not really?"

"He said he was with his friends. You know men always go drinking with their buddies."

"Sure do. Do you know if he is seeing someone? I mean a female friend."

"Not that I know of. But she is a jealous type and constantly nagging him. Maybe there is someone. I don't know."

The cop turned to Cice. "Did your daughter say anything to you that might explain this tragedy?"

"No but I sensed something was wrong with their marriage."

"How do you know that?"

"Mother's instinct, I guess."

"How long have they been married?"

"Seven years."

"Any children?"

"None."

"Did your daughter mention why they were not having children?"

"Well, she does not want to be strapped with kids. She always wanted to maintain her figure too. She was very conscious of that."

The cops raised his eyebrow. "Did your son-in-law want children?"

"I presume all men do. What's that got to do with anything?"

"We are just trying to figure out if they were happy not having children. We are looking for all angles that caused this tragedy," the cop said.

He then turned to the medical examiner.

"Anything important?" he asked.

"Looks like she took too many drugs and alcohol too," the medical examiner said.

"We have to do an autopsy."

"Yes."

He turned to Cice.

"Mrs. Cook, we have to take the bodies to the town morgue and take an autopsy."

"But why?"Cice asked.

"Crimes have been committed and it is our job to take an autopsy." Cice started crying hard again. The maid had to calm her down.

The cop told the maid, "She might need a sedative."

The maid nodded and the cop left them to take care of business.

# Chapter 22

Emma was in front of St. Patrick Cathedral waiting for Victor at the appointed time. He was late for their rendezvous. She waited for half an hour but there was no sign of him. She walked across the street to Saks and went in the store for ten minutes and went out again, looked at the southern steps on the side of the cathedral. He still was not there. She crossed the street and wandered for another half hour wondering why he was late. He was usually on time. This was not like him to be late. He was usually there when she arrived. She was the one who was always late. He was always earlier than she but never late. What was causing his delay? She began to worry. Perhaps it was his wife again giving him problems. Or maybe he changed his mind after all. Maybe he came to his senses that it won't work and decided to end it all. It was just as well.

She wandered at a newsstand. She scanned through the magazine and newspapers. Then she saw the headline "Murder/Suicide in Long Island." For nothing better to do, she picked up the newspaper and bought one. After she paid for it, she walked away from the newsstand and scanned the article. The first paragraph gave her a chill. She stared at the writing and could not believe it.

*"Daughter of wealthy food entrepreneur and her husband were found dead possibly murder/suicide at their home in a posh neighborhood in Long Island.",* the first sentence read. She continued reading. Her vision started turning blurry. Victor and his wife were dead.

"Oh my God!" She could not believe what she was reading. She put her hand over her mouth and tears started rolling down her check.

Anna allegedly killed Victor with his gun and then committed suicide. There was no witness. She felt sick. She steadied herself and tried to comprehend what happened. She folded the newspaper and started walking aimlessly. She walked until she reached Central Park oblivious of what was around her. She saw a bench near the Bethesda Fountain. She sat down, looked at the newspaper again. She was still numb from the news. It could not be possible. She had a hard time believing it.

She remembered the day she and Victor walked here hand in hand. He seemed very happy and asked her to marry him. She did not give him an answer. He promised to get a divorce to be free from Anna. She was not sure then if she wanted to marry him. There were complications. She wanted to marry Todd Prescott. She was just having fun with Victor.

She stayed for quite a while thinking of what to do next. She tried hard to focus on what she wanted to do. She was debating whether to go home, then decided not to. She had to talk to someone. But who?

Lorna. Yes, her best friend, Lorna. She could confide in her.

She walked out of the park. She walked down Fifth Avenue toward Lorna's grandmother's place in Chelsea. It would be a long walk but she needed time to think. She walked down Fifth Avenue without thought of what she was doing. She knew she would find her friend at her grandmother's house. Lorna was still busy getting her grandmother's house for sale and packing to move. She braced herself. She had to tell Lorna about her affair. It would not be easy but there was no one else to talk to. She felt guilty about what had happened. At least no one knew her affair with Victor. She could not possibly be implicated. Besides, the papers said murder/suicide. Her head was spinning. Suppose the police got wind of her involvement with Victor. She hoped and prayed it would not come down to that. Her family would be scandalized. Her parents and Spencer would never forgive her.

Emma reached Lorna's place and knocked at the door. Mr. Menton opened it. Lorna was on top of the stairway wanting to know who the unexpected guest was.

"Oh, Emma," She called from the top of the stairway. She ran downstairs and welcome her friend and sister-in-law.

She turned to Mr. Menton, "Can you bring us some tea, Menton."

"Surely, Mrs. Wentworth," he said and went to the kitchen.

"Come on, Emma. Let's go to the parlor. You look weary. What's up?" Lorna asked.

"I need your advice," Emma said. She knew she could trust her friend.

Lorna looked at Emma who seemed worried. Lorna had not seen her that way before and she did not like it. Something was bothering her gravely. Emma was usually vibrant, always bubbling with energy. Something was wrong. She could feel it. Emma sat glumly on the settee.

"Emma, what's the matter? You look troubled. Tell me." Lorna noticed the newspaper that Emma just placed on the table. She picked it up and saw the headline. "Oh, my God. How awful!" Is this what's bothering you?"

Emma nodded. "I don't know what to do," Emma said softly. Lorna raised her eyebrow and looked puzzled.

"I don't understand. Do you know them? I don't recall meeting them at all." She started reading the article. She still did not know them. "Who are they?"

"She is the daughter of Mr. & Mrs. Cook, the owner of Cook's Emporium and one of Wentworth Bank's big depositors. I met her and her husband last year when we got invited to their dinner party. Spencer first refused to go then finally agreed with my father that it was good for business. Spencer asked me to go with him for company in case he got bored."

"Spencer never mentioned the family to me but then we never talked about any of his clients either. But I still don't get it. How does that affect you?" Lorna wanted to know.

"It's a long story." Emma sighed. They heard a tap on the door and Mr. Menton came in with the tea.

"Thank you, Menton."

"Anything else, ma'am?"

"This is fine. Thank you."

"Very well, ma'am," he said and backed to the door, closed it quietly and left. Lorna started pouring the tea. She handed Emma a cup and poured her own. Emma took a sip.

Lorna looked at her sister-in-law. "You said it is a long story. Well, I'm listening."

Emma took a deep breath. "I don't know how to tell you this. I hope you will understand and not judge me harshly."

"Emma, you're my best friend. You helped me in my time of trouble. I'm here to help you whatever was bothering you."

"I know I can trust you." Emma breathed a sigh of relief.

"Of course, you can trust me. Come on now. What's the matter?"

"I feel guilty about what happened to Anna and Victor," Emma said in anguish. She tried to hold her tears. She was not the crying type.

"Why?" Lorna did not understand why Emma felt guilty. She suspected something but she wanted to hear Emma confirm her suspicion.

"I had been having an affair with Victor the last few months." Emma lowered her gaze. She did not want to see the expression on Lorna's face. She knew Lorna would be shocked. She was right. Lorna's mouth opened wide not believing what she heard. She stared at Emma. She recovered quickly.

"Does Spencer know? How about Todd? I thought you wanted to marry Todd," Lorna said trying to comprehend what she was hearing.

"Spencer does not know. Nobody knows as far as I know unless Victor mentioned it to someone. We were very discreet. I have not seen Todd for a couple of months. He was too busy at work. I missed Todd and it was probably the reason why I fell in the arms of Victor. Oh, Lorna, I feel wretched. I feel I was the reason why Victor's marriage was in shambles and why his wife killed him and then committed suicide."

"How did it start? I mean your affair with Victor. I could not see how you two met again since you are not in the same social circle."

"It was a chance meeting. I had not seen Todd for a couple of weeks. He was buried in work at his uncle's law firm. I was on my way to go shopping at Saks when I literally bumped into this fellow by accident among the crowd on Fifth Avenue. He was very annoyed at me. We had some harsh words. I did not recognize him. I kept on walking but he recognized me and followed me after the initial shock. He caught up with me and apologized. It was around noon and he asked me to have lunch with him, sort of compensating for his rude behavior towards me. I should have said no but I didn't. I saw no harm in having lunch with him. As a matter of fact, I thought it was a novel idea, having lunch with a Polish man. One lunch led to another and then dinner and in no time, I was having an affair with Victor. I found myself heavily involved with him. He was irresistible and I was very attracted to him. He promised to marry me although I was doubtful about my feeling towards him. It was not love at all. It was lust, plain and simple. I'm sorry to shock you. I still want to marry Todd."

"What a mess!" Lorna took a sip of her tea. She tried to think. "Do you think you should tell Spencer about this?"

Emma stood up and went close to the fireplace. Lorna waited. "I thought long and hard. When I saw the news, I wandered and walked to Central Park thinking hard what to do. I was supposed to meet him in front of the cathedral but he was late. I wandered to a newsstand and bought a paper. I saw the headline. My heart sank. That's when I walked to Central Park. I sat by a bench at Bethesda Fountain and stayed there for a while. I could not think straight. That's when I decided to come here. I don't want to tell Spencer. He would be furious. And my parents. It would kill my mother."

"Yes, Spencer probably would. Your parents I'm not sure. How about Todd?"

"I don't know. He might walk out on me if he finds out I had an affair with Victor. I don't want to lose him." Emma's voice cracked and she stood up and went towards the window. She did not want Lorna to see that she was in the verge of tears. She stared into the distance and shook her head.

Lorna was watching her and felt sorry for her friend. She went to her and said, "Emma, Todd is different from your brother. He is more pragmatic whereas Spencer is so old-fashioned. Todd would probably get angry at first but he might understand you better than your brother. You were lonely and Victor was there while Todd was too busy with work. He might blame himself for what happened too."

"I am afraid he might not take it that way. I don't want to take that chance."

"But if he found out later, it would be worse. You have to be honest with him. You have to tell him."

"I have to think about it. I'm sorry I was so stupid to get involved with a married man. What was I thinking?"

"You were lonely, that's all."

"And he was a great lover," Emma said.

Lorna was not quite sure whether to laugh or to get shocked at her sister-in-law. But then Emma was always so direct in her manners. She would say such a thing. Emma saw the reaction of her sister-in-law and she began to laugh. "Did I shock you?"

"No. With you, nothing shocks me anymore. Remember, we are best friends and I know you better than anybody. I'm just worried about Spencer when he finds out."

"Well, let's just hope he does not. Forget I told you. I don't want you to get messed up with my problem. I might tell Todd when the time is appropriate. I don't know when at this time. In the meantime, I'm still worried about the scandal. I hope Victor did not tell anyone about it. That is my biggest worry."

Lorna hugged her friend and did not say anything. She was worried too that it might leak to the press and then the family would find out.

## Chapter 23

It was the end of the summer. Emma, Spencer and Lorna decided to come down to *Wentworth Hall* and spend the Labor Day weekend in Long Island. The days were getting shorter and the night air was cooler. There was an autumn feel in the air. The majestic color of the trees on the ground of *Wentworth Hall* was beginning to turn and it was a sight to behold. It was a great day to spend in the country. Lorna was nearing her term and both she and Spencer were happily anticipating the arrival of the baby.

On the other hand, Emma was still worried about the murder/suicide of Victor and Anna. After the private funeral which was closed to the public, the news started to dissipate. The authorities had two theories on the case. Since burglary was prevalent in the area at that time, it could be an accident shooting with Anna thinking the man was a burglar and shot him in darkness or they had an argument and Anna got hold of the gun and shot him and then committed suicide. Since there was no witness and Anna was still holding the gun when police came over, it was decided to have the case closed. The news was finally buried on page 5 with the economy occupying the front pages of the papers. Emma was relieved that she was not implicated and spared the family much embarrassment. Still her conscience was bothering her. None of the family members seemed to know and Spencer never mentioned any of it. He was too preoccupied with the financial condition at the bank and the upcoming arrival of the baby.

At dinner on Friday night, Emma sat quietly at the dinner table while conversation focused on what was happening in the country. She was thankful for that. Nothing was mentioned about the murder/suicide. There was a bank run at the bank and Spencer was more worried about that than anything else. One of the customers withdrawing was Sally's parents. He did not think it had anything to do with the economy. It had more to do with his breaking his engagement off with their daughter, Sally. It could not be helped and he had to suffer the consequences. He just hoped it did not turn into a bank panic.

A bank run is the sudden withdrawal of deposits of just one bank. A bank run, also known as a run on the bank occurs in a fractional reserve banking system when a large number of customers withdraw their deposits from a financial institution at the same time and either demand cash or transfer those funds into government bonds, precious metals or stones, or a safer institution because they believe that the financial institution is, or might become, insolvent. As a bank run progresses, it generates its own momentum, in a kind of self-fulfilling prophecy as more people withdraw their deposits. The likelihood of default increases, triggering further withdrawals. This can destabilize the bank to the point where it runs out of cash and thus faces sudden bankruptcy.

A banking panic or bank panic on the other hand is a financial crisis that occurs when many banks suffer bank runs at the same time as people suddenly try to convert their threatened deposits into cash or try to get out of their domestic banking system altogether. In a systemic banking crisis, all or almost all of the banking capital in a country is wiped out.

"How is the situation at the bank?" Margaret asked Spencer. She read in the paper that Wall Street was not doing too well.

"There is always a long line at the bank nowadays," Spencer said as he put down his fork and looked at his father.

Margaret turned to George and asked, "What about?"

"They are withdrawing their money. People are getting scared. The line stretched outside the bank around the corner and into the next block," George said.

"Oh my! That does not sound good. I guess people are panicking and the newspapers are not helping the situation."

"You're right at that. The public lost faith in the banking system and are hoarding more cash at home," Spencer said.

"Are we heading for a big crash?" Margaret asked.

"All the signs are pointing that way," George said.

"I agree with you on that," Spencer said.

Emma was quiet. She was not paying attention to the conversation at all. While Spencer was agonizing on the situation at the bank, Emma was worried about her own predicament. Lorna was watching Emma and knew what was going on in her mind. She was caught in the middle worrying about Emma and also about Spencer. Things were not going well at all at the Wentworth household. She hoped it would not get worse than this.

After dinner, Emma excused herself and feigned a headache and decided to go upstairs to bed.

"Goodnight, dear," Margaret said as Emma turned towards the hallway to go to her room.

"Goodnight," Emma said to everyone.

"I think I'll go up too," Lorna said.

"I'll join you later," Spencer said.

Emma and Lorna went upstairs together. As they walked down the long hallway to their rooms, Lorna asked Emma, "Are you OK?"

"I'm fine."

"Are you sure?"

"Yes, I am. Really."

Lorna hugged her friend. Emma said softly, "Thanks for being supportive."

"Don't worry. You can always talk to me. I really mean that."

"I know."

Emma opened her bedroom door and walked in and Lorna proceeded to go to the end of the hallway to the master bedroom.

After Labor Day, Lorna and Spencer decided to move back to the city and wait for the baby's arrival in the city. Lorna was getting big and got tired easily. They brought enough staff to handle everything in the house. Paul Conley was now in residence in the city just in case he was needed and was at the ready to take them to the hospital. Spencer thought they would be better off in Manhattan where medical facilities were close by. Her doctor was also in the city. As the month progressed, Lorna got busy getting the nursery ready. They hired a private nurse to take care of the baby after it was born.

It was early morning of Sept. 26, 1929 when Laura felt her water break. Lorna got dressed. Spencer was already dressed getting ready for work. Instead, he had to rush Lorna to the hospital. He rang the bell and Mr. Clarkson, the New York butler, came into their bedroom.

"Clarkson, can you tell Paul to get the car ready. We have to take Mrs. Wentworth to the hospital now."

"Right away, sir. Do you need Sarah to help Mrs. Wentworth?" Clarkson asked.

"I don't think there is any need for her. Mrs. Wentworth is about ready," Spencer said.

"I'll go see Paul now."

"Thank you, Clarkson."

Mr. Clarkson closed the door quietly and walked hurriedly to the servant's quarters. The servants just finished their breakfast. Paul was having his coffee. Sarah was preparing the breakfast tray for her mistress. All stood up when he entered the room.

"Paul, Mr. Wentworth needs the car now. They are going to the hospital as soon as Mrs. Wentworth is ready," Mr. Clarkson said. He turned to Sarah.

"Sarah, there is no time for her breakfast. They are leaving for the hospital now."

"Right away. I'll be in front of the house in five minutes," Paul said, took another sip of his coffee, put on his hat and ran out of the house to the garage.

"Frank, I need you upstairs. And you too, Sarah."

Mr. Clarkson went back upstairs with Frank and Sarah. When they reached the door to the master bedroom, Mr. Clarkson knocked softly.

Spencer called out, "Come in."

Sarah attended to Lorna. Frank picked up Lorna's suitcase and headed downstairs to bring it to the car. Paul was waiting already in front of the house. Spencer walked downstairs slowly with Lorna and down the front portico. Paul opened the car door and Lorna got in followed by Spencer.

They reached the hospital in no time. Her doctor was already waiting. Spencer had called the hospital before they left the house. Lorna was wheeled into a private room while a team of doctors and nurses attend to her medical conditions. They timed her contractions.

Later on, she was wheeled into the delivery room. Spencer was sent down to the waiting room. Like an expectant father, Spencer was worried sick while Lorna was in the delivery room. He paced the floor up and down in the waiting room and could not sit still. It seems like forever, he thought. By lunch time, she was still in the delivery room. The nurse came by and told him it might take a lot longer. She was nowhere near delivering her baby. She advised him to get some lunch and she would probably be still in the delivery room when he gets back.

He went outside the hospital. It was good to get some fresh air. He strolled to the nearest coffee shop. He was not feeling hungry so he just ordered a cup of coffee. He sat at one of the small round table by the window and drank his coffee. He felt funny sitting there by himself but there was no other place to grab a quick drink. He also wanted to be close to the hospital so he could go right back. He quickly drank his coffee and headed back to the hospital.

As soon as he got there, he asked the nurse at the nurse's station if there was any news yet.

"She is still in labor," she told him.

Three hours later with Lorna exhausted from the ordeal, the nurse came to the waiting room. He saw her coming.

"Any news?" he asked anxiously.

"Congratulations, Mr. Wentworth. You have a beautiful baby boy." Spencer could not be happier. It was the best news. He had a son and heir.

"Is she all right? Can I see my wife and the baby now?" he asked eagerly.

"They are both fine. We are just getting him cleaned up. You can see your wife now if you want."

Spencer did not waste any time and proceeded to the private room where Lorna was. Lorna was still groggy when he entered the room.

"How do you feel, Darling?"

"Exhausted. Did you see the baby?" she asked with a faint smile on her face. She looked wan and tired. Just then the nurse handed him his newborn son. He was a little bit apprehensive but it was good to hold his baby in his arms. He looked at him adoringly.

"He is so tiny. Who does he look like? I think he looks like you," he told Lorna.

"No. I don't think so. He looks like himself." She smiled.

The baby started to cry. Spencer gave the baby back to the nurse who put the baby in the bassinet. He came to Lorna's bed and gave her a kiss on her forehead.

"Thank you. Thank you very much for giving me a son," Spencer said.

Lorna gave him a warm smile. "I love you," she said.

"I love you too. We are now a family as I told you before." He picked her hand and squeezed it. He noticed she was tired and sleepy. "I'll let you rest. I'll be back later. I have to go to the bank and tell everyone." He gave her a light kiss on her lips. "Bye, Darling. Take a good rest."

She smiled and waved him goodbye. As soon as he left, she closed her eyes and went right to sleep.

Spencer went straight to the bank. Everyone was eager to know about Lorna and the baby. As soon as he walked into the office, he announced the birth of his son. There was a loud cheer among the employees. Cigars were passed around and there was a joyous atmosphere in the executive office.

The euphoria did not last long. There was a financial audit going on and Philip Nelson, a partner at the accounting firm of Harold and Stewart who was auditing the bank books wanted a meeting with Spencer and George. They set up the meeting for the next day after lunch. Spencer and George were not anticipating any problem. This has been a practice done every year after the audit. It should be just a formality as had been done before.

After work that day, Spencer went back to the hospital and checked on Lorna and his son. Lorna looked much better. He arrived when Lorna was feeding the baby. Spencer could not be happier seeing his wife was nursing the baby. He did not know much about baby care but from what he heard, babies who were breast fed fared better than bottle fed babies. What did he know? But if it was, he's proud of Lorna, taking the initiative to do the right thing for their son.

The next day found Spencer busy at the bank with more lines outside taking their money out of the bank. Things were not looking good. He wondered when this happening would stop. Someone had to do something. People's confidence was eroding and they were afraid of what was going on in the economy. He had a light lunch at his office and then proceeded to the conference room with his father. Philip Nelson was there already with some paperwork scattered on the table.

"Do we have to read all that?" Spencer asked Philip as soon as he sat down across the table from the auditor. His father was already sitting at the head of the conference table.

"Not really unless you want to. I summarized the whole thing so you can just listen to what I have to tell you."

"Good. Do we need William Storms to be here?" George asked.

"No," he said abruptly. The tone of his voice gave Spencer a shiver. Spencer looked at his father who gave him a quizzical look.

"OK, I have no objection," George said.

Spencer was wondering why William Storms was not included in the meeting. After all, he was the VP-Finance of the bank.

"So is the bank sound?" George asked.

"I'm not quite sure," Philip said.

"What do you mean by that?" Spencer asked suddenly, getting concerned.

"There were some discrepancies in the bank accounts."

"Like what?" Spencer raised his eyebrows. He looked at his father who also seemed surprised at the revelation.

"The checkbook and the bank account do not agree. We traced each transactions and it seems like some checks were written and paid to outside vendors that do not exist. Some checks were paid to investment banks for stock trading and yet the stocks were not recorded in the investment account," Philip Nelson said.

"Did you talk to William about it?" George asked.

"No. Not yet."

"Why not?" Spencer asked.

"As far as I know, only William could sign the check and only one signature was required."

"What are you implying? That William Storms was the one doing this," Spencer asked.

"I don't believe he is capable of doing that," George said.

"He is the only one who has access to the checkbooks and can sign the check without being questioned. We checked with his stockbroker and he said he was investing heavily in stock last year," Philip Nelson said.

"Oh . . ." Spencer looked at his father. He looked aghast at the implication.

"You mean to say, he was stealing the bank money to invest in stock for his own account," Spencer said. He turned to his father again who nodded, then shook his head.

"Seems that way. He probably thought the market would keep on its climb and then he could make a bundle and then he could straighten out the books and pay the bank without anyone noticing what he was doing. Unhappily, the stock market is not on his side. As you know the market is on its downward spiral," Philip said.

"I know. What was he thinking? I can't believe this," Spencer said. Suddenly he was furious. He could not believe what he was hearing. His father trusted William Storms and now this. He stood up and started pacing the floor.

"What do you recommend we should do?" George asked Philip Nelson trying to control his anger. He still could not believe it.

"Let me continue on what we are doing so we have enough evidence to tell the authorities," Philip said.

"How long will that take?" Spencer asked.

"A couple of weeks."

"That's too long," Spencer said. He was agitated and wanted to settle this thing with William as soon as he could.

"We have to be thorough just so we have all the evidence we need to prove he is guilty," Philip said.

"What do we do with him in the meantime?" George asked.

"You can either watch him carefully or let him take a vacation. Does he have any vacation accrued to him?"

"I'm sure he does. He never takes a vacation. It's probably why," Spencer said.

"All right. I will talk to him," George said. "Do this carefully without arousing suspicion from other employees."

"I will do that," Philip said.

George stood from his chair and thanked Philip. George and Spencer left the conference room and headed to George's corner office. They closed the door as soon as they got in.

"I can't believe this," Spencer said as he slumped on the chair across his father's desk.

"I don't know what got into William to do such a despicable thing," George said.

Spencer was silent. He had an idea why. Greed. Same thing that he did. The only difference was he was borrowing money to finance his investment whereas William was stealing the money from the bank.

A couple of weeks later, William got back from his vacation. He was very reluctant to go but George insisted he take a break since he had not taken a vacation of late. When he got back, he was summoned to George's office. The police were called and they were waiting at Spencer's office. As soon as he got seated, there was a knock on the door and Philip Nelson walked in with a bunch of papers.

William Storms thought it was the usual conference with the auditor. George started the meeting. George looked at Philip who nodded.

"The audit was finished and here are the findings. Philip will tell us." He turned to Philip who opened his folder. William Storms looked worried. He tried to remain calm but his hands were shaking and George noticed it.

"We found out that there are discrepancies in the bank accounts," Philip said without preamble. They were watching William.

"What kinds of discrepancies? Did you check thoroughly?" William asked trying to act nonchalant but he was nervous inside him. He remained calm.

"You know that was the standard procedures. The junior auditor did the initial paperwork, then counterchecked by the senior auditor and the then the audit manager. All the details were thoroughly verified. The investment account was all awry too. Checks were being paid to non-existent vendors."

William was quiet. He did not really think he would get caught.

Spencer who did not say a word stood up and went outside to his office.

"I'm sorry for you William. I trusted you and you broke that trust. What were you thinking?" George was angry. "I want you out of here. Not just out. We called the authorities." George dialed Spencer's extension.

Spencer answered his phone. "Hello," he said.

"Now," George said on the other end of the line and hung up.

Spencer stood up and with the two policemen went into George's office. They went right in without knocking. William was rooted in his chair and could not speak.

"William Storms, you are under arrest for grand larceny," one of the policemen said. The other policeman put handcuffs on him and escorted William Storms, the Wentworth Bank's VP-Finance out of George's office in handcuffs. William Storms walked out of the bank with head bowed down. The number three man at Wentworth Bank fell out of grace. The policemen took him to the police station to be booked.

## Chapter 24

It was a nice fall day in October when Todd decided to go to *Wentworth Hall* to pay a visit to Spencer and Lorna and see the new baby. The trees were now beginning to turn colors to its majestic hues of autumn – golden yellow, burnt orange, fiery red, scarlet and magenta. With each passing breeze, the leaves were falling down and carpeting the ground. Days are getting shorter and the air was getting cooler, a distant cry from the hot, humid summer. He knew Spencer and the new family had just returned to *Wentworth Hall* and it was perfect for Todd who still lived at his uncle's place in Oyster Bay Cove to go and visit Spencer and his family. He had not had time to see them in New York because of his busy schedule at the law firm. Besides, he also wanted to see Emma. He missed her too and it was about time he talked to her seriously about their relationship now that his position at the law firm was secure. It had been on his mind all this time but he wanted to make certain of what he wanted to do.

So on one Saturday, he pulled out of the Prescott's driveway in his new car and headed down to Meadowbrook. He just bought a new yellow Düsseldorf in August just after his promotion to a partner at his uncle's law firm and he wanted to show it to Emma. Things were looking good and his future prospects were promising. Now he wanted to do something with his life. He wanted to surprise Emma who he had not seen for a few months. She probably had forgotten about him but he had not forgotten her. She was always there in back of his mind. She was the reason why he was working so hard. He wanted to earn enough money to be able to marry her. It was the reason he was holding back. He knew she loved him. They always had fun together. Now that he'd got his promotion, he knew it was time to ask her to marry him. He could now provide her with things she was accustomed to.

As he rode through the streets of Oyster Bay Cove with the vibrant foliage color adorning the trees along the way, he began to enjoy the fall colors around him and the cool weather. He felt a bit nervous on what he wanted to do. But with the new car, he sure would make an impression on Emma and her family. Not that he needed their approval, he was positive they would like him to be a member of her family. They had known him long enough and he had a good rapport with Spencer who was very close to Emma. He did not see any problem marrying into the family. His uncle and George were close friends too. They would certainly approve of the match. He hoped so. He looked at the package on the passenger's chair. There was a package for little George. He smiled to himself. That was the excuse. His real reason for going to *Wentworth Hall* was to see Emma. He had a small box in his pocket from Tiffany for her. He realized he really missed her and it was time to do something about it. Now that his future looks promising, he thought it was time.

He got to the gate house and the attendant saw his brand new car. "Hello, Mr. Prescott."

"Hello."

"What a fancy car you are driving today, sir?" the attendant said.

"Thank you. I just got it two months ago."

"Quite fancy."

"I suppose so. Thank you."

"I presume you want to see Mr. Spencer."

"Yes, I do. Is he home?"

"Yes, sir. He did not tell me you are coming."

"I want to surprise him. I have a present for the baby. Is Miss Emma home too?"

"Yes, sir. They are all home."

"Thank you." Todd put the car in gear and waved the attendant goodbye.

The long winding drive was magnificent with some areas where trees of vibrant colors lining the drive on both sides. Out in the distance, there were more trees. He did not realize how pretty the place was during autumn. The first time he was here was in winter and even then it was so pretty with all the snow on the ground. Todd reached the courtyard and parked the car. He picked up his present and walked up the front steps. He knocked at the door and Mr. Yates opened the door.

"Oh, Mr. Prescott. Come on in. Let me tell Mr. Spencer you are here."

"Thank you, Yates." Yates took Todd to the drawing room and then proceeded to go to the library and informed Spencer that Todd was in the drawing room. Spencer stood up from his desk and went to see Todd.

As Spencer opened the door to the drawing room, Todd came to meet him. "What brought you here? Glad to see you. We haven't seen you for a while," Spencer said.

"I came to see the little one. How's he doing? And Lorna?"

"He's fine. Keeping us awake all night. The rascal. Lorna is doing well. Thank you."

Todd smiled. "Babies do that you know. It's their revenge to you for bringing them into the world."

"Wait till it's your turn," Spencer said with a grin on his face.

Todd ignored the comment. "Well, can I see him now?" Todd said.

"Let me get Lorna and the baby. I'll be back in a minute." Spencer went upstairs to fetch them.

As Todd was waiting for Spencer to come back, he heard some footsteps coming in the direction of the drawing room. He went toward the window knowing it might be Emma and he did not know how to approach her after not seeing her for a long time. He was a bit nervous like a school boy facing a new girlfriend. Just then the door opened. Emma gasped as she saw Todd.

"Hello, Emma," Todd said and approached her.

"I'm sorry," she said. "I did not know you were here."

"You looked like you saw a ghost," Todd said and smiled.

"I was not expecting you. That's all."

Todd came closer to her and gave her a kiss on the check. She felt a shiver. She wanted to push him away and yet she wanted to hug him. Todd noticed her reaction.

"Emma, what's wrong?"

"Nothing."

"I want to talk to you about our future. I just got promoted."

"Congratulations," she said coldly.

"Well, now that I know I have something to offer you, I would like..."

Emma stopped him. "Don't say it Todd. Please."

"Why not?"

"Because if you know something, you'll hate me," Emma said. Just then, they heard Spencer walking down the corridor with Lorna and the baby. They both fell silent.

Spencer opened the door and let Lorna in with the baby in her arms. Todd looked at the little bundle Lorna was holding and peeked through the blanket. A tiny handsome fellow smiled and waved his hand.

"Look, he seems to like me," Todd said. Todd took the baby's little hands and the baby gripped it.

"Amazing how they know who to like at that young age," Lorna said.

"Say hi to Uncle Todd," Todd said to the baby. The baby shook his hand. Everyone was laughing including Emma who forgot her problem and joined in the merriment.

They all sat down. Lorna handed the baby to Spencer. Todd took his present and gave it to Lorna.

"Open it," Todd said. It was a robin blue box from Tiffany. Inside was a silver rattle and a silver piggy bank.

"Thanks, Todd. They are lovely," Lorna said. She handed the baby the rattle which he shook vigorously and made the baby smile. "And the silver piggy bank is just wonderful. It will start him on the right track, saving for his future." She handed the piggy bank to Spencer.

"Thanks, Todd. You are so smart." Spencer nodded to his friend. "Now that you have met little George, I think he should take his nap. Lorna went near the fireplace and rang the bell. In no time, the nurse came in and took the baby up to the nursery.

"We have not seen you for a long time," Lorna said to Todd, then glanced at Emma.

"I've been extremely busy. But it did pay off. They just made me a partner."

"Well, a celebration is in order," Spencer said. "You're staying for lunch, I hope," Spencer asked.

Emma was quiet. Todd took a glance at her and nodded. Spencer stood up and pulled the bell. Mr Yates came in the room.

"Yates, can you tell Mrs. Conley that Mr. Prescott is joining us for lunch," Spencer told Mr. Yates.

"Yes, sir. Anything else sir."

"A nice cake will also do for dessert. We're celebrating his promotion," Lorna said.

"Very well, ma'am." Mr. Yates turned to Todd and said, "Congratulations, Mr. Prescott."

'Thank you," Todd said.

Mr. Yates then turned towards the door. He closed it quietly. After Yates closed the door, they caught up on the news.

Then Todd wanted them to see his new car. They all went outside. They scrutinized the car. Spencer was thrilled. Then Lorna excused herself and dragged Spencer inside. Emma was left with Todd admiring his new toy.

"Why don't I take you for a spin?" Todd asked.

"I think we better not. Spencer might want to talk to you." Emma was not sure she wanted to be alone with Todd after what she started telling him in the drawing room.

"He can wait. We won't go far, just to Jericho and back," Todd said. He wanted to be alone with her as much as she did not want to be alone with him. Knowing Todd won't take no for an answer, she finally gave in and they went for a short ride.

They drove down the long winding driveway and passed the gatehouse. The attendant waved at them. They drove slowly to town. Todd was busy telling her that he always wanted to own a

Düsseldorf. When he got his promotion, he decided to treat himself to owning one. After making a round in town, they went back to *Wentworth Hall*. They parked the car in the courtyard but did not go in. They had half hour to spare before lunch. Todd wanted to talk to Emma in private.

"Can we take a stroll in the rose garden?" Todd asked Emma.

"We don't want to be late for lunch," Emma said.

Todd looked at his watch. "We have half an hour. Besides, I'm sure they will wait for us."

"OK." Emma said reluctantly. It seemed like she could not win with him. But in spite of her fighting her emotion, there was that desire to be with him alone. She had not seen him for so long and she wanted to enjoy his company again.

They strolled in silence for a while with each of them busy with their own thoughts. They got into the rose garden and in the middle of the garden was an iron gazebo with climbing roses. There were few blooms left. They sat on the bench. After a short while, Todd stood up and leaned on the post and stared at a distance. Then he said, "You said a while ago that if I knew something, I would hate you. What does that mean?"

"I'd rather not discuss it," Emma said.

"Emma, I want to know. My feelings have not changed. I know I have not seen you for a while but it did not matter. I still love you and always will. Something has happened to you. You're acting strangely."

Emma sat silently. She wanted to cry on his shoulder but she could not do that. She felt humiliated. She could not bear the thought of him hating her. She did not feel like baring her soul to him. The thought of losing him, even just his friendship was too much for her. Now, she realized Todd was really the only person she loved. She made a terrible mistake and she was ready to take the blame.

"Emma, talk to me. Please. You started it and I want to hear the rest of it." Emma looked at him and she could not stand the anguish on his face.

"Oh, Todd. I wish things were different. I wish I could turn back the clock. It was my fault."

"What are you talking about? What was your fault? You're being mysterious. Trust me. I will understand whatever is bothering you."

"It's not that simple." She paused. Todd looked at her waiting. She looked down trying to avoid his gaze.

"Emma, please tell me what is bothering you."

"I committed adultery," she blurted out. She could not control her tears. Todd stood transfixed. He was not expecting this. He was not comprehending what he heard.

"How? Where? With whom?" Todd asked in succession.

Emma wiped her tears with her sleeve. "Do you remember the news a month ago of a murder/suicide?" Emma asked.

"Vaguely. I don't read the sensational news."

"You should. The victims were Anna and Victor Winiarski. You know them. We met at their party last year."

"Yes, I remember. What's that got to do with you?"

"I had an affair with Victor before he died. I felt responsible for the breakup of their marriage."

Todd was dumbfounded and suddenly got angry with her. "What made you go to bed with Victor knowing he was married?" Todd was furious.

"I don't know. I saw no harm in going out with him at first. I was lonely."

"And you went for a Polish man and a married one at that. I don't understand you, Emma. How could you?"

"I missed you and you were too busy with work." She twisted her fingers. "I bumped into this man near Saks while I was shopping. He was very rude. Then he recognized me and apologized and asked me to lunch. I did not know it would lead to more meetings and such a thing. It was lust, Todd. I then realized I didn't love him at all. I wanted to end it. We quarreled that night before he went home." Todd remained quiet. He turned the other way.

Emma continued, "When I saw the headline the next day, I felt sick. I felt responsible for their deaths." Her voice quivered. She was holding her tears. "I'm sorry. I really am. I know you're going to hate me. I'm ready for that. I deserve it."

She stood up from her seat. Todd stood motionless, still facing the other way. He could not say a word or look at her.

"I hope we remain friends. Goodbye, Todd. I'll see you at lunch. Spencer does not know. I told Lorna." She started walking. Todd remained transfixed for a few seconds then he ran after her.

"Wait. Not that fast," he grabbed her arms. Emma turned around. Her tears started flowing. Her vision blurred.

"I love you, Emma and my feeling has not changed. It's over between you and Victor. He's gone and he's not going to hurt us anymore." Emma looked at him with teary eyes. He pulled a box from his pocket, knelt down and held her hands, "Emma, will you marry me?"

Emma looked at him puzzled. She wiped her tears. "Are you serious? After I told you about my affair?"

"It does not matter. Yes, I'm serious. It has been on my mind for some time. Now, I ask you again, will you marry me. Say yes, Emma."

Emma hesitated for a short time. Todd waited anxiously and remained kneeling in front of her. Then she smiled and said, "Yes, I will marry you, Todd Prescott."

He handed her the blue box from Tiffany. "Open it," he said.

"It's beautiful. It must have cost a fortune," Emma said.

"You're worth it." He took the ring from the box and put it on Emma's finger. Then he stood up and kissed her. Emma put her hands around his neck and kissed him. Todd brushed her hair and as if by magic, all her anguish faded away.

She pulled back and asked, "Are you sure you want to marry me?" She looked him in the eyes and saw a deep love in there.

"Certainly. I worked very hard to get to this point. I want to give you the things you deserve. I love you, Emma and always have since I first saw you at that party at Overlook."

"Let's not talk of Overlook again," Emma said. "I love you, Todd, always have and always will." Emma looked up and Todd kissed her once more.

They walked back to the house hand in hand with a broad smile on their faces. Lorna and Spencer were in the drawing room and waiting for them. As they entered, Todd had a broad smile on his face. Lorna knew something happened.

"We just got engaged," Todd announced.

"What? Just like that?" Spencer asked and slapped Todd's shoulder.

"Yes. Just like that." Todd turned to Emma and said, "Show them your ring, Darling." Emma raised her hand and showed them her big rock.

"Well, congratulations to both of you," Lorna said and hugged Emma and then Todd.

"Congratulations and welcome to the family!" Spencer shook hands with Todd. "That calls for a drink." Spencer went to the sideboard with Todd.

The ladies excused themselves and went upstairs to freshen up for lunch. As soon as they entered Lorna's room, Lorna asked Emma, "What happened? Did you tell him?"

Emma nodded her head, "Yes, I did."

"Everything?"

"Yes, everything."

"How did he take it?"

"He was shocked and angry at first. Then I told him I just hope we remain friends and then I walked off. He ran after me and told me not that fast and first thing I knew, he was on his knees and asking me to marry him. I could not believe it at first but he asked again. When I said yes, he took out a Tiffany box from his pocket and asked me to open it. Oh Lorna, I loved him more than ever at that instant."

Lorna hugged Emma. "I'm glad it worked out. You are brave for telling him the truth."

"I followed your advice. You're right. If I hid it from him and he found out, it would be worse. This way, he knows the truth. He was wonderful, Lorna. Just wonderful."

Lorna gave her best friend a big hug again.

"Thanks, Lorna. I'm glad I followed your advice," Emma said gratefully.

"Let's go back downstairs and join them," Lorna said.

## Chapter 25

After the birth of their son in late September, Spencer was extremely happy and looked forward to coming home after work to see his son. It gave him great pleasure to see the boy after a stressful day at work. Lorna was adjusting nicely as a mother. If only things were better at the office, then it would be a perfect world. But such was not the case. In back of his mind, he was worried sick that things were not what he hoped to be.

The condition on Wall Street was getting worse. The market was coming down daily. People on Wall Street were in panic. In prior years, stockbrokers keep on buying stocks on credit. They thought the boom was going forever. Then the market started on its spiral dive.

In Wall Street, the market had been on a nine-year run that saw the Dow Jones Industrial Average increase in value tenfold, peaking at 381.17 on September 3, 1929. On October 24, 1929 ("Black Thursday"), with the Dow just past its September 3 peak, the market finally turned down, and panic selling started. The market lost 11 percent of its value at the opening bell on very heavy trading.

Several leading Wall Street bankers met to find a solution to the panic and chaos on the trading floor. They chose Richard Whitney, vice president of the Exchange, to act on their behalf. With the bankers' financial resources behind him, Whitney placed a bid to purchase a large block of shares in U.S. Steel at a price well above the current market. As traders watched, Whitney then placed similar bids on other "blue chip" stocks. This tactic was similar to one that ended the Panic of 1907. It succeeded in halting the slide. The Dow Jones Industrial Average recovered, closing with it down only 6.38 points for the day. But, unlike 1907, the respite was only temporary.

Over the weekend, the events were covered by the newspapers across the United States. On October 28, "Black Monday", more investors facing margin calls decided to get out of the market, and the slide continued with a record loss in the Dow for the day of 38.33 points, or 13%. The stock market closed at 260.64.

The next day, "Black Tuesday", October 29, 1929, about 16 million shares traded. The Dow lost an additional 30.57 points, or 12 percent at 230.07, amid rumors that U.S. President Herbert Hoover would not veto the pending Smoot-Hawley Tariff Act, a bill to raise taxes on American imports by about 20 percent. The volume of stocks traded on October 29, 1929 was a record that was not broken for nearly 40 years.

To demonstrate to the public their confidence in the market, William C. Durant joined with members of the Rockefeller family and other financial giants to buy large quantities of stocks. But, their efforts failed to stop the large decline in prices. Due to massive volume of stocks traded that day, the ticker did not stop running until about 7:45 p.m. that evening. The market had lost over $30 billion in the space of two days which included $14 billion on October 29 alone.

During the Crash of 1929 preceding the Great Depression, margin requirements were only 10%. Brokerage firms, in other words, would lend $90 for every $10 an investor had deposited. When the market fell, brokers called in these loans, which could not be paid back. Banks began to fail as debtors defaulted on debt and depositors attempted to withdraw their deposits *en masse*, triggering multiple bank runs. Government guarantees and Federal Reserve banking regulations to prevent such panics were ineffective or not used. Bank failures led to the loss of billions of dollars in assets.


The bank was not doing well and money was getting tight. Spencer could not keep up with the household expenses. There was now a notice that the house in New York would be foreclosed if he could not pay up. *Wentworth Hall* was not faring any better. He had to sell one or the other. He could not keep both.

Spencer sat at his grandfather's desk in the library and pressed his hands to his face. He was tired, exhausted and sick with worry. He had a hard time sleeping at night. His insomnia was nothing new. He seemed to be cursed with it these days or rather these interminable nights. Even when he resorted to drinking three, sometimes four large shots of port after dinner, and vintage port at that, the wine did not act as a sedative. He would sleep for several hours, a drugged and heavy stupor descending upon him, but then he would awaken suddenly in the early hours, perspiring or shivering, depending on his nightmares. His mind a turmoil of painfully analytical assessments of his life, which did not please him. It had not for a long time except for the birth of his son.

Lorna had no idea what was going on at the bank or in the economy. She was busy with her newborn baby and the house and was not aware of Spencer's problems. Spencer was terribly worried about their finances but it was not the thing he would discuss with his wife. He did not want Lorna to worry about his finances. There was no point to it.

As they got ready for bed, Lorna noticed the worried look on his face.

"Spencer, something is the matter. You're not yourself the last few months. You have to tell me what it is," Spencer remained silent. Lorna continued, "I married you for better or for worse. I want to share your burden. You cannot bear it yourself. You have to trust me," Lorna begged him.

Spencer sat on the edge of the bed, looked at his wife, put his hand on her shoulder. "I'm sorry," he said.

"Sorry for what?" Lorna looked into his eyes. She saw the sadness in them. "What's wrong? Please tell me."

Spencer was debating whether to tell her what was the problem. Lorna was insistent so he decided to tell her the truth after all.

"You know the bank is not doing well. The stock market is collapsing. We're about to lose our homes, this house or the one in New York. I can't keep up with the household expenses with this type of economy."

Lorna was speechless. She stroked his head and embraced him. He found strength at the gesture.

"I was not aware it's that bad. I should have known. What are we going to do?" she asked.

"We can reduce the staff which I hate to do. These people need their job. They have been very loyal to the family for years," he said sadly.

"I know what you mean," she said.

"If we have to sell, I much prefer to sell the New York place. I would rather keep *Wentworth Hall* even if it is more expensive to maintain. I love this place and it's my inheritance and I mean to leave it to our son. We cannot keep both houses though. It would be impossible. Even with one, it would be stretching our finances. I'm sorry," he said.

Lorna could sense his agony and she embraced him and patted his back. She tried to think. Then a bright idea popped into her head. She quickly decided on what to do.

"OK. If we have to sell, we can sell the New York place but I want you to keep *Wentworth Hall* as you said. I love this place too and it's your and our son's legacy. We should keep it. I think I can help you," she said brightly.

"How? You're not going to work. I won't let you," he said.

"I could work but I'm not going to. I have to take care of little George," she said.

"So what are you talking about? How can you help me?" Spencer asked.

"When my grandmother died, she left me the house on Fifth Avenue. Knowing that I won't need the house anymore since I'll be living here forever, I sold the house for a great amount of money. The money is in the bank."

"But . . ."

Lorna stopped him. "I said I married you for better or for worse, didn't I? Also, I believe what is mine is yours now and with the baby, what is ours is also for the baby."

Spencer nodded. Lorna continued, "There is also the house in Pittsburgh and some commercial buildings that Grandmother owned. They all went to me."

"I haven't heard of any commercial buildings owned by your grandmother. You didn't tell me this."

"You never asked and I did not want you to know. Nobody can accuse you of marrying me for my money."

"True enough but people thought it was the other way around." He kissed her forehead. "I did not know your grandmother had money."

"Nobody did. Also, Grandmother had five million dollars in the bank that I received outright when she died. It's all in the bank in cash. Grandmother never believed in stocks. My grandfather also left me with quite a bit of money through a trust fund he set up for my mother. He owned some coal mines in Pittsburgh. When he died, he left a trust fund of another five million dollars for my mother which she would receive when she turned 30 but she passed away before that so I got all that too."

"Holy smoke! What else are you hiding from me?" Spencer asked.

"You know the property in Bar Harbor. That is also mine now. I'm not hiding anything from you. You never asked so I did not tell you. There's a big difference. I'll call my attorney tomorrow and I can arrange to settle all your bills."

"Lorna, I don't know what to say. I can't believe this."

"So don't say anything." She smiled warmly and kissed him. "We'll be fine and *Wentworth Hall* is safe for little George."

## ABOUT THE AUTHOR

ROSALINDA R MORGAN is a multifaceted talent. She has been a C.P.A., a real estate agent, a businesswoman, an active community volunteer, a gardener, a writer and an author. She also has a degree in Art and Antique Appraisal. Her short story, "The Pink Slip" and numerous gardening articles have won awards. Since retiring to Charleston, SC in 2011, with her husband, Matthew Morgan, she has published *BAHALA NA (Come What May)* and *The Iron Butterfly*. *The Wentworth Legacy* is her third novel.